COMING
UNDONE

COMING UNDONE

LAUREN DANE

HEAT | NEW YORK

THE BERKLEY PUBLISHING GROUP
Published by the Penguin Group
Penguin Group (USA) Inc.
375 Hudson Street, New York, New York 10014, USA
Penguin Group (Canada), 90 Eglinton Avenue East, Suite 700, Toronto, Ontario M4P 2Y3, Canada
(a division of Pearson Penguin Canada Inc.)
Penguin Books Ltd., 80 Strand, London WC2R 0RL, England
Penguin Group Ireland, 25 St. Stephen's Green, Dublin 2, Ireland (a division of Penguin Books Ltd.)
Penguin Group (Australia), 250 Camberwell Road, Camberwell, Victoria 3124, Australia
(a division of Pearson Australia Group Pty. Ltd.)
Penguin Books India Pvt. Ltd., 11 Community Centre, Panchsheel Park, New Delhi—110 017, India
Penguin Group (NZ), 67 Apollo Drive, Rosedale, North Shore 0632, New Zealand
(a division of Pearson New Zealand Ltd.)
Penguin Books (South Africa) (Pty.) Ltd., 24 Sturdee Avenue, Rosebank, Johannesburg 2196,
South Africa

Penguin Books Ltd., Registered Offices: 80 Strand, London WC2R 0RL, England

This book is an original publication of The Berkley Publishing Group.

This is a work of fiction. Names, characters, places, and incidents either are the product of the author's imagination or are used fictitiously, and any resemblance to actual persons, living or dead, business establishments, events, or locales is entirely coincidental. The publisher does not have any control over and does not assume any responsibility for author or third-party websites or their content.

COMING UNDONE

ISBN 978-1-61523-900-9

PRINTED IN THE UNITED STATES OF AMERICA

I write about family a lot because I believe in connections. I believe connection to community is what makes us human. This one is for those people in my family (the one I was born with and those who've grown into the family of my heart) who have loved and supported me, pimped my books, critted for me, talked me off the ledge and squealed appropriately over good news. You know who you are.

ACKNOWLEDGMENTS

As always, I'm thankful for the support and love of my wonderful husband and best friend, Ray. Thank you so much for being you.

Laura Bradford, my friend and my agent, thank you for never giving up on me!

Leis Pederson, editor most wonderful, thank you thank you for the work you do to make my books the best they can be.

I love ballet, and this book gave me the chance to watch countless hours of dance with my daughter tucked into my lap. My daughter who knows the difference between a *fouette* and a *pirouette*, LOL. The obsession seems to have infected the next generation—dancers, choreographers, orchestra, all: thank you for providing me with so many hours of enjoyment. I refer to the National Ballet Theater, but I mean the American Ballet Theater and their many years of beautiful, well executed, always amazing programs, as well as all the local companies nationwide, like the Pacific NW Ballet and the Anaheim Ballet.

A huge shout-out to those authors who've become my friends, my mentors, my advisors and my sounding boards: Megan Hart, Anya Bast, Ann Aguirre, Jaci Burton, Maya Banks, Sylvia Day—you all rock my world like *whoa*. Bradford Babes—what a fabulously talented group of authors Laura has brought together. Thank you all for your friendship.

Last but most certainly *not* least, my readers! Thank you for all your kindness and support, thank you for the feedback—much of my success is due to you all. Renee and Mary, thank you for all you do at my message board and for all the beta you've done for me. I appreciate you more than you can ever know.

COMING UNDONE

1

Even at the close of the day, the sun was enough to make the ride home from work totally perfect. He took the scenic route, settled onto the seat of the Harley he'd splurged on the summer before at Ben's urging. Best impulse buy *ever*.

The joy of it was enough to bring him the long way home, down surface streets, a bit south and then back north again. He leaned back, the weight of his body balanced just so. The warmth on his thighs, against his back, eased him away from work and into leisure. The light of the often absent sun after the darkness of winter gave him an easy mood. Happy. Satisfied. The thrum of the engine vibrated, humming into his bones.

Late spring in Seattle and people began to emerge from their squall jackets and endless layers. The city came alive with color as flowers burst from ground that had been barren for months; the trees exploded with leaves and blossoms.

Other than early autumn, this was his favorite time of the year. He loved the glimpses of feminine skin as women started going bare-legged again when they wore skirts; loved the emergence of cleavage. He liked winter for all the vibrant, tight sweaters. But in spring and summer, women went softer, showed skin, wore dresses and floated around in his vision. All these things made every day a fine day in his life.

He'd go home, drink a few beers and sit on his back deck to watch the sunset. Maybe he'd even order a pizza if he could be bothered to get up and deal with the front door. Having made his mind up, he stopped in at the grocery store to pick up some hard lemonade for his sister, Erin, in case she showed up. Knowing his siblings, he expected one or both to roll in and demand food, so he liked to have the things they enjoyed on hand.

The slow ride down his street enabled him to catch all the activity on that early evening. People did yard work and washed cars and boats. He hoped they were all using that special soap to do their washing, or Mrs. Cardini, accompanied by her dog, would storm over and yell at them for being irresponsible with the environment.

The woman was in her nineties, and she ruled the entire block— both sides. She and her dog—one of the ugliest things he'd ever seen and always decked out in some special dog outfit—would make their way up one side of the street and down the other, her doling out advice and lectures as she saw fit.

He grinned when he pulled into the driveway and keyed the bike off, only to hear her lecturing his immediate neighbor to the right about the shabby state of his trash cans. Grabbing the groceries from his side bag, he waved quickly and headed to his door before she got to him. God knew he had to be responsible for some kind of violation or other.

Once inside, he kicked off his boots, hung up his jacket, put the groceries away and turned the stereo on. It was fully time to get his leisure on, and his deck and the sunset beckoned. He cracked open a beer and shuffled out toward his favorite spot to unwind.

Brody arched his back, stretching himself as he reclined in the big, comfy Adirondack chair. He'd had a lot of clients that day in his tattoo shop, and he was getting old. Old enough and been tattooing long enough that his body reminded him at the end of each day.

The sky burned soft and bright in shades of blue, purple and bright, nearly neon orange as the sun set. He relaxed into his chair and tipped his bottle back, letting the cold beer ease his day and his back strain. His eyes drifted closed as he simply let the twilight settle in.

"Thought we'd find you back here."

Raven. A friend who used to be more way back when. While there'd been times on and off since they'd ended up in bed during her visits, they'd kept their relationship to just friends. Despite her quirks, she'd become a part of his extended family. He knew her in ways she'd never allow others. He wished she would soften a bit, let someone in. But it was her way and he respected that.

"Got enough for me?"

And his sister, Erin.

He smiled, his eyes still closed; for a few moments he held in his mind the vision of the cotton candy clouds bathed in an explosion of color. He'd known not to expect solace for very long. It was rare when he didn't see one of his siblings at least once a day. He liked that he was a touchstone for them both. They certainly were for him.

"You know where the fridge is."

He listened to the happy sound of his sister and Raven chattering away in his kitchen and making their way back out to his deck.

"Why are you here?" he asked, opening his eyes and looking to his sister.

Erin dropped a kiss on his forehead. "Thanks for the lemonade. Am I so transparent?"

"I knew I'd be seeing you one night this week, so I wanted to be sure you had lemonade to drink."

Her teasing smile softened. "You're a big, huge marshmallow. I won't tell anyone, but just know that I know. As for why I'm here, I wanted to see you. Duh. Todd says hey. Ben may be over in a while. I ordered pizza. Meatball, green pepper and mushroom, so don't get that face."

All that without an extra breath. Brody had always been amazed by his baby sister's boldness, the way she took life on. Still, a man had standards when it came to pizza. "Pagliacci?"

She snorted. "Where else?"

He nodded, approving her choice. "Don't tell anyone I said so, but you're made of awesome." Today her hair was fire-engine red with yellow streaks. On any other woman it would have looked ridiculous, but on Erin it worked.

She laughed and kissed him again before sitting next to him, squeezing into the space he gladly shared.

Totally and utterly content. His life was good. His business was solid, profits were up, enough that he could take fewer clients himself and actually have a day off every week. His house was finally where he wanted it. His sister was happy with her unconventional life and two totally devoted men, and his brother was on tour and had just celebrated yet another record going triple platinum.

"Your garden is nicer than mine." Erin began to prattle on about her day, and he thought about smoking a cigarette, just half even, but then reconsidered. Raven would complain and Erin would give him that sigh of hers. Yeah, it was bad for him, but a man needed a few vices.

Instead, he listened to two of his favorite women talk and occasionally grunted or responded. All the while, he drank his beer and half-listened to Kings of Leon as they floated through the air from the stereo in the house. Not a bad way to spend the evening.

Forty-five minutes later, the pizza arrived, so Brody let himself be lured inside by the scent and his growling belly.

He stood for a moment, looking around. His dining room table was large enough for twelve—more if he put the leaf in. Even though his siblings were out on their own, Brody enjoyed that his was the place they sought when they needed to reconnect. His couches were comfortable and worn. The media center was state-of-the-art, because while his brother and sister made the music, they weren't the only ones who loved listening to it. A big flat-screen plasma hung in his television room downstairs, where he could play on the Wii or the Xbox, and he'd recently picked up a very fine pool table at a garage sale.

In truth, his wilder days had passed and he found he'd rather hang at home in comfort than at a club. If he needed a woman, he could find several with a few calls. If he needed company, the same applied.

Brody enjoyed that most people saw the broad shoulders, the tattoos and the wary eyes, and thought him a rough-and-tumble bad boy. In reality, he liked to watch movies and eat popcorn with his baby sister. One of these days he'd bounce nieces and nephews on his knee and teach them bad habits.

"You're pretty mellow tonight," Erin said as she slid a plate laden with pie toward him.

"I have it good. Why not be mellow? Pretty women to my left

and right, good music, good beer and good friends." He tipped his beer toward Ben, who'd wandered in a few minutes before, not so miraculously, when the pizza had shown.

She smiled. "Good. By the way, I thought of a new tat I want you to do."

"Whatever you say, baby girl." He shrugged, happy to do it. He'd done all her inkwork and trusted it would continue that way. Raven handled the piercings and that was fine by him. But Erin's tats were special, like she was, and Brody wanted to be sure no one he considered inferior ever did work on her.

The predictable argument broke out between Erin and Raven about why Brody should do it instead of Raven, while Ben and Brody looked on before returning to their dinner.

Ben rolled his eyes at the exchange and looked back to Brody. "We need to go for a ride on Sunday. You up for it? The weather should be good. I thought a trip out to the Olympics? We can stop and eat some crab before we turn around."

Brody respected the man who cared so much about his sister. The guy was good people, and he'd come along at a time in Erin's life when it would have been a hell of a lot easier to run in the other direction. That went a long way in Brody's book.

Sunny weekend with bikes and friends? "Yeah, that sounds damned good."

2

Pain sliced through her as his fist connected with her jaw, sent her flying back against the table they'd bought years before at a flea market. Wood splinters rained on her as she slid to her knees, bright points of light painting her vision as breath tore through her lungs.

He hauled her to her feet, but her right leg buckled and she fell again. He'd used a baseball bat on it. Somewhere in the back of her mind she knew it was broken. Knew she'd never dance professionally again. But her mounting fear had nothing to do with that.

Blood marked the pale tile in the entry, and had smeared where he'd hit her and dragged her while she screamed and fought. And then he'd hit her until she couldn't fight much anymore. Handprints, spatters, smears—all ominous portents of just how far the situation had deteriorated over the past nearly three hours.

In the midst of the beating, of the verbal abuse, of being sick from the pain and of watching him tie off and be unable to find a vein for long minutes at a time, she'd tried to focus on a plan. Time had passed; he'd dragged her from room to room, becoming increasingly agitated. He broke things, like he wanted to break her. He wouldn't.

The clock on the living room mantel chimed four times. Her baby was due home soon. She knew he'd harm her daughter. Knew he had to be stopped before he could get his hands on Rennie. She only had herself to count on, but no one was going to hurt her child. Not while she still had breath.

Elise pulled to a stop in her driveway and looked into the backseat. Rennie was asleep, her well-loved blankie curled against her side, pillowing her head, pale blonde hair spread around her face.

An ache, both sharp and sweet, spread through Elise's chest at the sight of the unlined forehead, the trouble-free face of sleep. Seattle had been very good for the both of them. Hard, yes. A long way from the life Rennie had known and Elise had been supported by. There'd been no choice; there was nothing left but pain for them in New York. But, wonderfully, they'd begun to place roots there in the Northwest. Rennie was settling in, making friends. Rennie even expressed an interest in sports. Her baby girl—oh hell, not a baby anymore; the kid was nearly seven, going on forty—was coming out of that dark place they'd both been in.

More than that, Elise felt *safe* for the first time in a decade. That was more precious than she cared to even contemplate for very long. The price had been higher than she'd ever imagined. But, she thought as she bent to ease Rennie from the seat and carry her into the house, there was no way but forward, no direction but up.

As she made herself a late dinner, she took in the space they now called home. Over the weekend she'd hung up the art she'd stuffed into the van they'd driven out from New York. The couch, on sale at a local store, had come a few days prior. *Red.* Red with white cushions. Just looking at it made her happy.

The area rugs she'd collected over the years as she'd traveled the world covered the shiny wood floors. The house was earthy, colorful and warm. A big change from her silver and pale blue Manhattan condo.

A *needed* change. Warm and earthy suited her, damn it, and it would keep on that way. Rennie's recent artwork splashed the refrigerator doors with color and lent that extra bit of home. One positive she got from her father.

Shaking her head, Elise moved back to pleasant things. She made a mental note to thank her friend from the NBT who'd hooked her up with some local people and gotten the word out about her school. That word had given her enrollment numbers a huge boost. The bills would be paid, and in a year or so they might even be turning a profit.

Rennie appeared to be making friends in her summer camp program, which kept her busy during the day and worked most of her energy out, much to Elise's relief at bedtime. They'd gone furniture shopping and gotten new beds for each of them. Their nightly routine included grabbing some groceries and heading home.

Glorious and totally, utterly normal.

The fact that she lived without fear occurred to her in the same way you notice when crickets suddenly start up in the summer. Life springs around you and you realize it's going to be okay.

Her *left* leg was fine. Elise could still dance better than 95 percent of the population, but she'd never be a primary dancer again. She'd never dance with any major company, because her body would not hold up under the stresses of that life. Age was a factor now, but mostly it was the damage to her right leg and the multiple dislocations of her shoulder. Her balance wasn't as precise, her strength not quite enough.

In that, Ken had won. He'd taken that dream from her.

But simply by standing there, happily enjoying a rage-free home and a glass of wine, Elise had won. And she had absolutely no intention of feeling guilt for surviving. Rennie needed her. Moreover, Rennie needed to see her mother as a woman who stood tall instead of wincing in fear. Who took what life had to offer with both hands and forged a place for herself instead of waiting for someone to provide it for her.

Through it, Elise knew she'd be a better person for herself too.

Elise worked in her front yard, cleaning out the flower beds and getting some new plants in. As she did, it wasn't like she couldn't take a look from time to time as a new, hot-looking bad boy rode up on a big motorcycle. For someone so big and sort of scary-looking, that guy who lived across the street was pretty hot. His friends too. Apparently Elise had a thing for bad boys. Hmm. Well okay, so that wasn't so much of a surprise, but hopefully the bad on those boys was the good kind.

And since this was just a conversation going on in her head and all, it was nice to know that after two years of having sex with no one but her hand or her toys, her libido could still rev up at the sight of something so spectacularly male. She could look, store up some fantasy fodder for her dates with her hand and also know men like her neighbor were totally out of her league.

But *holy shit*, all the hard thighs encased in faded denim, the tight asses, the tattoos and general bad-boy air going on was more than enough to overcome any discomfort at being on her knees in the dirt. She had on sunglasses and a ball cap, so it wasn't like they could see her ogling them or anything. She could objectify and fantasize to her heart's content. Mmm.

The earth was warm, the scent dark and rich as she dug and

planted, tore out and worked. It felt good to make a physical change with her hands. To create a difference in her environment.

"Momma, we need more pink flowers. We don't have enough pink."

Grinning, she looked up the filthy legs of her monkey of a child and into a face dirtier than her clothes. "I'd be challenged to find a spot on your body not covered in dirt. Honey, have you been *eating* dirt?"

"Ew! As if! But a girl has to get her hands dirty when she's working in the garden. That's what Gran says."

Elise laughed, thinking of her mother saying exactly that, though usually as she ordered someone else around to do the gardening for her while she watched.

"We can go to the garden center later today, if you like. Then you can pick out the flowers you'd like to plant. Maybe after we get some lunch. What do you say? A girls' lunch date and then some shopping?"

Rennie's big blue eyes lit. "Awesome."

"First, you need to be cleaned up and changed. Good Lord, I should just hose you off out here."

Rennie squealed as Elise grabbed the nearby hose and gave her daughter a squirt. The squealing rose in volume and pitch as Rennie grabbed the watering can, tossing the contents at her mother.

"Oh, I'm gonna get even with you for that!"

Rennie hooted some smack-talk her way as she streaked through the freshly painted arbor over the opened backyard gate, her mother in hot pursuit.

Ben looked up from his bike and toward the noise across the way and then back over to Brody. "Dude, when did you get a new neighbor? I thought an elderly couple lived over there."

Brody caught the sight of two females, one grown chasing a smaller one, laughing, water spraying from the hose. He smiled briefly at the idyllic scene and the flash of pale blonde hair as they rounded a corner. "Dunno. I noticed a new car in the driveway, but whoever they are I haven't met them yet. Maybe a young family or something."

"Maybe a hot single mom," Cope, Ben's younger brother, added. "That would be nice."

"I'm not looking for hot single moms. I don't need any baggage or ex-husbands hanging around." Christ, why would he? There were plenty of single women without kids and exes around. Anyway, she probably had a husband, not that he'd noticed one way or the other.

Cope snorted and got on his bike. "Not for *you*, dumbass. For me. You can get your own pussy, I'm not your pimp."

"Don't fuck anyone in my neighborhood, Cope. The last thing I need is to be involved in a situation where some woman is brooding over you when you dump her. Don't fuck where I sleep."

"You wish I'd fuck where you sleep." Cope raised a brow, smirking before he slid his shades up over his eyes.

"Ha! If I liked men, yours wouldn't be the ass I coveted. You're too short. I couldn't fuck you without bending my knees and straining my back. Plus, you're not as hot as your brother, who I'd totally fuck if my sister wouldn't kill me."

Ben laughed, tossing a towel at his little brother. Considering that Ben was fucking not only Erin but her husband Todd, who was also Ben's boyfriend, Brody wasn't too far off the mark. Both on Ben's attractiveness and his sister's willingness to kill anyone who tried to filch one of her men.

"I'd be fucking *you*, old man."

Brody barked a laugh. "Now it's you wishing. Stop harassing

my neighbors and their children and let's get this show on the road."
Brody snorted, shaking his head as he climbed aboard his bike and
keyed it on. He slid the strap of his helmet home, tightening it,
and adjusted his ass on the seat. A new splurge, comfortable for
long rides just like the one he was about to take.

Six of them roared down the street, toward the freeway and a
day of riding out in the gorgeous weather. Freedom.

After getting Rennie down to bed, Elise had puttered around the
house, folding laundry and returning some phone calls. Then, at
long last, she locked the door, ran a bath, grabbed a book and a
glass of wine, and settled in for a nice soak.

The bathroom had been remodeled some years before, so it was
larger than it would have been for a house this age. It was one of
the reasons she had bought the place. Huge jetted tub with a garden window and a skylight. Just the place for an aging dancer to
soak away the day's stresses.

And, she thought as she soaped over her nipples and they stood
at attention, a nice place to masturbate too. Her eyes drifted closed
as she thought of him. Of the dark-haired giant across the street.

His voice would be low, she decided, low and gravelly as he
talked dirty in her ear. He'd bend her over a desk, or a table, kick
her ankles wide to spread her open just for his cock.

Hard. His body would be hard against hers as he fucked her. Fu-
riously, deeply, so much so that little grunts of air would emerge
from her lips each time he slammed home.

Her soap-slicked hand slipped down her belly, finding her pussy
ready. She teased around her clit as she continued to think of him.
Of how he'd pull out and pick her up, depositing her on the table-
top and settling in between her thighs.

Ken had hated oral sex—the giving of it anyway—but it featured mightily in all Elise's fantasies. She'd loved it when the men before him had done it for her. Wet, slick mouths on her pussy, tongues working against her clit. So intimate to be touched that way. A man like the guy across the street would do it and he'd love it.

Her middle finger slid back and forth over her clit as she imagined his tongue would move. She'd arch up into his face, unashamed, demanding more. And he'd give it to her, making her come before straightening to slide his cock back into her, even as her inner walls still jumped from climax.

She would be able to do nothing but lie there, rolling her hips to take him deeper as he fucked into her body. His eyes would burn into her like a caress until he got closer to climax.

Her breath came shorter as she neared her own climax, imagining how his neck would tighten, how the muscles on his forearms would cord as he gritted his teeth and came into her, hot and so wet.

She let go, coming, and sliding beneath the water as she could still imagine the scent of the sweat on his skin.

3

Elise enjoyed the early afternoon quiet as she used the long-handled roller to spread paint up and down the section of fence just to the left of her porch. Rennie played with Barbie and My Little Pony on the porch, singing one of her numerous made-up songs that made Elise grateful to have birthed so fabulous a person.

On a Saturday in the early summer, the street was rife with activity, everyone in the yard or dealing with a car. Children riding bikes or roller skating. None of it was overwhelmingly loud, just a quiet hum of activity. Soothing rather than jarring.

The hottie from across the street walked toward his mailbox at the curb, and Elise paused to watch the lope of his strides. Long and sure. Today he wore a black T-shirt and jeans so faded they were pale against the flip-flops on his feet. She wondered what his hair would feel like. Soft?

Close-cropped, it only highlighted the bold lines of his face. Some men were so handsome they were pretty, but this one was . . .

not pretty. He was hard. She blushed as she remembered the nights of the past week, using her toys and her fingers to make herself come as she thought of him.

Wow, that guy was going really fast for a residential neighborhood. Elise straightened, checked back over her shoulder to be sure Rennie was still on the porch and out of harm's way before she looked back out again, only to see the dark sedan careen to miss a trash can and, instead, clip the hottie, tossing him against his mailbox as the car peeled away.

Adrenaline filled her, spurring her to action. "Rennie, get the cell phone and the first-aid kit! Now!" she called as she ran toward where he'd fallen.

Rennie quickly obeyed, pressing both into her mother's hands just moments later. One-handed, Elise dialed 911, relayed the information and handed the phone off to Rennie, whom she'd ordered up onto hot guy's lawn, out of the way of a return trip by the hit-and-run driver or the arrival of the aid vehicles.

Elise wasn't a stranger to first aid triage. She held the memories at bay and pretended to be someone else while she stanched the bleeding on his forehead and checked him for other injuries. Her hair had fallen from where she'd had it loosely knotted, but she didn't want to let go of the pressure on his wound, so she let it fall into her face.

His eyes flickered open here and there as he fought unconsciousness, but he never seemed to focus on her at all. During one such moment of his partial consciousness, she smiled down at him, hoping she was at least somewhat comforting. "Hold on. You're going to be all right. Help is on the way."

He licked his bottom lip and closed his eyes again, God help her, the sight tightened things low in her gut.

It wasn't too much after that when the sound of a siren punctuated the afternoon and paramedics pushed through the crowd surrounding them.

She reassured him quietly, keeping out of the way as best as she could. And when he opened his eyes, focusing them on her, seeing her for the first time as the paramedic knelt beside them, she felt the connection all the way to her toes.

Her pulse jumped as he blinked thick, sooty lashes shading big, brown eyes. He smiled, crooked through the neatly trimmed goatee and mustache. "Angel."

She laughed. "Not so much. You're going to be all right, Mr. . . . Um, yeah, I don't know your name."

"Brown. Brody Brown." No slurring, so that was good. A bit of tension in the words, probably soreness and pain. But his pupils looked fine.

A cop stood to her left and she multitasked, speaking to the officer about the car, the license plate and other details while making sure Rennie kept her booty away from the street.

The paramedics got him onto a board as she kept her eye on them, making sure they didn't jar him. He grumped at the paramedics, bitching about being bumped around. She smiled down at him, touching his cheek, sliding her fingertips into the surprising softness of his beard. "Okay, Brody Brown, stop fussing and let them take care of you. I'm talking to the cops right now. I've got it handled. Do you want me to call anyone for you?"

"You're not real."

She laughed. "My electric bill says otherwise. I'll lock your house up for you, all right?"

"On my phone, in the hall, push one. My sister."

She nodded. "All right then. I'll go now."

They told her where they were taking him, and she stood watching as they drove away, then she headed into his house.

She didn't expect what she saw inside, even just from the entry near the phone. Neat. Lived in, but neat. Hmm. Elise grabbed the phone, steeling herself for a call she was frightfully glad she wasn't on the other end of for a change.

Erin groaned and leaned over Todd's body to grab the phone. Late nights under his talented hands were more than worth the sleepiness the next morning.

"Hello, Brody. Why on earth are you calling my house at ten on a Saturday?"

"I'm sorry to wake you up. I'm Elise Sorenson. I live across the street from your brother. First let me tell you he's fine."

Erin sat up, awake instantly. Todd stirred, his handsome face creasing with the concern he must have felt when he saw her reaction.

"Is everything all right?" Nausea swamped her, her heart pounded.

"He's had an accident. They're taking him to Harborview right now. He asked me to call you."

Erin scrambled up and began to get dressed as she held the phone to her ear with her shoulder.

The woman on the other end gave her details but kept her cool. Erin really appreciated that level voice as the fear threatened to tear reason from her head.

Ben came in carrying a cup of coffee and wearing nothing more than a smile. Sweet baby Jesus, was he pretty to look at. Even better, when he saw the look on Erin's face and Todd getting dressed, he simply put the mug down and began to dress as well.

"Thank you, Elise, I appreciate you calling and locking up Brody's house too."

"Not a problem. He's going to be all right. He was conscious enough to be grumping at the people getting him in the ambulance and to tell me where the phone was to call you." She paused. "If you need anything, please feel free to call me. I'm just across the street."

Erin liked this Elise Sorenson. The woman was no-nonsense and calm, two qualities Erin needed and appreciated right then. She hung up after giving Erin her phone number and offering to help if she could, kindly waving away Erin's profuse thanks.

"What's going on, gorgeous?" After she dressed quickly, Ben handed her the coffee, now transferred to a travel mug, and the three of them headed to the door.

Thank God for them. Her men, her everything. She rose on tip-toe to kiss Ben and then Todd. "Brody got hit by a car. They're taking him to Harborview. His neighbor called. She says he's all right, but I'll feel a lot better when I see for myself."

Todd nodded, taking the keys. "I'll drive. You call Adrian on the way."

Ben put an arm around her as they drove to the hospital, and Adrian was, thank goodness, just getting back from an afternoon television appearance in New York.

"I'm coming back right now. I'll just head straight to the airport."

"Brody will be so pissed if you come back here without making sure there's a reason to. Why don't you wait. Sit tight and I'll call you the minute I know anything else."

"Um, let me see. Hmm, what to say, what to say? Oh, I know. Fuck you. I'm coming back. Do you think for one second he'd just hang out in the city to be interviewed and get blown by hot chicks if one of us got hit by a fuckin' car? If I didn't know you were only trying to manage everyone and keep us all happy, I'd be insulted. You call me the second you hear anything. I'm in the limo and on the way right now."

"I told you the just-stay-in-New-York-unless-we-hear-bad-news thing wasn't going to work for him. You Browns are all stubborn as hell." Todd looked at her in the rearview mirror. "He's going to be all right, darlin'."

Which she knew, of course. But this was her brother, and she'd feel a hell of a lot better when she was able to see it for herself.

Brody was in X-ray when they arrived at the hospital, but the nurse didn't seem too worried. Another hour passed, Erin stepped out to leave a message on Adrian's voice mail, and finally they got to see Brody.

"Christ a'mighty, why are you here looking like someone kicked your kitten?" Brody was grumpy in his paper gown, but Erin saw him fight a smile when she fussed over him. "I almost said 'ate,' and then I remembered who I was talking to."

She rolled her eyes. "*Someone's* had some pain pills. From the sound of it, they gave you the good stuff. Now, do kindly shut up. You're coming to our house for a few days, where I can keep an eye on you."

"*You* shut up. I'm older and I'm not going to your palace of decadence and deviance." He made a raspberry sound and Todd burst out laughing.

She didn't feel like laughing. Erin wanted to punch someone for his scaring the crap out of her. What on earth would she do without Brody? The very thought of him not being around had left her sweaty, grumpy and slightly depressed despite the evidence that he would recover completely.

"You got *hit by a car*. I'll be the judge of where you go. A hit-and-run. Oh my god. Your neighborhood is so nice. What the hell is the world coming to?"

Brody squeezed her hand. "Baby girl, I'm fine. Some bruising, a bump on my head, but nothing broken. I'm pissy, I'm hungry, and I feel like someone ran over me with a car. I want to go home. I want to eat and take a few more of these very fine painkillers, and I want to watch *The Matrix* in bed."

"Adrian is on his way back. I told him to stay in New York but he said bad words to me."

Brody barked a laugh as he signed the release papers. "You gonna want me to kick his butt? You're on your own there. The two of you are the exact same. Full of shit. It's a wonder all my hair didn't go gray after seeing you through teenagerdom. Now, let's get me home. I want to stop at Red Mill."

That was a good sign. "If you want to eat burgers, you must be feeling better."

Carefully they helped him into the shirt Ben had been smart enough to bring along and led him to the car.

Despite the official okay to leave, Erin worried. She kept at his side, her hand tucked in his even as they drove back. She didn't plan to let him out of her sight for the time being. The scent of the hospital had been bad enough. If he hadn't been holding her hand, it would have been shaking.

He brushed his lips over the top of her head. "You all right? I know how much you hate hospitals."

Being understood that way made her love him even more. This man who, at seventeen, had stepped in to raise his younger siblings. A man who never complained about giving up his dreams to make sure theirs came true. And here he was, bruised and damaged from being hit by a car, and he was worried about her feelings.

"I'm fine. You're here. Thank God you're here and okay." How very blessed she was to have so many wonderful people who loved her.

He sighed and pulled her close. "I sure do love you."

"Back atcha. By the way—Elise? Your neighbor who called? She sounds really cute. What's she like?"

Ben burst out laughing. "Honey, let the man get his stitches out before you start trying to play matchmaker, why don't you?"

Erin blew raspberries at Ben. "What? She seemed very nice. She has one of those soft, gentle voices, but she must have her shit together enough to deal with some stranger covered in ink and blood. I like that. Who's to say she's not hot? And looking for a nice man? Sheesh. You have to grab opportunity with both hands when it comes."

Brody just shook his head and groaned when a wave of dizziness hit. "I'm not looking for a nice woman. I'm not looking for a woman, period. I think she's got a kid anyway. Probably a husband too. I don't do married women."

"Leave him alone, gorgeous." Todd chuckled, and Erin made a snuffling sound. Brody knew his sister; she did what she wanted to do, accident or not. God knew he was helpless against her most of the time.

"Thank God, we're home." Good thing, before his sister had him engaged and choosing silverware patterns with the woman across the street.

Hell, all he could remember of her was the pale hair and the sweetness of her smile. She was probably covered in spots and had buck teeth. He'd had a head injury after all; his memory was most likely faulty.

4

"Go the hell home. You've been here nearly twelve hours now."
Raven pointed toward the back door and glared. "You just got hit
by a freaking car a few days ago. If Erin or Adrian find out I've let
you be here this long, I'll never hear the end of it. Especially from
Adrian, who already thinks I'm evil incarnate. Now go."

He bent and kissed her soundly. She allowed it for a few moments until she gave his bottom lip a hard nip.

"You wound me."

She laughed. "Now go home, please. You look pale. Do you
need me to come over and bring you dinner?"

Raven, the woman he'd once loved until she'd broken his heart,
and then he'd come to like her and realized *like* was better. Safer.
She summered in Seattle and worked in his shop, helped him run
things when it suited her. Most of Raven's life was about what
suited her, he had realized some years before. At one time it had
hurt him deeply, but now he just accepted it as part of who she was.

Still, he knew she cared about him in her own way. And she was right. He had a headache from concentrating on the fine line work in a full sleeve he'd spent hours on that day. His back ached, his eyes were dry. The constant buzz of the needle machines, the scent of the ink, of skin and disinfectant—of his shop—was usually a comfort, but it was getting on his nerves today.

"I'll get takeout. I'd guess Adrian is still camped in my house anyway."

Raven laughed. "He's still refusing to go home?"

"Eating me out of house and home. I'd forgotten how much that lean body could tuck away morning, noon and night. Thank God he can afford his own groceries now. The man has his own freaking palace with a view and he insists on sleeping in one of my spare rooms. I'm fine. I keep telling you all that."

"If you got in the habit of calling it a guest room instead of *Adrian's* room, I might believe you were annoyed by his presence. They want to do for you the way you've done for them, time and again. Now stop your pussy-assed whining and go home."

Tenderness burst through him and pride as well. His siblings had grown into such exceptional and gifted people. He'd had a part in that and it made him smile, even as they were overprotective and annoying.

"Yeah, yeah. I'm going now. Thanks for holding down the fort while I've been out."

"What out? Puhleeze, Brody. You've been here every day but the one where you were hit. Sheesh." She swatted his ass and he laughed as he left.

He pulled into the driveway, and on his way to the front door, he spotted her. The woman he'd begun to believe he'd dreamed up.

She struggled to her front door with an armful of bags, and he found himself sprinting over there, heedless of his aches.

"Hey, let me help you."

Her head snapped up and she paled, stepping back. His smile slipped from his face as he was offended for a moment. Was she shrinking back from him because of the tattoos?

Her smile came then, shy but genuine, and his confusion was replaced by other, more immediate and pleasant feelings. "Oh, you startled me. Brody, right? How are you feeling?" A child came streaking around the corner, hugging a soccer ball to her chest.

"Yep, Brody. Can I help you with those?" He gestured at the bags. He tried not to loom or be scary. He wasn't looming—well, he was, but it was only due to the fact that she was so small.

After a slight hesitation, she nodded and handed him two while she opened her front door and led him inside.

"Momma, who's that ginormous guy in our kitchen?"

"Sweet Christ," the pretty blonde, obviously the mother to the little girl, muttered, and Brody tried not to laugh.

"Irene, this is our neighbor. You remember? Mr. Brown is the man who got hit by the car on Saturday. Also, try to remember your manners." She turned to Brody. "This is Irene, my daughter."

Big, deep blue eyes blinked up at him, and her smile showed a gap where she'd lost a tooth on the top. All in all, a pretty cute kid as far as kids went. "Oh, yeah. You didn't look so huge when you were on the ground. I brought over the first-aid kit and the phone for Momma to call the police."

He put the bags on the table and grinned down at the miniature version of the larger woman. "Hey there. I'm Brody. Thanks for helping me this weekend."

"Anytime. Momma says we're part of a community, and community means you help each other."

He nodded. This kid reminded him a lot of Erin. Firecracker. He wondered what the mother was like. He looked back to her, she of the very soft voice and the scared rabbit nerves. Thank God those had seemed to calm a bit; her eyes had stopped darting all around, but her small frame still held tension.

As he'd thought of Erin, he also realized he recognized the look on his savior's face. The fear there wasn't of him personally. Someone did something to her or she saw something to make her react that way. Anger, unbidden, washed over him a moment at the idea of anyone harming a woman—this woman.

He held his hand out and she took it. Soft skin to go with the voice. Small, fragile even. An urge to protect her washed over him. He tried to bury it. "I wanted to thank you too. Did you tell me your name was Angel?"

She laughed, blushing. "No." He let go, but his skin felt her touch for long moments more. "You called me angel when you looked up at me. The hair maybe? The sun behind me? You were pretty out of it. I'm Elise."

He grinned. He liked the blush, and the lack of a wedding ring on her left hand as well. "You do have that sort of face. Angelic. Beautiful. My sister wants to thank you too. She's pretty protective and she'd have been a lot more upset if she'd gotten the call from the hospital instead of you. So I thank you for that also."

"I'm glad you're all right. Did they catch the person who hit you?"

"Not yet. They have his identity, thanks to you and your sharp eyes. But he's on the run. He's got a long history of DUI, and this is apparently one of those last-chance things. It's probably why he didn't stop."

"Either that or he's the kind of thoughtless jerk who repeatedly drives drunk, gets stopped, arrested, set free and drives drunk again."

Her mouth twisted and he saw something in her eyes, just for a brief moment, before it slid away again.

"Could be. Sorry, I was having a glass-half-full moment."

"Join me on the dark side. We have cookies to go with our half-empty glasses of milk."

He started and then laughed. "I do like cookies."

She blushed again, and he knew he'd be back, because he had a bit of a like on for the very charming, blushing Elise. Like was a good thing between two single adults. Especially if it entailed naked and horizontal moments.

"I'll see you around the neighborhood then, Elise. Thank you again, for everything." He stepped back, and he didn't fail to notice the way her spine lost some of its tension.

She walked him to the door, and he waved, winking at Irene before he turned to amble on back to his place.

Elise managed to hold off fanning her face until she'd shut the door and locked it . . . and sneaked another look at a man who looked damn fine from the back. He'd startled her, but she'd learned enough from the neighbors to know he wasn't a man prone to violence or harm.

On the ground as he'd been the weekend before, or from a distance, he hadn't seemed so huge. But *christamighty*, he was gigantic. For a moment when he'd first reached her, he'd towered over her. Fear had washed through her, evoking that fight-or-flight response, and it had been a hard-fought moment to get herself back under control.

He must have sensed something, because he stepped back, not quickly and not really slowly. But he gave her space and it allowed her to breathe again. And that's when she really began to see him.

He was . . . Well, there wasn't any other man she could compare him to really. His hair was close-cropped but tousled. If it had been longer she'd have bet he'd have had thick curls. Dark as night. The neatly trimmed goatee and mustache worked for him, framed a mouth she was quite convinced would deliver some devastating goodness. He wasn't going to hurt her, she knew that much.

No, she was threatened on a whole different level. Like a sensory bomb had gone off as she'd stood there, resisting the urge to rub herself on him. So alluring, this man. His voice, oh good lord, his voice was like suede. Deep and rough/soft. When he wasn't on the ground, out of it and bloody, he was hot. Up close, he was . . . a bit overwhelming. More than handsome— he was too hard-edged to be handsome—he was compelling, magnetic.

She needed to keep her distance until she figured it out. She was suspicious of her response to him. When she'd met Ken, it had been lust at first sight. He had been a big personality too. He'd taken over every conversation, had managed every detail until she'd been in so deep it was all she could do to tread water and not drown.

When it had been good, he was a force of nature. Funny, solicitous, affectionate, intelligent and creative. But he had demons, and instead of dealing with them appropriately, he'd self-medicated, and it had turned those demons into pain for everyone around him.

No, she couldn't be trusted, couldn't know if her attraction was to someone real or to some idea. God knew she couldn't survive another Ken, and until she got a mental handle on herself and what brought about certain choices in her life, she'd forgo relationships.

She had Rennie to raise and a business to run. She knew she'd have sex with someone in the future—she was a woman in the sexual prime of her life, and there was only so much masturbation she could engage in. After a while, masturbation felt empty. It met her need, but it was not the same as having a man above you. However, *love* was out of the picture. *Romance* was out of the picture. She didn't have the time and she didn't know if she had the heart anymore.

Sex with Brody Brown? Well, now, that wasn't such a bad idea. She hadn't dated in a million years, but she remembered enough to recognize the attraction in Brody's eyes, the way he lingered, his gaze snagging on her mouth.

Enough of that for the moment! She'd turn into a puddle of goo if she kept thinking along those lines.

"Rennie, let's get those groceries unloaded and then we'll make dinner and you can call your grandmother before your bath."

Rennie froze a moment, panic on her face. "No."

Alarmed, Elise knelt before her daughter and took her hands. "Noodle? What's wrong?"

Her normally good-natured daughter crossed her arms over her chest. "I don't want to. You can't make me." Her bottom lip trembled.

"Take a bath? You're a mess, you'll feel better after you get all cleaned up."

"I don't want to call them. I don't want to talk to *her.*"

Had Rennie and Martine had some sort of falling out? Rennie would have said, or her mother. Elise had just spoken to her mother the day before, and there had been no mention of a problem. "You never have to talk to Gran and Pops if you don't want to. I thought you'd like to tell them about your day, but if you don't want to, that's okay."

"Gran? I thought you meant the other one. Momma, I don't like talking to her. She's not nice and she never wants to hear about school. She only wants to hear about what you're doing and saying. She makes my tummy hurt."

Holding back a sigh, she took Rennie in her arms and smoothed a hand up and down her spine. Helplessness washed through her at her inability to excise these damned people from her child's life. "I'm sorry. I wish I could . . . You have to talk to them once a month. The court says so. But the fifteenth is next week, so you don't have to talk to them until then. I can be with you, in the room, when you talk to them if you want. You can snuggle on my lap."

"I can?"

"Totally. That's what my lap is for. Now, go on upstairs, wash your face and come back down to help me put away the groceries, okay?"

Rennie perked up. "Okay. Be right back!" She ran upstairs, her footfalls a thunder above Elise's head as she headed into her bathroom.

God, she hated that her child got so upset over the calls from the Sorensons. She hated being powerless to protect her from it. Hated that it was the lesser of many evils so they had to endure it in exchange for those people staying out of Rennie's life on any greater level.

Her upset forgotten, Rennie charged back downstairs, ready to help. Her normal demeanor was back in evidence and Elise relaxed a bit as they began to unload the groceries.

Rennie danced around the kitchen, singing a song from her endlessly changing repertoire as she spun and put things in cabinets. The kid not only had her father's eye for painting and drawing, but also the natural grace of her mother. Elise was proud and wary of that power and talent. It took so much energy to guide her daughter in the right direction. Rennie needed the stimulus, thrived on experience and affection as any child would. There were times when Elise wondered if she was enough.

A wave of longing for her family hit her so hard she gripped the counter. They'd been such an integral part of her life, of Rennie's life. Elise missed that connection.

Tug, tug, tug on her shirt hem. Elise looked down into blue eyes very much like her own. She couldn't help but smile. "Momma, can we have tacos?"

Thank God for Rennie. Something to keep Elise from wallowing. She swallowed back her loneliness and nodded. "Sure thing. I got avocados for some guacamole too."

"Wheeee!"

With a laugh, Elise began to assemble dinner, her heart a bit lighter.

5

Brody rode his bike up the driveway and turned the ignition off. When he slid his sunglasses down his nose, he watched Elise get out of her car, and smiled at all the crap she wrestled from the trunk as the kid bounced around the yard.

He saw her trash cans at the curb and thought, *Why not?*

Hailing her with a call of her name and a smile, he took one can per hand and carried them up toward where she stood. "Can I put these somewhere for you?"

"Um. Yeah, the garage. Here." She bent into the car and hit the garage door opener. He didn't fail to see how flexible she was, and a brief flash of what she'd look like naked, sweaty and beneath him, flitted through his brain.

He hurried past and put the cans inside, stepping out as she closed the door again.

"Most people park in their garage." He grinned.

"I will soon enough. Pete and Emmabeth—the couple who lived here before? They're friends of a friend. They sold me this house on very short notice and asked if they could leave their furniture here in the garage until the fall. They went on a trip to see their kids and then to Europe."

"Oh. I was wondering what happened to them. They were nice people. I'm glad they sold their house to another nice person."

"Wow. You're really good, aren't you?"

She cocked her head, and he realized she'd relaxed around him enough to actually joke, partially even flirt. Christ, her mouth, those eyes . . . He swallowed back the tide of longing, the urge to lean down and brush his lips over the curve of her cheek.

Instead he struggled for nonchalance. "I do try."

"Thank you for bringing my cans in. How are you feeling?"

"Much better. No soreness anymore. My brother finally went home, and he and my sister only call to check on me twice a day. The bruises on my side"—he raised his T-shirt to show her—"are all gone. They arrested the guy, by the way. The one who hit me. He confessed it to several people. They tell me he's going to make a guilty plea and go to rehab."

She touched his side, a quick breath of a touch, and pulled back, blushing. "I'm sorry! I didn't mean to touch you. I didn't think."

"It's okay. I'm pretty sure my innocence is unsullied."

She grinned. "Oh. Well, good. Um, listen, are you hungry? I was about to make some dinner."

The air between them charged, heated. He shoved his hands in his back pockets before he ended up reaching out to touch her like he really wanted to. By the look in her eyes, she'd have been just fine with that touch, and that drove him insane. Still, he liked that expectation in the air, liked the way it felt before either person made that first move.

There would be something between him and Elise. There was so much energy between them in the brief meetings they'd had, it would only grow the longer they knew each other. When the time was right, it would happen and he'd enjoy every single moment.

She licked her lips and he swallowed, hard, suddenly feeling like he was sixteen years old. He took a step closer and she didn't retreat.

Just then Adrian showed up, honking his horn as he pulled up to the curb in front of Brody's house. What timing his brother had.

He managed to bite back his groan of annoyance. "I'd love to, but my brother has apparently chosen now to stop over. Checking on me, I'd wager. It was Erin's turn yesterday. You know how family can be. I'm sure he hasn't eaten yet, so . . ."

She licked her lips again and little zings of chemistry buffeted between them. He enjoyed the intensity of it, the chemical soup of their connection.

"I'm making spaghetti. It's not like making it for two instead of four is a problem. I mean . . ." Again the blush as her pale blue eyes met his, cruised down to his lips and then away as she took a deep breath. "If you're hungry, Rennie and I wouldn't mind the company. We're new to Seattle, so it's nice to get to know our neighbors."

Rennie scampered up and nuzzled into her mother's side. Elise's arm automatically went around her daughter's shoulder, and it pleased Brody to see the easy affection there.

"Plus, we know you're not no mad killer or nothing. The lady next door to you, the one with the dog who has all the sweaters, told us you look scary but are sweet as pie," Rennie said.

Elise's eyes closed again as she fought a laugh. It wasn't like Rennie could help it; she was a blurter, much like her grandfather, Elise's father, was. "A mad killer or *anything*, darling. If you're going to insult our neighbor, let's use proper grammar to do so."

Brody's ridiculously big brown eyes danced with amusement.

The way his bottom lip slid against the line of his goatee made her sort of tingly. Sort of? That was a joke. The man had torched a freaking thousand-acre wildfire within her. Perhaps if she hadn't been masturbating to Brody fantasies so much, it wouldn't have made her all achy to just stand there near him. Pathetic.

"That's good to hear. Mrs. Cardini, the lady with the little dog—his name is Stoney, by the way—is a good judge of character. I also think Adrian, my brother, would love a home-cooked meal. Neither one of us is much for cooking. If you'll give me a few minutes, I'll go grab him and be back. That is, if you're sure it's not an imposition."

"No imposition at all. Go on. I'll get started. Oh, I guess I should ask if either of you is a vegetarian. I got sausage for the sauce, but I can make it without."

"Nope, we're both meat eaters. Be back in a few. And thanks again, Elise."

She pretended not to watch his ass when he walked across the street, but hello, the way his waist tapered down to such a spectacular behind, the way it all contrasted with the width of his shoulders and the powerful muscles of his thighs. The whole package was pretty stunning in that bad-boy-with-a-Harley sort of way.

Baby Jesus help her, when he pulled up his shirt, her mouth had actually watered. He had tattoos on his side and belly. His very flat and hard belly. What she could see there and on his wrist looked well thought out. Not a bunch of random stuff. What she saw seemed to have a Far Eastern influence. She wondered what he looked like under the clothes, under all of them. And not just for the tattoos either. He emanated power as he moved. Even when he stood still, the power rolled off him in waves of magnetism.

His eyes were wary and watchful, but once Elise had relaxed, he had too, and a light of amusement had come into them. No wedding ring and no women's names on the tats she could see. And yes, she had totally looked.

In short, he was fascinatingly sexy in a way she'd never really considered before. Rough edges, but the way his voice changed when he spoke of his siblings told her a lot about what he was like inside. He cared about his brother and sister and they clearly cared for him too. A very good sign of character.

A dinner couldn't hurt. She did want to make friends, and the neighborhood seemed rather close. And as Rennie had so helpfully pointed out, Mrs. Cardini had given him the thumbs-up after the ambulance had taken him off to the hospital. He'd brought in her groceries and now her trash cans. It was the neighborly thing to do. To thank him for his help. Her mother would want her to.

"He's kinda cute in his own way," Rennie observed as the two of them moved around the kitchen, pulling out what they'd need for dinner.

Elise laughed. "Sure. And he seems very nice. Why don't you set the table, please. Then you can go out in the back to play if you want."

Rennie finished the table and raced outside with her ball. She'd become obsessed with soccer, so they'd spent the evening before setting up a goal net in the yard.

Elise ran back to her room to freshen up. Just because she wasn't looking for a boyfriend didn't mean she couldn't look nice enough to inspire some wank fantasies for Brody, did it? She touched up with a tiny bit of lip gloss and brushed her hair, only barely resisting the urge to change into a sundress or something. He'd have to live with Capri pants and a sleeveless shirt.

Just as the scent of the sauce had risen enough to make Elise's belly growl, there was a knock on the door. She liked that he didn't just come in. It was locked anyway, but still.

She looked out the window just to the left of the door to make sure it was them, and opened up.

"Come in," she said, stepping back to allow both men to pass.

"I brought some wine and some sparkling water too." Brody handed two bottles to her and turned around to the guy who had to be his brother, and *holy cats*, his brother was Adrian Brown. *The* Adrian Brown currently on her CD player.

"This is my brother, Adrian. Aid, this is Elise Sorenson, and apparently she's already a fan." Brody's crooked smile put her at ease even though she knew her face was bright red.

"I . . . I'm so embarrassed! I didn't know, and I don't know if I should feel bad for not knowing or for having your music on and knowing you by sight. It's not that I've never been around artists before."

Adrian stepped forward and took her hand. He wasn't as large as Brody, but was still tall. He approached slowly, wearing a sexy smile. She wondered if Brody had noticed how freaked she was before and warned his brother.

"You shouldn't feel bad either way. Honestly. I'm flattered you like my music, and I'm really happy you invited us for dinner, especially now that I've smelled the sauce. Only so many bowls of cereal and take-out pizzas a guy can eat. It's nice to meet you, Elise. I've been wanting to thank you for helping my brother out." Christ, but he was charming.

"Of course I helped. I expect he'd have done the same for me. Well, come on through to the kitchen. I think I'll have a glass of wine now." Now that she'd babbled like an idiot.

"Where's your little girl?" Brody asked, looking around as he took the wine bottle from her. His fingers brushed the outside of her hand, just above the thumb, and sent shivers through her.

Time slowed like honey when he met her eyes, and every cell in her body responded. She watched as if in slow motion when his lips parted and his Adam's apple slid up and down as he swallowed.

Adrian cleared his throat, and the scrape of a chair as he pulled it away from the table brought her back to her senses.

"She's, um, out in the backyard. She's doing this soccer day camp thing this summer and loving it. We set up a net so she's kicking goals over and over. Which, well, let's be honest, is awesome for me because it runs her down and there's no three-hour battle to get her to sleep. She's pretty high-energy." She paused and laughed. "That's a nice way of saying she's hyper."

Both men laughed.

Brody held up the corkscrew and the bottle. "Shall I open the wine, then? Is it all right to have a glass in front of Irene? I brought the sparkling water for her if she likes it. Less sugar than soda and stuff."

Wow, he thought of her kid. "Thank you for asking, Brody. Yes, it's fine. I mean, I don't get snockered in her presence or anything, but my parents are European. Drinking wine with dinner is a pretty normal thing for her to see."

She bustled around as he watched her. The place was a surprise. He hadn't gotten a very good look the week before when he'd brought her groceries in. He'd been so focused on her, he hadn't really seen much of the interior.

He'd expected something either super-feminine, with lots of pink, or perhaps very cool and elegant. But the house was warm, with deep, earthy colors, art on the walls, a lot of photographs. It was comfortable, homey.

He handed her a glass of wine and she smiled, thanking him and clinking her glass against his and then Adrian's. "*A votre santé.*"

"To your health," Adrian said back, and she took a sip.

"Very nice. Perfect with the spaghetti." She drained the noodles, pulled out the garlic bread and put them on the table. She leaned out the back door. "Rennie, time to eat. Wash those hands."

Rennie grumbled, but scrambled quickly to obey. She returned shortly, holding her hands out for her mother to inspect.

"Fabulous. Sit now. Rennie, this is Adrian, Brody's brother. Adrian, this is my daughter, Irene."

"Hi there! You're cute. Do you have any girlfriends? 'Cause Gran says Momma needs a man in her life. Then Pops says, 'Pffft, Martine, the last thing Elise needs is a man!' But I think my Gran is right."

"Rennie, for tonight, let's play the think-about-what-we-say-before-we-say-it game."

Adrian tried to hide his smile behind his hands as he and Brody shared a glance. "Nice to meet you, Irene. Or should I call you Rennie?"

"My mom calls me Irene when she's mad. Irene Anne Sorenson when she's really, really mad. But mainly everyone calls me Rennie. Everybody but Gran. Gran calls me Irene 'cause that was her mom's name and she says it's more than good enough for me. Mom says Gran is in a category all her own, so you'll probably want to call me Rennie too." Rennie grinned up at Adrian, and Brody saw that his brother was just as charmed by the Sorenson females as he was. Well, he hoped not *as* charmed, because Elise Sorenson was a woman he didn't want to see his brother with. Selfish though that might be.

Brody took in the efficient way she filled her daughter's plate and then her own. Around that, she passed platters and made sure everyone had enough of everything they needed.

He liked to look at her. She was beautiful in a way he'd never seen up close before. Big, china-blue eyes, pale skin. Probably the type to burn like mad in the sun. Her features were delicate and nearly perfect. But at the same time, despite the outward fragility, she was clearly capable. Her manner with her child was the biggest indicator. A kid like Rennie would take a lot of energy to guide, to not overprotect her but also to give enough space for that sharp little mind to grow and learn. She was a free-spirited child, but not bratty. Keeping that balance, he knew, was difficult.

The long line of Elise's neck called to his fingers. Hard, flat muscle lay over her bones. She wasn't bulked by any stretch of the imagination, but clearly she worked with her body. Yoga maybe?

"This is really delicious." Brody dug in, enjoying every bite.

"Thanks. It's a standby recipe. Easy and fast. Lots of food groups represented." She shrugged. "So what is it you do?"

"I run Written on the Body, a tattoo shop about two miles from here. We know what Adrian does, when he's not clearing my pantry of all food items. What about you?" He looked around and saw the partial answer to how physically fit she was. "I see from the pictures that you dance. Do you do it professionally?"

"I used to. For ten years. I'm just teaching now. I started a studio just north of downtown. I do group classes and some individualized teaching."

"Who did you dance with?"

"The Ballet Theatre. Started in school with them when I was pretty young and landed in the company later on."

Her voice was soft, smooth, without the snags and burrs in his own. He realized he could listen to her for hours without getting bored. The sound of her was as soothing as the sight of her. Just beautiful, elegant lines and tones.

He wanted to ask her more but wondered if there was tragedy there. Had she been injured? Just gotten too old to do it? The life of someone who danced like that on a regular basis would have to be incredibly hard on the body. What if she just wasn't good anymore? That would suck. He didn't know her well enough to push, so he'd let her take the lead in how much she revealed.

"I don't have any tattoos. I've wanted one for some years now, but never got around to doing it. Are you any good?" She leaned forward, amusement showing in the cant of her mouth.

He laughed. "I've been told, yes."

Adrian interrupted, "What he's too humble to say is that he's one of the best tattoo artists in the country. People come from all across the States to get his ink."

Her face lit up. "That's wonderful. What a talented bunch you Browns are. So much artistic expression in one family."

"I'm going to be a painter one day."

Adrian and Brody looked to Rennie. Adrian grinned and asked, "That so? Tell me about it."

"My momma says I have the genes to be a great artist. I like it. But I might be a soccer player too. To have something to fall back on like Pops says. It's good to have something to fall back on."

"Her father was a painter. She comes by it honestly. Or as honestly as it gets for her. I'm totally biased, of course, but I think she's got an amazing eye for color." Elise pointed to a series of small framed paintings. "Those are hers."

Brody stood and examined them. Elise hadn't been bragging. The lines were bold, but the explosion of colors worked well together. He'd never have guessed a child did the work. "How old are you, Rennie?"

"Six years and three months."

He kept his face turned toward the frames so she couldn't see his smile. "Very nice. Your mom was right."

"She did those when she was four. My father had them framed."

"And what do your parents do then, to have spawned such artistic talent?" Adrian asked.

"Please, have more. I made plenty." Elise pushed the platter toward Adrian and Brody snorted. The man had to have a tapeworm
to eat as much as he did and be so damned thin. Elise caught Rennie's eye and nodded. "Yes, you can have an ice-cream sandwich and
watch television. Go on."

Rennie cheered and took her plate into the kitchen before grabbing her treat and scampering into the adjoining family room.

"My mom is a classically trained pianist. She played with the
New York Philharmonic. She's a piano teacher now. She likes to
scare children and boss people around. It's a gift." Elise shrugged.
"My father is a professor emeritus at CUNY Albany. Poetry and
literature. He just likes to be worshipped by young people." She
spoke with affection rather than sharpness or bitterness.

"Any siblings?"

"I had a younger brother who died five years ago."

"I'm sorry." Adrian shoved half a piece of garlic bread in his
mouth, and suddenly Brody felt like the father of a wayward teenage boy.

Manners must have held back any look of horror and disgust at
the way Adrian ate. Brody realized, not for the first time, that it
was a good thing Adrian was so handsome and talented. Rock stars
could eat like they hadn't seen food or utensils ever before.

Instead, Elise simply said, "I'm glad you like the bread. There's
more if you like." She said nothing else about her brother, and
Brody noticed she'd mentioned Rennie's father in the past tense, so
she must be a widow.

"Enough about me. What about you two? You have a tattoo shop
and your brother and sister have music careers. What else?"

"Parents died when I was eleven," Adrian answered. "Brody was
just ready to finish high school and start art school. Instead he got a

full-time job, finished high school around that and raised me and Erin. My parents instilled a love of art and music in us early on. Erin picked up a guitar when she was Rennie's age. I wanted to be like her, so I did too. You couldn't keep Erin off a stage, for a long time anyway." Adrian's voice went very soft, and Elise reached out to touch his hand.

"I remember the news reports about the kidnapping and the death of her daughter. I can't imagine what she went through." She looked through the open archway, toward her daughter, and Brody's insides tightened. He didn't want to examine his reactions to her very closely. Something about the beautiful widow Sorenson left him off balance.

"And now here you all are. It's nice that you're all in the same city." She looked back to Brody. "That's a testament to you, I think. It had to be hard at your age."

He shrugged. "It was what needed to be done. I did it. I love them, they needed me."

Her smile melted as she cocked her head. "Aren't a whole lot of men like you. Too bad."

"All the more of me to share." He grinned and shrugged.

She laughed, the sound delightful. He *liked* her. His other neighbors he enjoyed, some he tolerated, some he disliked, but he didn't really seek out any of them to hang with. It didn't hurt that she wasn't a chore to look at either.

He and Adrian hung out for another hour or so before standing to leave. Rennie had gone upstairs, and Adrian scampered quickly back to Brody's place, leaving Elise alone with Brody on her porch.

"Thank you for dinner."

She smiled up at him. "Thank you for coming to dinner. It was nice, having company. Rennie had a great time too."

He stepped closer as they stood in the shadows, a broad column near the steps shrouding them from the street. "Elise, I think I'm going to have to kiss you because I can't stop thinking about it."

She blinked up at him and nodded. "I think you should."

He wanted to lay her out on the grass, the stars above, the scent of lilacs heavy around them. Wanted to kiss her long and slow for hours, until he could do nothing more but slide into her body as she welcomed him.

But that was not going to happen. Not that night, at least.

Instead, he bent his knees as she tiptoed up. With no more than fingertips cupping her chin, he leaned down those last glorious inches and took her lips with his own. He'd meant to slide into it, to take it slow and give her a sweet smooch.

Instead, the moment her taste met his lips, a fire banked within him. He needed more and settled in, coaxing her mouth open, sliding his tongue along hers, only barely resisting his desire to cup one of her breasts, though his palm felt the phantom press of a wanton nipple.

Her breath chased her tongue into his mouth, her hands, small and soft, lay palm open on his chest. So fucking good, the kiss was so good he wanted to do it for hours and hours. Instead, he heard Rennie call her mother's name and she stiffened.

He stepped back with great regret. "Thank you again, Elise. Good night."

She nodded, looking sort of stunned. Which was good, because it meant he wasn't the only one feeling totally punched in the gut by desire. He walked down her steps and waved, catching her eye as she went back inside. She smiled, returning the wave, and then closed the door.

On his porch he turned and looked toward her place. The front windows were open, and he saw through to her stairs, where she jogged up, smiling, clearly talking back and forth with her daughter. The sight brought a lump to his throat.

"I like her. She likes you too." Adrian nudged the screen door open with the toe of his sneaker.

"She's so not our type." Didn't matter one bit to his cock, though.

"*Our?* I don't share women. Most certainly not with my brother. Anyway, she didn't look at me that way. She looked at *you* that way. I'd totally make a run on the very lovely Elise, but I figure you'd hurt me if I tried. Even when you're trying to pretend you didn't just totally make out with her on her porch." The look Adrian sent him made Brody want to laugh. Instead he rolled his eyes as his brother shooed him out of the way and locked up. "Call Erin. I'm going to take a shower."

Adrian strolled from the room and Brody realized that would be the end of his hot water for at least forty-five minutes.

"You have a fucking mansion! You're here eating my food and using my hot water!"

"You love it," came the faint, amused reply.

He grumbled the entire time he dialed Erin's number. Smiling.

Elise sat on her porch and read. It had been a very long while since she'd had the time and inclination to do it, but her life was different, better now, and she'd vowed to enjoy the quiet moments more than she ever had before.

Rennie was across the street two doors down, helping Mrs. Cardini. Elise's daughter and the neighborhood matriarch had created a bond. Rennie loved the elderly woman and that dog of hers. The three were currently pulling weeds, drinking lemonade and having a grand time. Elise knew she could trust Mrs. Cardini with her daughter; she'd visited enough with the woman herself to know she'd raised six sons, four of whom lived within a two-mile radius. But it was hard to let go, and Rennie could be a handful, so she gave them some space but kept close enough to intervene if a problem developed.

"I see Rennie has joined forces with Mrs. Cardini. Everyone better really watch out now."

Brody.

Elise put her book aside and looked up at the man who'd spoken. "Hello, Brody Brown. Yes, Rennie and Mrs. Cardini are pretty much the exact same person, only at different stages of life. I think they'll keep each other out of trouble."

He sat next to her on the porch swing and they both looked across the street. "You hope, anyway. But just in case, you're keeping an eye to be sure."

"Busted. I'm not judging or anything. Please don't think that. I know Rennie is fine and all. I just like to be around in case I'm needed."

He took her hand like it was the most normal thing in the world, instead of something that sent threads of pleasure through her each time his thumb slid over the sensitive skin at her wrist.

"I didn't think you were. First, it seems to me you're the kind of mom who wouldn't just let her kid go off with anyone she didn't trust. But also because it seems to me you take care of people. Mrs. Cardini is lonely; she gets just as much out of time spent with Rennie as Rennie does being with her."

It turned her stomach upside down to hear such praise from him.

"That's not good mothering, that's just basic parenting."

He bent his head, pressing a kiss to her wrist, and she drew in breath. Which didn't help because it was breath filled with the scent of him. He was so big, took up so much space. She should pull her hand away, should stand and break this contact before he dug into her life any deeper, before this need of him got out of control and she did something stupid.

Instead, she drew her fingertip along the shell of his ear and he shivered.

"I wish it wasn't full daylight. I wish we were alone," he murmured as he continued to hold her hand, slowly rocking the swing back and forth as he kept an eye on the street.

She wished it too, but knew wishes were something entirely apart from reality. He was more than she could handle. Even if she wanted, very badly, to handle him. Out of her league.

"School starts soon," he said, not commenting further on the previous statement.

"Yep. Hard to believe she's going to be in first grade." Like every mother, Elise felt as if the years had just flown by. One day she'd brought home a pink bundle from the hospital, and now that baby was outgrowing her shoes every few months and was going to be a first-grader.

She'd have time alone, more than she'd ever had before, even if it would be filled, more often than not, with work. Maybe even some time to sneak in a man here and there. Have some connection to someone that wasn't about parenting or work.

Admittedly, part of what attracted her so deeply to Brody was being seen as a woman, as a sexual being, by a man to whom she was attracted right back.

"I haven't stopped thinking about kissing you. One taste and I'm jonesing." He grinned, and it did all sorts of crazy to her belly. And other parts. God, this was dangerous, and so hot it made her want to throw caution to the wind and invite him inside.

"I haven't stopped thinking about it either." She shrugged. No point in lying about it.

"So, what are we going to do about that?"

Before she could answer, Rennie looked over and saw them. "Momma! Brody! Come over and see the flower bed."

Well now, that brought the fantasy in her head to a screeching halt. The man would probably run the other way now. She stood, waving back at Rennie. "On my way."

"I'll come as well." Brody stood and they began to walk toward Mrs. Cardini's.

"Sorry about that." She laughed.

"Never apologize for being a connected mom. It's your job. I knew we weren't going to go at it on your porch in broad daylight." He winked.

6

Elise bent and stretched, placing her palms flat on the floor. Stretching felt like meditation sometimes. Her body knew it so well, knew the movements, the positions, the limits of her range, she simply fell into the routine, like breathing. As she stretched, warmed up, she pushed away all the things on her to-do list—the new toe shoes she needed to order, the people she needed to call, the squeaky door on one of the lockers she needed to grease. It all fell away.

She put Goldfrapp's *Black Cherry* album on and began to move, letting the music take over as she spotted her first pirouette, and round again. Stepping back, she noted the lack of pull in her calves and noted it gladly.

It wasn't until she'd moved to *fouetté en tournant* that she noticed him standing in the doorway, watching.

Smiling and pleasantly surprised, she stopped and turned the music off. "Hi, I didn't expect to see you here. Is everything all right?" They'd left a lot unsaid the last few times they'd seen each other.

Brody cocked his head at her. "Wow. You're totally amazing. I've never seen anything like those twirly things you were doing just now."

Pride warmed her. She'd worked hard to get where she'd been before the whole thing with Ken. Most of her life had been spent in ballet class; she never regretted that time and dedication like some others had. She loved dancing and missed it a great deal, but this new stage wasn't all that bad. The feedback was nice, she had to admit.

"Thank you. That's called *fouetté en tournant.* Ballet moves are French so they sound awesome and graceful. *Fouetté* means 'whipped,' by the way." She laughed. "It's the whipping motion of the leg that propels the body into the turn."

"Ah, makes sense then. It sounds—and looks—pretty complicated. Speaking of looking pretty complicated, I looked around when I first got here. When you said you'd danced for the National Ballet Theatre, I hadn't guessed what that meant. Not really. You weren't a dancer there, you were *the* dancer there. I'm incredibly impressed."

A hated blush heated her cheeks. "Not *the* dancer. I was a principal dancer. There were two other female principals when I was with the NBT. I worked my way up over the years."

"Do you miss it?"

She paused. "Sometimes more than I want to. Brody, not that I'm unhappy to see you. I mean, look at yourself. Any woman with eyes would be happy to look up and get a load of Brody Brown standing in her doorway. But, why are you here?"

Brody looked down at her, this small woman with more muscle and balance than he'd ever imagined, a hand on her hip, staring down a man nearly a foot taller than she. She was surprisingly blunt, a quality he very much enjoyed. Still, he wasn't quite ready to say he couldn't stop thinking of her and had sought her out.

"I was at my bank. It's just a few blocks away. I go to this little Indian place for lunch afterward. Like a little ritual, I suppose. Anyway, I was there, eating way too much naan, when I looked up and saw your name on the door across the street. I wandered in, came up the stairs, looked at the photographs of you in all that ballet tutu stuff, realized you were like some ballet superstar. When I walked through and saw you, I just watched for a bit. I hope you don't mind."

She had all that glorious, pale blonde hair twisted into a high bun. Her graceful neck was exposed, set off by the straps of the leotard she wore. His hands twitched with the need to brush fingertips over the edge of her collarbone. She wasn't wearing a tutu or a skirt. He'd sort of been expecting that. Instead she wore a leotard with longer shorts over it and the prettiest shoes—toe shoes he figured, with the way they laced around her ankles. All that strength in such an elegant package. He found himself impressed and yet put off by it. She was culture and classical music, and he . . . was not.

"No, of course I don't mind. I had a morning class. It's a small one, but serious. These students are very good. I'm lucky to have them. I came to Seattle at the right time. A school closed and two of the preeminent teachers here have retired. My old dance partner at NBT, his mother was one of those teachers. I inherited many of her students."

"I imagine your history helps too. Can't be too many principal dancers offering classes."

She laughed. "Well, we dancers don't like to just walk away if we don't have to. I don't want to stop dancing. I just can't do it at the level I had before. So this is a wonderful opportunity for me. And yes, it helps that I was at the level I was when I . . . retired."

The weight of all they left unsaid hung between them. "Will

you dance for me? I've only seen *The Nutcracker*. My mom, she took us every year. I didn't see much of you when I came in."

"I'm not . . . not what I was in those pictures. My right leg was broken in two places. I'm older now. I'm not her anymore."

He stepped closer, so close she scented the soap he'd used that morning. "You're you. Please. I'd very much like to see you dance."

She paused, taking his measure. "All right. You can sit over there if you like. How about something a little nontraditional? Before I left, one of the choreographers did something for me. It's one of my favorite pieces."

"I'd like that."

She moved away and he settled into a nearby chair. She bent in half, and he had a brief but very vivid image of bending her over just that way and sliding his cock into her from behind. Christ, the woman did things to his mind.

But when she hit the remote and moved into position, and a few moments later Tito Puente came through the speakers, he was a goner.

Shoulders rolling, she moved slowly, sensuously, across the hardwood floors. She opened herself up to the music, to the movements, until it was all one thing. Like breathing. She was the dance. The beat was cha-cha, so the choreography was all about sensuality, grace, balance and movements from the toes up. So many times every day she failed to find the words, but when she moved she didn't need words, she spoke with her body.

His eyes on her were a brand. The tension between them was taut, exciting. She felt him watch her, his gaze a heated caress of her neck, her arms. In his eyes, she felt beautiful and sexy. Elise was, right then, a siren, a seductress with her body and her grace. It was rare to feel that anymore, and the confidence of it roared through her. She knew her leaps were beautiful, her grand jetés precise and her pirouettes spot-on. Part of her wanted him to see how good she was, wanted him to realize she was more than a broken dancer who'd run from the spotlight, but a dancer who'd held it for good reason for many years.

It burned within her, that recognition, that beauty, until she stepped back on her left foot, rolling her shoulders to set her head when the music died.

Time slid by as she stood tall and met his gaze. Silence, thick, charged, hung between them. Everything unsaid, everything said and done, it was all there in his gaze, in the one she returned. Oh, how she wanted this man. He simply continued to watch her without speaking. He stared for so long, she wondered if she'd misinterpreted those looks from him as she danced.

"I've never seen anything like you before." He moved to her slowly, not gracefully; he was too big for that. But enough to let her step back or run. The heat in his eyes, the memory of his lips on her wrist, of his taste on her tongue, held her there, rooted to the spot.

"Is that a good thing, or a bad thing?"

"To be honest with you, Elise, I don't know. Here's what I do know. I can't stop thinking about you. Thinking about those kisses we shared, about the way your pulse at your wrist beat against my lips. The hollow of your throat." He drew a fingertip over that very sensitive skin and she drew in a shaky breath. "The way you smell. Christ, so feminine. Not flowery, not vanilla, but so female. Drives me crazy." He leaned in and took a deep breath, his lips hovering just above her shoulder.

"I probably smell like female sweat just now." She tried to joke, but his nearness put her on edge. Not with fear but with desire, with wanting things she'd never imagined she'd want. Of wanting him to give her exactly what he said he wanted to deliver. Of wanting him to *take*.

"You smell so fucking good, I want to take a big bite. I want to lick you from the tips of your toes to the tops of your ears."

His words left her gaping like a goldfish in a bowl. She gave in to the feelings, let go and let her fingers thread through that thick hair of his. It was softer than she'd imagined. The strength of him under her hands, as he bent to her, sent a tremor through her. Oh, she wanted this, wanted the power of his body against hers, sliding skin to skin.

"I want you, Elise, and I think you want me too. No. I know you do. I can see it there in your eyes. I tasted it on your skin."

She nodded as he stood back, straightening. His hands remained at her waist, the heat of him, the weight a reminder of what they could have.

"We're friends now, right?"

"Yes."

"You're busy, I'm busy, but I want you so much it drives me to distraction." So much he'd found himself at the bank on a non-banking day. Made himself go to the little restaurant so he could look at the door to her studio. Finally let go of what he should do and let himself go to her.

What a surprise Elise Sorenson was. Not just any ballerina but a principal dancer. The pictures and news clippings he'd seen on her walls as he'd climbed the stairs, the prestige of what she'd been and accomplished, hadn't really come as that much of a shock. Despite her size, he was quite convinced she was a strong and driven person. But when she danced she was magic.

He was nearly forty; he'd seen a lot in his life, had done a lot. Until he'd met Elise, he'd been quite sure nothing could surprise him anymore. Until she kissed him back on her porch that night after dinner. Until she'd moaned, just a whisper of sound as he'd done it.

Until he'd seen her dance for him just moments before. He'd never paid much attention to ballet. He didn't hate it or think it was too froufrou; he realized it was incredibly difficult. He'd just never taken much interest. But the strength she emanated, the grace and fluidity, it was achingly beautiful and keenly athletic all at once. And it made his want for her simply unbearable. That one person could move with such utter confidence of grace and timing simply shook him. He didn't quite know why it touched him so deeply, moved him so, but as he'd watched her, the need had crawled over his skin.

"And?"

"We have chemistry, Elise. We fit. Given the way I nearly came just from kissing you for five minutes, I think we should expand our friendship to friends who have sex."

She was silent, chewing her bottom lip until he began to think he probably shouldn't have said a damned thing.

She met his gaze without blinking. Nodding. "I agree."

Oh. Well, he . . . All right then. He raised his hand to touch her, but she caught it, halting his movement, but keeping her hand on his.

"I have some ground rules."

He grinned. "I promise to make you come every time."

She laughed, her blue eyes dancing with a light he hadn't seen before. It was then he knew for certain they'd be dynamite in bed.

"That should go without saying. My rules are that you can't sleep over. I'm sorry but I really need stability in Rennie's life. I won't be dating for a while yet and I don't want to have men overnight to confuse her. And if we do this, I'm the only one you sleep with. I realize you're not offering me your frat pin or anything, but I want to be careful, and frankly, I think I deserve that one nod to fidelity."

He'd never let on that he found her so fucking cute when she got demanding, or that he hadn't wanted another woman since he'd felt the touch of her fingers on his cheek that day he'd been hit. He'd been with a lot of women, but he couldn't seem to recall a time when he'd wanted a woman more than he did Elise. Plus, it certainly wouldn't be a chore to fuck her and only her as long as they had this little arrangement.

"I agree to both conditions. I respect your putting your kid first and I respect you too."

"I don't have another class for two hours. What I do have is a very large couch in my office and a door downstairs that locks."

And yet more surprises from her. Boldly sexual too. "I'll be back in a sec." He dashed downstairs, flipped the sign to closed and locked the door.

She called after him, "Don't break anything! Those stairs are steep and I'm not going anywhere."

He stalked to her, burning for her now that he'd been freed to touch. "Neither is my need for you. Come here. I've been wanting to kiss you since about thirty seconds after the last time."

She went to her toes on those glorious satin shoes and took the kiss he offered. Her mouth was sweet, just as he'd remembered, but the need there was a stronger flavor. It met his own, challenged his own, tested the limits on his control.

Her arms around his neck were strong and sure and held him in place against her lithe body as she squirmed to get closer. This artlessness, the sort of innocent need she showed as she clung to him, surprised him as much as her total confidence of movement when she danced. What a package of contradictions and layers she was. How utterly delightful.

"I want to lay you out and reveal you inch by inch," he gasped, pulling his mouth from hers.

She took his hand and led him down a side hallway and through a door at the end. Her office held a large desk, a big, cushy couch and lots of windows high up on the walls so the room was filled with light but held privacy.

"I want to see you," he murmured as he slid a strap of her leotard from one shoulder, kissing the spot he'd exposed.

"I'm . . . I've been dancing. I'm sweaty . . . Oh god that's . . ." Her head dropped back as he swirled his tongue across her shoulder and to the spot where it became her neck. Her breast, small, pert, fit perfectly in his hand, her nipple pressing against his palm like he'd pictured a thousand times since he'd met her.

"Stop it. I'm licking you right now and you taste salty-sweet. That's my favorite flavor combo. Chocolate-covered pretzels, popcorn and M&M's. Elise Sorenson. I love it and I can't wait to lick more."

She exhaled, shaky and with a tense groan behind it. He simply looked at her upper body when he pulled the top of the leotard down around her waist, exposing all that pale, creamy skin, the acres of toned muscle, the shape of each beautiful breast capped with a pale pink nipple.

Unable to resist, he leaned down and licked over one and then the other. He picked her up, placing her cute ass down on her desk. "That's better. How flexible are you, Elise?"

Giddiness flushed Elise's system. Her actions this entire morning had been totally unlike her. How wonderful to be a woman she'd never imagined being! *In a positive way, for a change.* In reply to his question, she swung her leg up, the tip of her shoe near his shoulder.

"Very."

"You're going to kill me, but it'll be worth it." He groaned and took her ankle in his hand, wrapping strong fingers around it. "These shoes are very sexy, but they need to be off so I can finish getting you naked." He paused, looking. "Where's the tie?"

She laughed and moved so her leg was bent, foot in her lap. "A dancer's bane is the way the ribbons on toe shoes come undone all the time. If I were performing I'd go as far as to sew the knot in place, but today I just used a clear Band-Aid." He bent and watched while she quickly peeled the bandage off, untucked the knot and loosened it to take off one and then the other toe shoe. She hoped he was impressed with the rest of her because a dancer's feet were anything but pretty.

He was there again, standing between her thighs as he pulled her shorts down and off and the leotard followed, until all she had left were her tights. The air of the room was cool, but heat rolled from him, blanketing her as she leaned forward to press her face against his chest.

The muscles in his sides jumped as she slid her hands under the edge of his shirt. He was warm and hard, and suddenly she needed to see him so badly it hurt.

"You're too tall this way. I can't reach you."

He simply picked her up, and she knelt on the top of the desk, peeling his shirt off, exposing his upper body. She studied him for long moments, taking in the hard muscle, the twist and curl of ink, the silver barbell in his left nipple.

"You're making me nervous," he said, sounding a bit agitated, so she smiled at him.

"You're gorgeous. I can't decide what I want to touch first. But I want to touch it all." She traced along a spectacular dragon, from the swirl of a tail around his belly button up to the head that took up his entire shoulder.

He closed his eyes a moment as his vision swam. Her hands on him, her eyes greedily taking in the sight of his body, did something to him. Damn it, made him even harder—if that was possible.

"Touch whatever you want." He shivered when she brushed her fingertips over his nipple and the bar.

"Did I hurt you?" She started to draw back, but he took her wrist and put her hand where it had been.

"Not at all. Your hands on me feel good. I want more."

That's when she licked from his belly button to the barbell and he saw stars. Like he'd never had sex before. And then she said, "You taste yummy. Thank God I'm not on a diet."

"Christ." He pulled the tights down her legs until she lay back on the desk, spread out there like a sweet treat. So petite and perfect and ready. He saw the glistening lips of her cunt, smelled her on the air. He wanted more.

She wailed when he dropped to his knees. "Wait, no! Your pants off."

"If I take my pants off, I'll want to shove my cock into you until we succeed in knocking everything from the surface of this desk. I want to do this first." He spread her thighs as he pulled her toward his mouth and latched on.

She hissed an appreciative sound, followed by an entreaty. But her taste drowned him and he surrendered to it. So sweet and unique. He took a long lick, swirling his tongue to catch her honey and take it in. Her moan in response was low and throaty, such a contrast to the soft sweetness of her voice.

Her body writhed beneath him, responding head to toe to his touch. The triumph of that, of bringing pleasure to this woman, rang through him. He wanted more of her, wanted her climax and then many more. He wanted to lose himself in her for hours on end. Nothing else mattered then but her, but the two of them.

She cried out, the hands buried in his hair yanking tight as she came on his tongue, a climax so beautiful he felt it low in his gut with each sobbed wave of her release. He fell then. He just wouldn't know it until later, until it was far too late to turn back.

He stood, toeing his boots off as she sat up. "Let me," she said, hopping down, her hands going to his belt and then the button and zipper of his jeans. "Your body is so sexy. So beautiful." She pressed a kiss to his side. "I've never wanted a man like you before. You're overwhelming."

She pulled his jeans down as he tried to puzzle over what she'd just told him. Should he be offended? Why, when he felt the same? His women had tended to be big and bold, tatted and pierced. They inhabited his world. This woman was not that on any level, and yet, beneath the exterior, he definitely felt a sort of kinship with her.

She nipped at his belly button and caressed his thighs and calves as she helped him from his jeans, boxers and socks.

"This is very, um, impressive," she said of his cock, and he was the one who blushed for a change.

"Thank you," he said, laughing.

A laugh that died when she angled toward him and licked across the head. Dear sweet god in heaven, her mouth was right. Hot and wet and eagerly sucking him. His balls crawled up close to his body, and he grabbed the back of the chair behind him to keep from tearing her hair free of that perfect bun and fucking her mouth.

The way she held him, held his cock gently, told him a lot. The caveman who lived in his gut liked that she didn't seem super experienced. Obviously enough to have had a child, and she knew her way around a blow job. But she didn't venture away from his sac or gobble him down to the root or anything. A stupid thing to be pleased about, he realized, but there it was.

"You have to stop," he said around clenched teeth, "or I will come in your mouth, and I want to be inside you when that happens."

She pulled back and stood up, running her hands all over his torso, and yes, she made him feel desired and attractive in a way that made him want to puff out his chest and strut around. It was then he remembered the condom thing.

"Shit." He bent and grabbed his pants, pulling out his wallet. "Please let there be a condom in here," he mumbled, and a startled laugh bubbled from her.

He pulled out a lone condom, checked the expiration date and breathed a sigh of relief. He'd need to make a donation somewhere that afternoon when he left, to thank the universe for that luck.

One-handed, he rolled the condom on before drawing her to the couch where he'd first sat. "You can control everything this way," he explained and she scrambled onto his lap.

"It's okay if you say something about the size of your equipment. I know I'm petite. But at the risk of sounding like a line from a bad romance novel, I'm pretty sure you'll fit."

He reached between her thighs and slid his fingers up into her gate, stretching her a bit. "You're still so wet and hot."

"I want another part of you in there." She moved his hand and replaced it with the head of his cock as she rose up on those powerful thighs and then fell inch, by slow inch, surrounding him with heat and tightness that stole his breath.

"I don't want to hurt you," he managed to say, fighting the nearly overwhelming need to slam his cock into her, balls-deep. "Are you all right?"

"I'm *more* than all right. I'm not in pain—well, a good kind of *full*. It's just been a while. But everyone should break their fast with something this good." She opened eyes that had been half-lidded, and he felt that zing between them. "No one should be as pretty as you are."

She settled with his cock in her body totally. Elise had to admit she liked the look of strain on his face, liked knowing he was as on the edge as she. She hadn't felt so good in a very long time. Years.

Leaning backward, she braced her hands on his thighs, just above his knees, and began to slide up and down his cock, slowly at first, as her body got used to him and because it felt too good to rush.

"No one has ever said I was pretty before. Should I be offended?" He wore a grin so cocky it should have been illegal. Instead it just added to his overall sexual appeal.

"You're stunning. The tattoos, the wary eyes, the messy hair, those broad shoulders—it all works in a way I find quite unexpectedly hot. And yes, pretty, but in a manly way, of course."

"Pretty can't hold a candle to what I'm looking at. Watching my cock disappear into you over and over, coming out all shiny with your juices. You're so long and lithe for someone so petite. All that gorgeous pale skin." He skimmed his palms up her belly and cupped her breasts. "These are, Christ, they're lovely."

She blushed, there was no way to hide it. "They're very small. Men usually like big breasts."

"Yes, yes, like that. Oh, that's sweet," he ground out as she rolled her hips once she'd taken him inside totally. The length of his cock stroked over her clit when she did it that way. "Men like breasts. Period. Full stop. Yours are pert, your nipples stand up so nicely." To emphasize that, he dragged his thumbs over them, bringing a gasping cry from her. "I also like that you make noise. That's hot."

She bit her lip and levered herself forward to change the angle and increase her speed. Above him, she looked down into his face before lowering to kiss him, tasting herself on his lips. A groan came from deep inside when his thumb, one that had been teasing her left nipple just moments before, found her clit, stroking from side to side just as he had with her nipple.

Sensation rose within and she knew he'd make her come again. He swallowed every sound she made as he played over her clit and began to thrust up to meet her body as she slid down. So good, so damned good.

She tore her mouth away as she climaxed and he nipped her bottom lip. The sting washed through her, sharpening the pleasure as her body clamped down around his cock. Two orgasms in one session? Clearly she'd made the right choice when she'd agreed to this *friends with benefits* situation.

"Yeah, motherfuck, yes." He thrust up hard and deep and held her there. Within her body, she felt his cock jerk as he came; she watched his face, the tightening of his glorious mouth and then the total relaxation as he exhaled long and slow.

7

"Hey there, Rennie! Where are you off to all dressed up?"

Rennie, ever pleased with attention to her clothing choices, turned to face Brody with a wide smile. "Hi, Brody! It's the first day of school. Do you like my new dress? We got it last weekend." She twirled to show the full effect and Brody clapped. Elise smiled at him too. How could she not?

"I like it very much. That's the same color as your eyes. What grade are you starting today?" he asked, knowing full well it was the first grade because he and Elise had discussed it before.

"First. My teacher is a Mister!" Rennie's eyes widened at the very idea of a male teacher. Sometimes, at moments like this one, Elise just wanted to hold her daughter and soak up all that wonderful and never let go.

"Wow. What's his name?" Brody had moved to a crouch so he could see eye to eye with Rennie.

"Mr. Alexander. He was nice at the orientation. He kept looking at Momma."

Brody's lips quivered a bit as he stifled a smile. "Well, she's awful pretty to look at. I can't blame him."

Oh good lord. "Yes, well. Time to go," Elise said. "We've got to get going if we're going to get there on time. We have all these bags of supplies to take, so we want to be early to get it all unloaded."

Brody stood. "You guys walking?"

"The school is three blocks away, it's a sunny day. I figured it would be good to do it while we could."

"True." His eyes were shaded by dark glasses, but she knew amusement lit them. He was a funny man, easily led to laugh or smile. They'd begun their sexual relationship just two weeks prior and had been able to meet only once more for another round of ridiculously hot sex. But they'd chatted many times in passing, and he'd seen her struggling with the bark and had come over, spending a good two hours helping her haul the bags and spread it.

"I'll see you later." The soul of a fifteen-year-old girl inhabited her body suddenly as a wave of giddiness hit her.

"I'll be around for another hour or so," he said quietly before he turned back to Rennie. "Have a great first day."

"Thank you! Come on, Momma." Rennie tugged on her hand and she laughed, walking alongside her daughter, while Rennie skipped and chattered about school. All around the neighborhood, other parents were walking their young children toward the school, and the feeling of community and common purpose made her warm inside.

As it happened, one of the little neighbor kids was also in Rennie's class, and they became fast friends on the short walk. The girl's mother was nice enough, full of curious but friendly questions, and Elise answered them as they walked.

The little desks were different from the tables of kindergarten, and with a pang, Elise realized how fast the time was passing. She helped Rennie label things and put them in their proper place, all the while wrestling the bittersweetness of the moment.

"Bye, Momma. See you at three." Rennie hugged her, gave her a kiss and sat back down, happily chatting with the kids to either side, and with that, Elise was dismissed.

Brody had watched them walk away in the morning sun. The pale-moonlight hair of the mother, drawn up into a ponytail, and the more golden blond of the daughter in her little first-day-of-school dress.

He'd seen the look on Elise's face as she watched Rennie tell him all about school. His parents had been a lot older when they had kids. Brody had been the one who walked Erin and then Adrian to school for their first day each year until they were too old to need the escort. Sometimes he saw Erin so much in Rennie that it made him want to grab his phone and call to check in with his sister.

All thoughts of anyone either young or related to him flew out of his head when the knock came at his door.

"Morning." He dipped his head to grab a kiss when she walked through his front door.

He liked the way she craned her neck to look at him better, licking her lips. "Mmm, morning. You taste like coffee."

"You can have some when I'm finished with you."

She dropped her bag and took his hand. "Finished, hmm? You have plans for my body?"

"Oh yes, yes I do."

"All right then. Do me."

The last two times they'd been together it had been at her studio. Now he had his bed and an hour. More than an hour, since he really didn't have to be at the shop until ten. There was a lot a man could do with a fresh box of condoms, an hour and a big bed with a beautiful woman lying on it.

"I like it." She looked around the room as she unbuttoned the front of her dress and stepped out of it, naked but for tiny panties. The morning light through the filmy curtains glowed off her skin.

"I like that." He indicated the beauty of her body.

"Now you." She tipped her chin at him and began to work on his belt and the button and zipper on his jeans.

Grinning, he pulled his shirt off and took over getting naked as he moved toward the bed. But she put a hand out to stop him. "Wait, I want to really look at you." He shivered at her touch as she traced over the firebird on his back, up the line of his spine where her lips pressed a kiss. "Who does this for you? Obviously you can't do your own back tattoo." She ducked around him and kissed his belly, sliding her palms up, exploring his body.

"I don't do any of my own tats. I'm not that much of a control freak, no matter what Erin says. I have a friend in Portland. He and I trade services. I do his work, he does mine. Works out that he's really good."

She tiptoed up and licked over his nipple, the one with the ring.

"Not as good as you though?"

He liked the shape of her smile, liked that she was relaxed enough to tease.

"Well, not everyone can be as good as me." He laughed. "But he's good."

"If I decide to get a tattoo, would you do it for me?"

He paused, touched. "I'd be honored to do it."

He picked her up and she wrapped herself around him, bringing her nakedness up against his. Christ, that felt good. One-handed, she reached up to pull her hair free of the ponytail, and a shower of soft, pale hair cascaded down her back and over her shoulders. He hadn't seen it down until that moment; it softened her, tousled her just enough that the need pulled at him even more.

He lay her back on the bed, crouched above her as he took her in. "You're so fucking beautiful." He meant it. Her nipples pressed toward him and he dipped to lick across one, delighting in her soft sound of desire.

She arched up into his touch, her fingertips digging into the muscle of his biceps. He cruised over to the other breast, licking and nibbling there until she began to writhe in earnest. Her scent, rich and spicy, painted the air between them.

The muscles in her belly jumped as he licked his way down, past her ribs, past her belly button, past the scar marking the birth of her child. Everything about her outside was soft. Her skin was soft and sweet, her taste, everywhere but her cunt, was sweet as well. Here, he thought as he slid his tongue through the slick furls of her pussy, here she was spice and tang. Here the muscles of her thighs might have trembled when he licked over her clit, but there was strength and resilience.

He could see, like the aftereffects of a camera flash, the ink on her skin. Starting at her hip bones and curling around her back, up her spine. Roses and ivy, strong and feminine, soft and thorny. He'd love to do her inkwork.

Right then, though, he wanted to make her come and then fuck her. And make her come again. Her taste was a lure, the feel of her against his tongue, filling him with sensation clearly all her. She was everything he felt just then.

Elise dragged in one breath after the other as she struggled not to drown in everything Brody Brown was. She liked sex, especially oral sex but Ken hadn't been that crazy about doing it and as a result, wasn't that good at it. But even a bad blow job was better than most things, so she'd been happy when he overcame his reluctance and did it.

But *this* man loved pussy. He loved his mouth there, doing all those deliciously wicked things, and it showed. She felt it straight to her toes. He owned his intensity in a quiet way. He was so . . . in charge and yummy.

Each time his tongue dragged down and speared up into her gate, she shattered just a little bit more. Slipped down toward climax inch by inch, and then he'd move back to her clit and make her work to get back there all over again.

Until he tried it again, and she grabbed two handfuls of his hair and hauled him back to her clit with an insistent sort of moan. He chuckled against her skin, sending shocks of pleasure through her, but kept at it. Thank God.

And it hit. Hard and without surcease. She came and came and then she came some more, until her muscles were fluid and warm and she just sort of twitched and sighed in its aftermath.

"Do the words 'reverse cowgirl' mean anything to you?" he asked, that deep-velvet voice pulling her back from that quiet, pleasurable place she'd been floating in.

She smiled and got to her knees, watching as he put a condom on, and she realized he could make anything look sexy. "I think I can figure it out. Are you an ass man, Brody?"

One of his brows winged up and he grinned. "I like the line of your back as well as your ass. But I like that I can lay here and watch you in that mirror over my dresser too."

She looked up then, saw herself and blushed at how disheveled and sexed up she looked.

"Stop that. You look hot. Now, I'm here all alone. You wanna keep me company?"

She straddled his hips and angled him to meet her body as she slid down. His entry hit lots of lovely spots within her and she sighed, happily full.

"Open your eyes, Elise. Look at how beautiful you are as you fuck yourself onto me."

She did, mainly because he told her to and his tone had tightened her nipples. But once she had, she couldn't tear her eyes away from the sight of his cock disappearing into her body over and over. His hands looked so large as they lay against her hip bones, his skin tone olive to her pale—the contrast striking.

Her hair had grown a lot over the past two years, and she felt the cool tickle of it against her lower back. She tipped her head back, arching, taking him deeper, knowing too that the tips of her hair brushed against his lower belly.

He made her feel like the sexiest woman in the universe, bold enough to look at herself in the mirror and hold her gaze there. She still liked her body; she looked good for her age, fit, even as parts of her were broken down.

But the way he looked at her made her feel like a movie star.

She straightened and inched forward, experimenting with her range of movement to keep him within her while she moved. His hands on her hips tightened, so she supposed he liked what she was doing with the small swivel of her hips as she slid back, her body taking his cock deep each time she moved all the way back.

"Touch my balls," he groaned, and she did. Experimenting with holding them, still sticky and warm from her own juices as she'd been on top of him. To judge her progress, she listened to his breathing and the sounds he was making. "Yes, that's nice." He groaned when she ran the edge of her nails across the skin of his sac ever so gently.

She wanted to know more. Wanted to know what pleased him.

Wanted to know everything, and at the same time felt like such a novice for not knowing everything already.

"Touch yourself for me. Touch your clit. Make yourself come while I'm inside you."

She burned, turned on and embarrassed all at once. It wasn't like she'd never made herself come. Just never for another person, not while they were watching!

"It's okay if you don't want to."

She'd be an idiot not to want to. She was naked, bent over him, fucking him for goodness' sake! It wasn't as if it would be inappropriate for the situation or anything.

Watching herself, she dipped her middle finger to slide around where they were joined, and dragged that lube up to her clit. They both hissed at the contact. Ripples of pleasure rolled through her body and she fell into that, shoving her embarrassment away.

"So hot. There's nothing hotter in the world than watching you, with your fingers working your clit, your cunt sucking my cock inside, your tits jiggling just so. Damn, you're sexy."

Her gaze let go of her hand and moved to meet his eyes in the mirror. They remained that way, even as orgasm stole over her and took him just moments later. Something passed between them, addictive and sweet, sticky and heady, and like an addict, she wanted more.

"I like your hair down," he said, handing her a cup of coffee.

"Thanks. It gets in the way, so I usually have it up. I should just cut it, but old habits die hard." She smiled, settling into the chair across from his.

"Don't. It's beautiful. What do you mean about old habits?"

"Dancing. It's easier to keep out of your face if it's long enough to be up. I've had long hair for as long as I can remember. For a while it was shoulder-length." Her gaze went hooded, wary, and he wondered what that was about. "This is the longest it's been in years though. Rennie likes to brush it at night." She shrugged. "It's sweet mom/daughter time."

"So how long have you been dancing then?" He sipped his coffee and watched the precise way she held her mug, drank, placed the cup down and ran the pad of her finger over the handle before letting go.

"My mother put me in this artsy type preschool program and I took to ballet right away. I was three."

"Artsy family. Your parents and you. Your brother too?"

She took a deep breath. "He sang. Opera. Had a voice—my god, his voice was something else. My parents were convinced he would be a superstar one day."

"What happened?"

She paused, licking her lips. "He could have been a superstar. He was that amazing. So much talent. He had so much inside. You'd cry to hear him sing because his emotion rang so clearly, or laugh—whatever, he was evocative because he felt everything so much. Which was his problem as well as his gift. He liked drugs. He liked women. He liked fast cars and living on the edge. Being with him was exhausting sometimes. He just sucked everything he could from life, but it made him"—she licked her lips, taking a sip of her coffee, and he pretended not to see the tears she blinked back—"it made him unstable. He had problems and he attracted other people with problems. Went to rehab more than once, began to ruin his voice; you can't smoke heroin and cigarettes and not hurt yourself." She shook her head and sat up. "He overdosed and died alone because he'd estranged himself from everyone. We didn't know for a week. Finally, his landlord called me. I was in the middle of a storm of my own. I didn't see it had gotten that bad. Or maybe I didn't want to see. Coulda, shoulda, woulda."

"I know what it's like to see someone you love fall away from you like that. I know that helplessness." He took her hand. "I'm sorry. How long ago was it?"

"Five years."

"I'm sorry. When we lost Adele—that was my niece's name—when we lost her and nearly lost Erin, Adrian and I at least had each other to rely on while we did our best to keep Erin from sinking."

"My parents are good people. They didn't deserve what we brought to them. They deserve peace."

Oh man, there was a story there. "You wanna tell me about it?"

She exhaled sharply and drained her mug. "I've got to get going, so I'll spare you my sob story. I've got a class this morning. These girls are advanced, so they keep me on my toes."

He let it go and hoped she'd unburden herself sometime. Whatever they did in bed, he was still her friend. Or he wanted to be. He liked the widow Sorenson a great deal.

"Let me walk you out then." He took her hand and they walked across the street. She tossed her gear into her backseat and climbed into the front seat. How oddly normal the moment was.

"See you later, Brody. Thanks for this morning. My muscles are nice and warmed up."

"Would that every day started off this good." He kissed her quickly and stepped back to watch her drive away.

8

Elise looked through her front windows to catch sight of a bunch of cars out in front of Brody's place. Crap. She didn't want to be out there with Rennie and have him think she was watching him or something suitably creepy or stalkery.

"Let's go, Momma!" Rennie balanced on her inline skates. The day was gorgeous; it was now mid-fall, so there was a chill in the air but the sun was out. Perfect for skating.

She tightened Rennie's helmet and made sure her kneepads were on tight enough. There would be no avoiding it, and if they moved quickly, they could head to the park and he wouldn't even see them.

"Let's go to the park. It looks like there's a lot of traffic out here today."

Rennie squealed her approval of that idea, and they headed out carefully as Elise locked up the house and they descended the steps.

"Hey there! Elise and Rennie, how are you?"

Damn and double damn.

"Hi there, Adrian!" Rennie called out, looking both ways and then skating across the street where Brody's brother stood at the edge of the lawn.

"Good afternoon, Adrian. It's a pretty day, Rennie and I are headed to the park." *Let's go before Brody comes out.*

"Wait a sec. Before you two go, I know Erin wanted to meet you." He turned and bellowed his sister's name, and Elise managed to get her helmet off, hoping she didn't look too bad.

"Yeah, no one would ever know you can belt it out to the back rows with that yell," a woman shouted as she came through the back gate toward them.

"Wow, your hair looks like cotton candy. That is wicked awesome." Rennie's voice was tinged with awe.

"You must be Rennie and her mom, Elise." The pink-haired woman had to be Erin. Elise recognized her features from the CD covers she'd been on. She also saw the pain, chased by tenderness, in the woman's eyes when she'd looked at Rennie. "I'm Erin. I'm glad to finally meet you two so I could thank you for helping Brody."

Elise shook Erin's hand and smiled. "It wasn't like I could just leave him in the gutter. Really it wasn't a big deal." She tried to edge away, but Rennie was fascinated by that cloud of pink hair and stayed in place, staring up at Erin.

"Momma, I want my hair to look like that. Can I get it pink? Please? Pink is my favorite color and so that would be really cool."

"You can have it pink in the summer when you aren't in school if you still want it pink then." She looked back to Erin and Adrian. "It was nice to meet you, Erin, and to see you again, Adrian."

"Anyone seen Erin?" Brody called from inside the backyard.

"Out here!" Erin called back.

"Well, we really should be going and let you guys get back to your day."

"Elise and Rennie. Just the ladies I wanted to see." Brody walked out the open gate, and Elise saw quite the crowd gathered back there.

She waved, but Rennie hobbled over on her skates to give Brody a hug before starting to chatter. Brody, to his credit, appeared to be listening and nodded in all the appropriate places.

When Rennie finally slowed down, Brody looked up and caught Elise's attention. "You two busy today? We're having a barbecue. Adrian just went triple platinum, so we thought we should celebrate. We've got burgers, dogs, salmon and even veggie burgers if you're so inclined. Cream soda and ice cream for later too."

He was just so, *gah*, she shouldn't let herself be so attracted to him, but that pull, that draw they both clearly felt, zinged between them.

"Ice cream? Momma, can we?"

"I don't want to intrude on your family celebration."

Erin took her hand and squeezed it. "We'd love to have you. There are a few other kiddos back there for Rennie to play with too."

"It's a ragtag group. They'll fall out of their chairs when you come through. So pretty." Adrian winked at her, and Brody moved closer, bumping his brother with his body.

"You wouldn't be intruding. I was headed over to invite you two anyway. I would have come by earlier, but I didn't know I was having a barbecue today until Erin showed up." He shot his sister a look and she simply shrugged.

Erin grinned, appearing totally unrepentant. "Your backyard is big. It's a nice day. Adrian's place doesn't have all the parking yours does. Plus, you know you love it."

He snorted and looked back to Elise. "So?"

"Okay. Okay. But you can't complain when she gets hopped up on sugar and starts talking a mile a minute."

Brody tucked a bit of her hair behind her ear and she nearly melted on the spot. "All right."

"Can I bring anything? I mean, I can toss something together." Great, her voice went all breathy and his sister totally noticed.

"Just you and Rennie will be fine."

"We just need to take off our skates and stuff. We'll be right back!" Rennie pulled on Elise's arm, so she followed her daughter.

"Just come through the back gate when you're ready," he called as they left.

"She's very pretty." Erin looked at her older brother as they headed into the backyard.

"And nice. Great kid." Adrian was *so* helpful.

"A girl would have to be blind or dead not to see the way you looked at each other. When did that start?" That her brother had never actually looked at a woman that way interested Erin greatly. When he'd tucked her hair back, so gentle and sweet, Erin had seen the chemistry between them written all over their body language.

Brody paused, looked at her and gave up. "About a month. She's got a business to build up, I have a business to keep afloat, she has a kid. We . . . It's very casual. I like her. She's a friend and we have chemistry. Like wicked crazy chemistry. She pushes my buttons in a big way. I gotta tell you, it's really good to be me right about now. It's not so much a secret, but we're keeping it mellow around the kid. She's a good kid."

"Reminds me a lot of you." Adrian pulled Erin's hair.

"This is exclusive?" Erin looked to Raven, who sat on the other side of the yard. Raven wasn't Brody's girlfriend, hadn't been for years, but they occasionally slept together, or had in the past, and Erin wondered how strong Brody's feelings still were for their friend. This brewing thing between him and the lovely lady from across the street had a lot of potential. Erin loved Raven like a sister, but

Raven left lovesick men and women in her wake, and Erin didn't much like it that Brody had been one.

"We're not dating. Not really. But we agreed to not have sex with anyone else. It's not too much to ask." He shrugged.

"I didn't say it was and I agree. I was just thinking you might want to, you know, keep some space from Raven if Elise is here. Elise may not be familiar with Raven's type and get the wrong idea."

"There are kids here, Raven'll behave."

Zing. Point went right over Brody's head like the dumb man he was. Brody having women he slept with was one thing. Raven wouldn't care about that. But Erin wondered how Raven would react to seeing her brother totally into another woman emotionally.

She looked to Todd, who sent her a shrug of his own. *Men.*

Rennie bounced ahead of her mother and Elise kept an eye out as she tried not to be nervous. Brody's backyard was filled with people, and true to Erin's claim, there were at least five other kids, all around Rennie's age, running around back there.

"Hi again, come on in," Brody called from his place up on the deck. Several people looked up to take her in. Erin waved and came over, grinning, holding hands with two kids.

"Hi, Nina!" Rennie began to chatter with the other little girl, and the boy bounced off.

"Rennie is in my class," Nina looked up to exclaim. "Come on, we're getting ready to play soccer."

"Bye, Momma!" Rennie scampered off, and Elise felt a tug in her chest where the other half of her heart lived. As lovely as it was to see her daughter make friends and like her new life, she was growing up at what seemed to Elise to be an alarming rate.

"They're good kids. Brody's yard is secure. Nina and Mase be-long to Arvin, he's the manager of Brody's shop. He and his wife live just two blocks over. The others, heck, Rennie probably knows a few more, as many of us live within a mile or so. Wow, you're a ballerina. That's awesome." Erin finally wound down, and Elise couldn't help but be charmed.

"Not as awesome as being a rock star."

An extremely handsome man came up to them, handed Erin a bottle of cream soda, kissed her gently and grinned at Elise. "Hi there, I'm Todd, Erin's husband. Can I get you something to drink?"

"Nice to meet you. I'm Elise. Um, sure. One of those would be good, thanks." She indicated the cream soda and he moved away to grab her one. "He's pretty."

Erin laughed. "He is. I have two of them, so I hope you're not offended."

"Two of what?"

"Todd is my husband, but Ben . . ." She paused, looking around until she smiled again and pointed out another man, this one big-ger than Todd but just as ridiculously good-looking. "Ben is ours too. Our husband but without the paperwork."

Was this a test? "Lucky you." Elise shrugged. "That one is pretty too."

Erin seemed to relax a bit. "I am lucky. They're both . . . Well, to find one person to love is special enough, but to find two and to be loved just as much in return, it's pretty amazing."

"Hello? Why are you bogarting my guest?" Brody called out, and Elise craned her neck to see him better. He grinned, a very close approximation of the smile his sister had worn just a few minutes before. "What can I get you? A dog? Burger? Salmon?"

Todd returned and handed her a cream soda. She thanked him

before heading up the steps to where Brody stood behind a fancy-schmancy grill.

"Any recommendations?" She looked over his arm to see the grill. "Swank."

He laughed. "Try the salmon. It has a miso glaze. Erin makes it."

"Some people have to hog up being good at stuff." She took the plate he handed her, a rush of sensation sliding over her when their fingers brushed. A taste of the fish only made it better. "Oh, this *is* good." She looked out over the yard to find Rennie running with the pack of kids, kicking a ball around. "I'd see if she was hungry, but I think she's a bit busy."

"I should have thought to introduce her to Nina and Mase this summer when you guys first moved in. She looks pretty happy."

Somehow, the way he looked at her daughter and smiled made her all warm. Good lord, she should not be having these little internal moments.

"Yeah, she does. Thanks for inviting us. Can I help? Get out of your way?"

He stepped very close. "You look so good. If Rennie wasn't here, I'd clear away that bit of cream soda from the corner of your mouth."

"You're not fair. I'm not sure my bra can hide how hard my nipples are," she murmured back. The up and down slide of his Adam's apple, the bead of sweat on his neck, the scent of his soap, all of it tested her control.

"I don't want to be fair. I want to put my hands on you. I want to put my mouth on your pussy and lick until you come."

She looked up at him as her skin tingled with awareness. He flipped her switch on such a primal level it was sort of scary. She thought about fucking him pretty much all the time. He set her on fire, had pushed her system into sexual hyperdrive, and she had to admit, she sort of dug it. She'd never been so hungry to be fucked in her life. It made her feel so alive! Sexy and desirable as a woman. It was liberating really.

"You keep looking at me like that, and I'm going to toss you over my shoulder and take you into the pantry." His voice was low, but she had to close her eyes a moment as the idea of what they'd do in the dark of the pantry flashed through her brain.

"If you want, I can take her off your hands. Since the burgers need turning and all."

Surprised, Elise turned and nearly smacked into someone. A very good-looking someone. Christamighty, where did all these hot people come from?

Brody put one hand on her shoulder while he flipped the burgers with the other one. "Yeah, I think not. Cope, this is Elise. Elise, this is Ben's brother, Cope."

"Ben is that one there, holding Erin's hand," he said, responding to her confused look.

At least the hotness made sense if he was related to that one.

"Ah, yes. Okay, Erin told me about him earlier, but I haven't met him yet."

"We're getting ready to play cards. Do you play cards?" Cope flashed a smile, complete with a dimple. This guy was a real bad boy. His grin was pure sex and he knew it. It charmed her.

That's when she saw the lush brunette approach. "Don't do it unless you're good. They're a very cutthroat bunch." Elise wondered just who this woman was, given the way Brody's body had tightened and he'd actually stepped closer to Elise.

"I spent a lot of time touring and waiting around backstage. I'm pretty good at cards and pool." She held out a hand after wiping the condensation from the bottle on her pants leg. "I'm Elise."

They shook hands and it was fine, but Elise's internal radar was flashing red. This was a woman who'd meant something to him once. Still did, if her presence meant anything, and she had no reason to doubt that. The people there were close-knit. They knew each other, this group. She got the feeling Brody Brown didn't do the important things halfway. He might come off as laid back to the extreme, but Elise saw his focus, saw the way he interacted with people. He'd be the type to take care of the things he valued. And the people. One of these days, he'd make some woman an exceptional husband and co-parent.

"I'm Raven."

The woman had a smile on her face, but if Elise wasn't mistaken, an air of challenge lurked there. Great, probably an ex- or not so ex-girlfriend.

"Elise and her little girl live across the street. She's the one who helped him when he got hit," Erin explained as she came up with Ben. "I saved us a table right there." Erin pointed.

Cope leaned back against a nearby ledge and sipped a beer. "Pool, huh? We play every other Friday at the pub just around the corner from the shop. You should come along sometime."

"Thanks for the invite. I don't have a lot of Friday nights free. I have a little girl, so I stick around home a lot." She didn't have the free time they did, but it was still nice to be asked.

"When she's not working in her studio. You should see her dance. It's pretty freaking amazing." Brody touched the small of her back. Just a casual touch, but it relaxed her a bit.

"Momma! I'm hungry. Can we eat?" Rennie led the charge of the pack of children she'd been playing with.

"I've got a platter of burgers and dogs right here," Brody called out to a cheer.

"I'll get that." She took it and looked over to the kids. "Why don't you all come over here to this table where the plates are so you can grab something?"

In the midst of the chaos of grabbing hands and pleased sounds from the kids, another woman came to help. "I'm Maggie, Arvin's wife. Those two are mine." She pointed out her kids.

"Elise." She motioned to Rennie. "That one is mine."

"I've seen you dropping her off at school in the mornings. If you ever want to take a morning off, or if you need to trade off, let me know. I teach at the school. Fourth grade. So I'm there anyway."

The two women, along with another mom and a dad, got the kids situated, and it wasn't until she'd moved back, standing in the autumn sunshine, that Elise realized it had been four years since she'd had a barbecue with friends, two since she'd really had close friends of any type.

Rennie and Nina had become fast friends in the way only girls their age could. A year ago, Rennie had been prone to nightmares about losing her mother. And now she could be in a backyard, eating freshly cooked burgers and giggling with a girlfriend. Elise had done the right thing to leave and move west.

"Here, you forgot this." Brody handed her the plate with her salmon, and he'd added some pasta salad on the side. "You'll waste away if you don't eat."

She looked up at him, knowing the smile on her face made it pretty obvious there was more between them than just being friends. But he made her happy and she genuinely liked him. Judging by his return smile and the way he squeezed her hand, he wasn't feeling too shabby either.

"I'm pretty sure I'll be okay, but I can't turn down lunch." She let him lead her to a table nearby where the kids had settled, and they both sat along with Erin and her two men. *Two*. Awesome.

"This is a great yard."

"Thanks. It's been a project for the last several years. I take something big each season and do it. The most recent thing was the water feature near the back corner. I like working with my hands."

Gah, she really wished she could control her blushes better. She may as well wear a sign that said, *Yes, we totally did it.*

Erin changed the subject. "I looked you up online. I admit it. I love dancing and I got curious when Brody had said you danced with NBT. I watched several clips of you on YouTube. I'm really impressed. You're an amazing dancer. You did Giselle several times, that's a big deal."

"It is? Why?" Brody leaned in for her answer.

Pleasure and pride flushed through her. "It's a plum role. The role you go up through school dreaming of dancing. Very dramatic story. Love, heartbreak, death, revenge, forgiveness. You're not only dancing but you're acting too. Technically it's very difficult, so many of the greatest dancers have taken up the role. To be among those names is a hope of many a young woman coming into ballet. It was most certainly mine."

"I'm so glad you got to live that dream. It's amazing, isn't it? To stand up on the stage and actually be doing what you'd fantasized about and worked for your whole life?"

Their gazes locked briefly and Elise realized Erin Keenan had a lot of depth.

"I don't know a lot about ballet, but I was so struck by the intensity of your grace and poise when you're dancing. It would have been wonderful to see you perform live."

"I've seen a bit, she's pretty amazing." Brody spoke in an offhand manner. Totally casual. And she melted a bit inside at the pride in his voice.

Erin's eyes widened, and then she sent Brody a decidedly teasing grin. Elise thought about her brother, thought about how much fun he'd been as they'd grown up. Erin still had that and Elise envied her.

"Thank you. I love to dance, I have for as long as I could remember. I'm not one of those people who was forced into lessons or whatever. I would have spent all my time dancing if I could have. But when your dad is a professor, you can't blow off school."

"Do you miss it?"

Elise paused. "Yes. But I'm getting older and I got hurt. Some things you can't come back from. So teaching is the next best thing." She needed to have that tattooed on herself. Some things you'll never come back from. But you can survive them and that's what she did.

Brody watched her in his yard, with his friends and family, and found that he liked her there. He had his circle, and they meant everything to him, so it meant more than he could really grasp to have her there and feel like she was *meant* to be there. Rennie fit in great with the other kids. Elise made friends in her own way, but she was sort of irresistible, this huge force of nature in such a deceptively pretty package.

He took some of the larger trays into the kitchen and began to clean them up as Todd packed up the leftovers.

"So what's that story?" Raven brought a tray inside and began to dry as he rinsed.

"Story?"

"Very tiny blonde lady in your backyard with the kid? Hello? I know you noticed her because you haven't taken your eyes off her for more than three minutes at a time. You've been stuck to her like glue and even gave Cope the stink eye when he started that game of cards and invited her to play."

He smiled at her, wondered what it was that had turned him so upside down those years before. When he looked at Raven now, he certainly found beauty; you'd have to be blind not to. But he saw so much more. Too much to ignore and continue to love her, but enough that he'd always hold her in a special place.

"She's a very pretty blonde lady who helped me out when I got hit by a car, and we struck up a friendship. I like her. I like her company. And as much as I'd get Cope's back in a brawl any day, I don't want anyone else to like her the way I'm currently liking her. Which is all I'm going to say about it right now."

Todd, who'd been ferrying things inside and back into the fridge, overheard and barked out a laugh. "You've got his number, but like Raven said, we'd all have to be blind not to have seen the way you two have been with each other all afternoon. Cope is a man whore, as Erin would say, but he's got ethics. He wouldn't poach anyone else's anything."

"Which is why he's out there playing cards with her and trying to see down her shirt and I'm not hitting him in the face."

"So have you retired your bachelor shoes?" Raven's tone was mocking as she leaned back against the counter, watching him.

"No. We're not going steady. But I'm an adult and I can like the people I'm with. I prefer it that way."

Raven snorted. "You'll get over it when the novelty wears off."

Brody shook his head and swatted Raven with a kitchen towel. "Don't be so negative. Jesus. You're going to get an ulcer or something. Try the half-full method."

When he went back out, Elise was in the process of trying to separate Rennie and Nina, and neither girl was having much of it.

"Why don't you guys have a play date soon? How's that?" Maggie smiled at both girls and then up at Elise.

"Okay! How about right now?" Nina said.

"How about soon? Do you have our phone number? You two can work out a few days and times and we'll work around it, okay?"

Elise held back a smile but Brody saw her fight it. He liked the way she was with Rennie. This wasn't a woman who had her roles confused. She wasn't Rennie's best friend, she was Rennie's mother. But she also seemed not so rigid that it harmed either one of them. It had to be tough, being mother and father.

The girls snatched up paper and pens and wrote numbers down while Elise chatted animatedly with Maggie. He liked that connection too. Maggie had been his first office manager back when she was working her way through school. Then Arvin had come in for a job, and within months the two had been not just a couple, but, like, cemented together. They were solid people. Great parents and wonderful friends to him. He enjoyed seeing Maggie have another mom to be close with, and it gave Elise another person in her life, helping her feel more at home in Seattle.

Elise turned to him. "Thanks for inviting us. We had a great time."

"Let me walk you two over."

She started to protest but closed her mouth and smiled instead. "All right."

Maggie hugged her, as did Erin. His sister didn't often click with other people, and certainly not as quickly as she had with Elise. But in truth, he had such great friends and family that it was sort of spooky how well their small group got along. Oh sure, they had their tiffs, people being pissed off at each other. That was natural given that several of them were married or siblings to other members of the group. But there was a sense of community and camaraderie between them all, of refuge and home. Standing there with his sister grinning at Rennie, and Cope chatting Elise up, he was at ease. He fit somewhere, with other people who were like him. And now Elise was one of them too, and he had the distinct feeling that her entry into his life would mark it deeply.

He told everyone he'd be back shortly and walked Elise and Rennie back home.

"Thanks, Brody! I had a great day." Rennie threw her arms around his waist and hugged tight. This kid was hard not to love.

"Anytime."

Elise unlocked the door and held it open. "Go on upstairs. Bath and pjs."

Rennie started to argue, but she must have seen the same look Brody had in her mother's eyes, and groaned. "Okay. Night, Brody." She ran off into the house and thundered up the stairs.

"Thanks again. I had a great day too." She took a deep breath and slid her palm over his throat and to the back of his neck. "I don't know what your plans are tonight. But if you're free in three hours or so and find yourself standing on my porch, I'd let you in."

"Are you inviting me into your parlor?" He wanted in her body right then. If it weren't for that kiddo upstairs, he'd be on her.

"Yes. If by parlor you mean my bedroom so we can have sex."

He laughed, dipping to kiss her quickly. "I'll make it a point to be standing right here in three hours."

"Okay then. I'll try not to keep you up too late since you have to work tomorrow and all."

"I've gone to work tired many a time; I can't think of a better reason than being worn out by you."

She smiled and stepped back, letting go of his neck, but he still felt her touch there.

He headed back home with a smile on his face.

9

Elise liked him. He was sexy and masculine and he made her laugh.
He was nice to Rennie, wasn't overly pushy, although he had alpha
male written all over him and she could see he liked managing
people. Elise didn't want to be managed. She'd had enough of that.
But they had great sexual chemistry. He always made her come. He
seemed to love oral sex and he had a great imagination. Not much
to complain about really.

So when she opened her door and found him standing on her
porch, she took his hand and led him back to her bedroom. They
didn't speak, not breaking the spell of the quiet house. She locked
her door and turned to face him.

"Hi," he said quietly, drawing her against him.

"Hi. You smell good. Like autumn. I love the way it smells here
at night. Like wood fires and cold air." She pressed her nose into his
neck and breathed deep.

"You feel good. I like this room. I'd like it more if you took this
off." He pushed the robe from her shoulders and it fell into a pool

of fabric at her feet. His hands, big and bold, swept down her back to cup her ass.

Instead of the normal, urgent, rip-off-clothes-and-fuck frenzy they'd had before, their pace was slow and sensual. His lips cruised across the swell of her cheek, to her ear and down her neck. His hands caressed, kneaded, seduced instead of demanded.

She gave to him, let him take, leaned her head to the side, giving him access to the hollow of her throat. A shiver of delight passed through her at the feel of his teeth grazing the hypersensitive skin along her collarbone.

God, he felt so good.

And she wanted more.

Pushing him back a bit, she managed to get his shirt up and over his head, and despite it not being the first time she'd seen the glory of his body, she still stopped to stare a bit. When her gaze reached his face again, he wore a smile, a knowing, male smile, and her own lips quirked up in response.

"You're hot." She shrugged. "What else can I do but stare a little?"

He laughed, startled. "Feel free to objectify me whenever you wish."

"Take your pants off and I'll do it some more."

He did, removing his shorts along with the jeans. He really was gorgeous. All barely leashed power just beneath the skin.

He drew in a shaky breath. "I want to take it slow and easy, but then you look at me like that and all I can think of is how good you feel wrapped around my cock when I'm inside you."

She'd never imagined anyone ever saying such a thing to her. So raw and beautiful, honest and frankly sexual. It was invigorating to have someone want her like that. Thrilling.

This man here before her was hers in a sense, in her bed, wanting her in his life both in his bed and out of it. That was a powerful lure. To be wanted that way soothed some jagged spot inside she hadn't known was rubbing her raw until his presence eased it.

She stepped in and licked up his side, over each rib, tasting him. The groan he made shot through her like a bloom of pleasure, knowing she made him feel that way. When he moved her hand to his cock, she nearly swooned at the feel of him, so hard against her palm.

She kissed his chest and down his belly until she got to her knees. Then her mouth went to his cock, tracing her tongue down the length of him and back up again. He cradled her skull in his hands as she continued to kiss and lick.

She took him back as deeply as she could and pulled away, over and over.

"Damn, you're so beautiful. I've never seen anything as beautiful," he murmured, his hands gentle in her hair, fingertips brushing against the nape of her neck.

She was like a butterfly, a bird, something magical and small and so very beautiful. The room smelled so strongly of her. Not perfume, not really; just an essential sort of sweetness with a small amount of spice. He'd had more skilled mouths on his cock, but this woman had something else, something ethereal that no one he'd ever touched had possessed.

Something surged through him from the balls of his feet, lodging in his chest. "Up here, beautiful. I want to lay you out, I want to be over you, inside you, when I come." He swept her up, kissing her before he laid her down on the bed and followed.

"I need you," she said in that soft voice, and it broke at his control like waves. "You didn't let me finish."

He kissed a nipple and then the other one. "Oh I'm going to finish. I promise."

"Hurry."

Her belly was warm and strong against his lips as he kissed it. Her scent, sweet/spice salted with the musk of her body, with the way *he* made her. "I have to taste you first. I think I'm addicted."

Her laugh was taut with need, and it melted into a sigh when he took the first lick of her. Such an intimate thing, his mouth on the center of her. She was rich and deep, and he couldn't seem to get enough, so he rejoiced that she seemed to want him as much as he wanted her.

Her thigh muscles bunched and relaxed as she rolled her hips, arching up to get more from him. He loved that. Loved that he made her needy and shameless when it came to taking her pleasure. Almost as much as he loved giving it to her.

When she came, he tasted it to his bones, felt the fine tremor of her body as she tightened and then relaxed on a stuttered sigh.

"Now that I've taken the edge off, we can get to the next part of the program." He reached down to grab his pants to fish out a condom from his pocket.

Elise looked up as he lowered himself over her. The blunt head of his cock pressed against her, pressing into her body as she made room, stretching slowly.

God, he felt good. He gave her just the right amount of weight, taking most of it on his forearms. She wrapped her legs around his waist, taking him in fully.

"Fucking you is much more fun than just about anything else I can think of. In fact, it's more fun than anything I can think of." He laughed, leaning down to capture a kiss as he began to thrust, slow and deep.

They didn't say much, but the silence wasn't heavy, it was nice between them, not needing to fill the space with words.

She felt every inch of him as she clutched his back, pulling him close, loving the way his muscles played against her palms. He held her gaze as he moved within her, held it as he changed his angle, bringing the line of his cock brushing her clit over and over, until she had to bite into his pec to muffle the sound.

He hissed, but not in pain. His eyes blurred and she felt him come as her body tightened around his cock.

Not wanting to crush her, he rolled to the side before getting up to deal with the condom quickly. When he returned, she'd lit a few candles and had stacked the pillows up at the head of her bed. The golden light from the candles licked at her skin, made shadows on the walls.

He kissed her because he could and he wanted to, as he settled in beside her.

"I enjoyed meeting your friends and family today," she said lazily, playing with his nipple ring. "This is beyond sexy, by the way."

He grinned. It wasn't that he'd never felt sexy or attractive. He did most of the time. He liked the way women responded to him. But when she said it, she said it with such artlessness, such genuine appreciation, it struck him deep.

"I'm glad you like it and I'm glad you had fun today. They all enjoyed meeting you as well, and I think Nina and Rennie hit it off. It's good for her to have connections in the neighborhood."

"It is. Girls her age can love their friends so much. I felt horrible moving out here, making her leave her friends behind. So I'm relieved she's making them here. Maggie is really nice. I like having connections here too."

He took her hand, raising it to his lips to kiss each fingertip.

"We're going to be down at the park next Saturday. A little grudge-match football game we have the weekend before Halloween. If you want to cheer and have the time off, you should show up. There'll be kids there for Rennie. Arvin plays, so Maggie will bring Nina most likely."

She blinked, surprised. "Thank you. I have classes each Saturday until two. If you're still there when I'm done, Rennie and I will stop by."

"Starts at three, so you should be good. If we start earlier, it goes on and on. So we decided a few years ago to get out there no more than two hours before sunset."

Laughter shook her very delightful breasts. "That's very cute."

He frowned and then bared his teeth. "Cute? I'm a badass, Elise. I ride a Harley and have tattoos."

She laughed even harder. "I-I'm sure you are if the situation calls for it. But you're a very sweet man beneath the tattoos."

"Sweet." He snorted, amused by her.

Rolling into him, she pushed him back to the mattress and kissed his face several times. "There's not a damned thing wrong with sweet. Sweet is very underrated."

He laughed. "Ha! Chicks only want sweet for their platonic male friends."

She sobered up and he traced the curve of her bottom lip. "Did I hit a nerve?"

Shaking her head, she dropped a kiss on his shoulder. "Old wounds."

Old wounds. Yeah, something like that.

She thought of those words as she worked over the next week. Wondered about how and when it had gone so wrong for her. Wondered if she'd ever not have her time with Ken hanging around her neck like a millstone.

Rennie sat at the kitchen table doing her homework while Elise folded laundry. The phone rang and she smiled at the number.

"Hello, Mama."

"Why didn't you tell us about this mess with Ken's parents?" her mother demanded.

"I'm gonna take these clothes up to your room and put them on your bed. You know which drawers they go in. I'll be back." She grabbed the basket and headed away from listening ears.

"What's going on? Have they been bothering you?" she asked once she'd gotten to Rennie's room.

"You answer my question first, Elise." Her mother's imperious tone made Elise smile. It was easy now, with a few thousand miles between them, to be amused.

"I didn't tell you because you two had enough to deal with. There's nothing you can do and it would have upset you. Now, what happened?"

"This is why you wanted us to stay in New York until Daddy had retired. I can't believe you didn't tell us! We're your parents. We have a right to know so we can support you. Didn't you know we would have helped in any way?"

"I did. I do. I swear to you. After Matthias . . . You just had so much to deal with, and then the murder. It's over anyway. Now, tell me." She sat on Rennie's bed, a froth of pink lace and stuffed animals lined up in an orderly fashion.

"She called today. That evil cow. Said you'd been refusing to let them have their monthly phone call with Irene. Said they'd sue us if we didn't help. Imagine my surprise to hear that they'd been threatening to ruin your new school and to take Irene out of the U.S. to raise her without her mother. Imagine *her* surprise to my response when she threatened to harm Daddy's professorship. People like them make me crazy. However, you not sharing drives me crazy too. I don't care what she says. You're our child, Irene is our grandbaby; they won't harm you through us."

Elise couldn't help but laugh at the idea of her mother telling off Bettina Sorenson. "I'm sorry. I just . . . Mama, these people are dangerous. You don't need it."

She *hated* them. Hated the Sorensons. Hated her kid getting sick at having to speak to them. Hated them for hurting her parents.

"Their son was the problem. Their son! I *don't need* it, *pish*. Elise, you don't get to decide what I need." This was followed by a two-minute-long, profanity-laced rant, all in French, wherein Elise was schooled on what her job was and how they were her parents so therefore Elise needed to obey them and stop hiding things.

Her father took the phone. "She'll be that way for a while. We're coming out for a visit over Thanksgiving. I know we invited you back here to visit, but your mother and I decided it's best to keep you two out west. I don't want those vile Sorensons anywhere near you or Rennie. We'll plan to stay for a week, during which we will be looking for a house."

Her head began to pound and tears of frustration threatened. "Daddy, really, it's not necessary. They're not a threat. I have sole custody and I haven't refused anything. They call at random and I say no. They upset her every time they call, so I keep it to once a month. She gets cranky, cries for no reason, gets stomachaches. I wouldn't do it at all, but I want to comply with everything so they can never have anything to use against me. I feel like I'm not protecting her, but I don't know what else I can do without making things worse."

"We're coming. You'll pick us up from the airport. Your mother says you have her services all week long at the studio. We love you, Elise. We miss you and we miss that baby. Your mother can teach piano anywhere, and I'm an old man who can find young people to adore him anywhere too. You need us. We need you."

She smiled through tears. She needed them so much; even at her age, she needed them. But Ken had been part of what happened to Matthias, had been part of that long slide into oblivion, and even though she and Ken had been estranged and Ken had been doing a stint in county jail when Matthias overdosed, the guilt of it still colored her perceptions.

"Momma, can I come up now?" Rennie hollered from the bottom of the stairs.

"I'm coming down," she told Rennie before turning back to her father. "Rennie knows you're on the phone, you want to talk to her?"

Her father laughed and her mother got on the other line. "I'm finished with the bad words now. We'll see you in a month and you well tell us the whole story when we arrive."

She handed the phone to her daughter and sighed deeply as she moved toward the rest of the laundry she needed to put away. It was a relief on so many levels to have that off her chest. To be able to share this with her parents. But on the other hand, she heard the anger in her mother's voice, had heard the barely disguised rage in her father's. She was done with all the violence and the threats, she simply didn't want her parents to be affected by the cancer the Sorensons were.

It was bad enough Rennie had to have a phone call from them once a month. It was more than generous, considering all the things they'd done, and in the end she continued to hope they loved Rennie enough to try. But she knew in her heart of hearts that it wouldn't last. They'd come after her again, so the longer she was established in Seattle, the more she grew roots in the community, the more

Rennie thrived and the longer Elise adhered to the rules of the agreement, the better off she'd be when they finally decided to act again.

"Pops told me to tell you I deserve a Fudgeicle," Rennie announced as she came back down to hang up the phone.

"Fudge*sicle* and why am I not surprised? Your grandfather's love of Fudgesicles is known far and wide." Elise rolled her eyes but rewarded herself and Rennie with one each.

10

"Oh, there you are!" Erin jumped up from the picnic table and headed toward Elise and Rennie.

Rennie, spotting Nina on the swings, gave Erin a hit-and-run hug and headed off toward her friend.

"Hi there!" Elise was surprised but pleased when Erin hugged her and dragged her toward the table.

"Sit and eat. Brody will be right back. He and his team have gone off to do whatever they do before the game. I suspect shots of liquor are involved. Probably porno magazines and stories of conquest. Or whatever they do when we're not around."

"More like sitting around, eating wings and drinking beer. Porn may be involved though." Maggie sat and put a bottled water within Elise's reach.

Erin laughed. "Oh, they're all so badass. Big bad cops and tat artists and stuff and they're all whining about their knees."

Elise grinned and dug into the bag of cookies after realizing she hadn't eaten much all day. Rennie played on the swings just to the left, so it was easy to chat, munch and watch the kids.

All the chatter faded into background noise when Brody came into view with several other men. His gaze immediately sought her, locked in as he strode toward her.

"Hey, you made it." His voice, that low, darkly sweet rumble, brought everything to attention.

"I did. How were the wings and porn?"

He looked straight to Erin and the women dissolved into laughter.

"All quite spicy, thanks."

Her phone started ringing. The cell she had just for dealing with the Sorensons. She sighed, digging it out, and sent a look to Rennie before getting up. "Excuse me, please."

She stepped a few feet away and answered.

"Hello?" She barely resisted the urge to answer with *Why the fuck are you calling again, you bitch?*

"It's Bettina Sorenson. You sound harried and scattered as usual. No discipline or drive. So middle-class. Since you're making me call you, yet again, please tell me why hasn't my granddaughter returned any of our calls."

And then she regretted her restraint. As if she didn't know who the bitch was. "You know very well why. You have a scheduled phone visit once a month. I'll have her by the phone on the fifteenth at the right time."

"You're difficult. Always have been. I told Ken that, but he had to have you. As if there weren't a thousand girls more suited to him. You've always tried to keep her away. You don't deserve her."

"We're done now. Do not call my family again about this. If you have a problem, you know my attorney's number. Deal with him."

"Your precious parents! Look at what they raised."

"I'll be sure to pass that on to them, and we'll try not to roll our eyes so hard we sprain something." She reined in her anger. There was no point in letting this woman get to her. She also had no idea if they recorded her, so she remained careful with what she said.

"Dude, what's that all about?" Erin asked Brody, who shrugged but watched Elise's body language change, tighten up. "I don't like it, Brody. Look at her. Something is wrong."

"Let's get playing!" Ben called from their makeshift field.

"Wait a minute." Brody motioned at Elise, and concern crossed Ben's features as they took her in. She paced, her free hand flapping around. "You can start without me. I'll be there in a bit." He moved toward Elise.

"I'm going to say it again just so we can be very clear. You have no right to call my parents. You have no right to call me on any day but the fifteenth at six p.m. Pacific time."

She paused, her jaw clenched.

"No, *you* don't understand. You make her upset every time you call. She has a schedule. A life. You can't interrupt it and I won't let you. I've spoken to my attorney about this. Stop now."

Her brow furrowed as she listened to whatever whoever it was on the other end said.

"I'm done. I'm hanging up now. Do not call again until the fifteenth." She flipped the phone shut and shoved it in her pocket.

The shoulder he put his hand on trembled and her eyes shone with unshed tears. He tipped her chin up. "Are you all right?"

She shook her head. "I'm just really, really angry. I can't talk about it right now. Rennie might see. Go and play. I'll be together in a minute."

He pulled her into a hug, and the tremor in her shoulders echoed through him as though it were a sob. "I'm going to hug you first. Then I'll play and take you and Rennie out for pizza afterward. Even better, we'll order in and have root beer floats. Root beer floats are made of win."

A ghost of a smile played on her lips. "No wonder you and Rennie get along so well. But you shouldn't worry. You're going to want to be with your friends. I'm all right."

He kissed her forehead. "You and Rennie *are* my friends. Now go sit down and be impressed with my athletic prowess." Keeping his arm around her shoulder he guided her back to the table, and then ran off to the field.

Erin handed her a cookie. "Looks like you could use one of these. I have a candy bar in my bag, wanna share it?"

Elise took the cookie and ate it, shoving her anger away. She'd become such a champion at shoving her anger away, at pushing it aside to get the job done, that she wondered about the effect it had on her body. And her mind. Still, right then it wouldn't do her any good and it certainly wouldn't help for Rennie to see it. "I'm good for now. I'm apparently having pizza and ice cream with Brody after this, so I'll eat too many carbs then."

Erin raised a brow and Elise wanted to laugh. "What?"

After several silent moments, Erin said, "Nothing. He does that to me too. When I'm having a hard day. He used to show up at my house with a fully loaded pie, a six-pack and some horrible movie with screaming and gratuitous nudity in it. He's a good friend to have. Or more. Or whatever."

Elise did laugh then. "You're not very subtle." She winced as Ben tackled Todd. "Oh, ouch! I thought this was flag football."

"Yeah, it is. But with tackling." Maggie looked back to the game again. "Hey! Don't break anything, I need him in one piece," she called out.

The kids made their way over, and Rennie settled in Elise's lap, eating cookies and clapping for Brody. It was wonderfully normal, and Elise sent a prayer of thanks that they had days like this now.

After the children had eaten their fill, they headed back to the swings and Erin turned back to Elise. "So when you toured before, did you bring Rennie with you? I'm curious. We brought Adele— that was my little girl—along on tour, but her father was our manager, so that was easy enough."

"My mother came along with us. She'd keep Rennie occupied while I was at rehearsals and on stage. I did have a nanny once, but Rennie and her gran are pretty tight, so neither of them liked it much. My mom had to fly to Australia to take over." Elise laughed at the memory. "I thought about quitting, but it was a steady source of income, and for a lot of the year I'd be in New York or a few hours' train ride away." She knew how much her parents had supported her; she'd have been lost without them.

"There are worse ways for a child to grow up than hearing a live orchestra on a regular basis," Maggie said.

"She was all about the costumes. Even when she was just a baby. Anything with sequins or feathers would catch her eye. She wanted to learn *en pointe* so she could have toe shoes because they're satiny and so pretty."

"Is she all set to follow in your footsteps, then? With dancing?" Erin asked.

"She likes dance, but she doesn't love it so much she's willing to live it. Which is fine with me, really. The kind of schooling she'd need if she really wanted to pursue dancing professionally would mean a lot less time together for us. She's not focused in the way she needs to be. But she's really artistic, it comes from both sides for her. Painting and drawing are more her thing than dancing. Watching her paint is an experience; she's all movement and color.

Her father was a painter, but he was her polar opposite when he worked. He went inside himself so deep he'd stare at a canvas for hours without moving. She's talking and dancing around, singing. She announced to me yesterday that she needs a studio of her own."

"Where was her father during all this? Staring at a canvas while you did all the work? God, sometimes men are such lazy assholes. They can spot a doormat a mile away. He had your number," Raven said.

Elise looked at her and wondered what her deal was. It wasn't that she was deliberately hurtful. But she seemed to just say whatever she wanted whenever she wanted without a thought. It wasn't cute. It rubbed Elise the wrong way. Part of that, she could admit, was that Raven clearly had some kind of connection to Brody. But just because you could say anything you wanted at any time didn't mean you should. Or that a little bit of thought before you spoke wasn't in order.

"Wow, Raven, did you forget to take your manners pills this morning?" Maggie asked.

"She doesn't mean to sound like a bitch. She just seems to lack filters," Erin explained of her friend.

"Was that rude? Clearly there's a father if there's a kid. I just thought I'd join in on the conversation." Raven truly did look confused, and Elise eased back on her anger. Still, Raven just *wanted to know*, so Elise decided to school her some.

"There was a father in as much as I had sex with a male who donated his sperm. In the whole of her life, she's probably only spent a total of a week with him. He was in county jail when she was born. In the end, it's a far better thing that I had to do much of Rennie's child-rearing myself." Elise hoped like hell all Rennie got from her father was his artistic talent.

The smirk on Raven's face fell, and Elise felt a stab of satisfaction. "Oh. Wow. I'm sorry."

"Me too."

Erin paused and sat forward, grabbing Elise's hands. "That wasn't him on the phone just now, right? If so, you need to record it and call the cops. Todd and Ben used to be cops, they know folks you can talk to. Or let Brody answer the next time. He'll set that fucker straight." Erin shook her head. "I hate abusers."

Ah yes, a reality check. After that call from Bettina it was hard to do. Things could be so much worse. It could be Ken, high and paranoid, screaming into the voice mail that he loved her and would kill her and Rennie so they could all be together. Compared to that, dealing with Bettina was a walk in the park. Besides, she'd gone head-to-head with Bettina and had won. Her child was out of their clutches. Even the phone calls could stop after Rennie turned ten, if Rennie so chose. They'd still controlled Elise to a certain extent as they played this little back-and-forth. But it was a waiting game and she'd do what she had to to be free of them forever.

Elise breathed out slowly. "No, it wasn't him. He can't call anyone, he's dead."

"Oh." Erin started to say more, but just then the game ended and chaos broke over the group as the guys came off the field and the kids ran over and the area overflowed with good-natured trash talk and lots of jostling and laughter.

Rennie headed not for her mother, but to Brody, who tossed her the ball, and she caught it before he gathered her up into his arms. The two of them laughed, and Elise realized she wasn't the only Sorenson female to have made friends with Brody.

He reached them, and Rennie scrambled from his arms, barreling toward Elise. "Momma! Brody says he's gonna get a pizza and we can all eat it in his living room! He said we could sit on a blanket on the floor and have a pizza picnic and he'd make root beer floats. Brody is totally awesome, he even invited Nina!" Rennie's eyes were wide, her face flushed, her hair a disheveled mess.

What a nice man he was. Nina and Rennie both seemed ecstatic about the whole thing. "Brody *is* totally awesome, you're absolutely right."

Rennie threw her arms around Elise's neck and kissed her cheek. "Momma, can Nina stay over tonight? I'm asking real quietly in your ear instead of asking in front of her and I got all my spelling words right this week. Can she, please?"

Elise nodded. "Yes. But let's okay it with Nina's mom too."

Nina giggled and Maggie nodded. "You sure? They could come to our house tonight. We're not going to the barbecue anyway."

"I'll do it this time, you guys next time. How's that?"

"You have a deal." Maggie looked down at the girls. "Let's go get Nina's pajamas and toothbrush. I'll bring them to your place in a few minutes?"

"Great. I'm on my way now. Be good for Miss Maggie, okay?" she asked Rennie, who nodded solemnly and then danced around, singing about crocodiles and monkeys. A sleepover? She was having an extra piece of pizza for this.

Elise looked around Rennie, up into Brody's face, and smiled. "I'm sorry about this. My house would probably be better since Nina is staying over."

"Makes sense. Next time we'll do it at my place. I just need to stop off at my house to grab the root beer and ice cream." He grabbed his bag and pulled a sweatshirt over his head.

"You sure you aren't supposed to go to that barbecue? Maggie mentioned it. I don't want you to babysit us instead of being with your friends. And you did just think it would be me and Rennie.

Two six-year-olds together? Whoo. You're going to have a headache when you leave." She laughed and sent an affectionate look at her daughter trailing off after Maggie.

"I've already told you, *you* are my friend too. I've known Nina since she was born, and Rennie and I are friends now. You three ladies are my dates for the evening. Imagine the kind of brag that'll allow me." He winked. "Now, come on." He began to tug her toward their street. "Honestly, I don't even want to go to this barbecue. It'll be loud and people will be drinking from plastic cups and tapping kegs. I want a quiet night."

"If you're sure."

"I'm sure I wish we had about ten more minutes, because you look good enough to eat," he said in a low voice that sent shivers through her.

"Instead you get squealing and giggling."

"And pizza. Don't forget pizza. Anyway, this isn't my first slumber party. I raised Erin through her teen years."

Brody sat back and watched how Elise was with the girls. Neverending patience, kindness, a vein of whimsy he hadn't imagined she possessed. She laughed as she helped him make root beer floats, she knew card tricks and she knew how to kick some serious ass on the PlayStation.

She was so very capable, which was beyond sexy. In his deepest heart, he could admit he found it sexy because she took care of her own shit. He didn't have to be responsible for her. She didn't need taking care of, though he did like it when she shared parts of her past with him.

He could enjoy her. He could enjoy their friendship and whatever else they had. He liked her, respected her. She was something he'd never really brushed up against before, so exotic and beautiful to his eye, to his heart.

And that kid of hers, wow. Irene was such a spot of sunshine. Bright, happy, loving. Whatever put that fear in Elise's eyes, she'd done something spectacular in shielding that little girl from it.

"You girls need to go upstairs and get ready for bed." Elise looked at the girls with a smile. "I'll be up in ten minutes to read a story, so pick one."

"Good night, Brody!" Rennie bounced over and gave him a hug, followed by Nina.

"Night, you two. Thanks for hanging out with me and your mom tonight."

Rennie fluttered her lashes at him, and both girls giggled as they ran upstairs.

"She's something else. Amazing kid you've got there." He looked up and caught the pride on her face.

"I don't really have much to do with it. She's been this way since the moment she came into the world. I'm lucky to have *her*."

"You want to talk about that call today?" He watched her carefully, not wanting to push too hard.

"I need to deal with them first. I can't unpack that wound just now." She put her hands on her hips, and he saw the cracks in her façade.

"I'll be down in a few minutes, if you want to wait around. I can't, well, I don't think tonight is the night for anything naked." She quirked up a smile. "But your company is nice and I like to look at you."

He laughed. "I'll be here. Unless you need my help up there?"

"Nah. They'll be hard enough to wrestle down. In fact, I'm guessing they'll be up most of the night."

"Okay then. I'll be here."

"Help yourself to whatever."

He watched her leave the room and liked what he saw. A lot.

"Oh man, I'm so full I may have to be rolled back to my house," he said after she came back down half an hour later. He'd made himself another root beer float and settled in on her very comfortable couch.

"I've got strong arms, I'll roll you." She tossed herself next to him, putting her feet up on the low table. He reached out and grabbed her feet, pulling them into his lap, starting to massage them. "Oh, you don't want that." She tried to pull back, but he held on.

"Oh, but I do. Woman, you do for people over and over. Let me do for you."

"Dancers have horribly ugly feet." She blushed.

"You have no idea what ugly is. Believe me. You're fine. Are the girls okay?"

She rolled her eyes, but let him work, even arching and groaning when he kneaded her insteps.

"I figured they'd be awake all night, but they're both conked out. I guess the game and the pizza and all that running around they did ran 'em down. The silence is so lovely."

"I like your voice."

"Thank you. You know, you give really wonderful compliments. As it happens, I like yours. It's like a hot toddy after being out in the snow for an hour. Warm and sinful, and it makes me all melty inside."

"Damn, now that is probably the most awesome compliment I've ever received."

She blushed. "Why tattooing? What made you do it?"

"I've always loved to draw, and for a time I was big into animation. I was headed to art school, but life threw me into another direction and I had to get a job. A friend of mine had a tattoo shop, and he hired me on to clean up the place at night and help out with whatever they needed. The hours were good, he let me work around when Adrian and Erin were in school. It really didn't take me that long to realize tattooing was an art and to get into it. Ron, the guy who owned the shop and pretty much taught me everything I know, let me apprentice. I was good at it right away. Probably because I was too stupid to be worried I wouldn't be."

"Or maybe, Brody Brown, perhaps you accepted it the way you accept that you're good at just about everything else I've seen you do. Some people are gifted. It's okay to be proud of that."

That struck deep in a place he seldom delved into. He took care of others. He was proud of Erin and Adrian and celebrated all their successes. But sometimes . . . sometimes he forgot he had his own accomplishments worthy of praise. And it was quite often Erin or Adrian who reminded him.

Interesting. Now it was Brody who blushed. Elise liked that, liked that she had looked long and hard enough and she'd glimpsed some secret part of him.

"Anyway, it went pretty quickly from there. Within five years I had my own shop when the owner sold to me. He's living in Hawaii now, surfing and watching hot chicks in bikinis all day. He deserves it. Believed in me when no one else wanted to take on an eighteen-year-old raising two siblings."

"I've seen your work on Erin. She showed me the tree of life on her back. It's amazing. You're really talented."

"I do okay, yeah. That one is special to me, of course. It started with small stuff and kept growing until it took up her entire back and we wrapped it around her hips too."

"Covers her scars, but memorializes what happened to her too. It's a positive thing."

He sighed. "I hope so. She's had a lot to deal with. More than anyone should. I expect, given the shadow in your eyes, you know a little bit about dealing with things."

She shrugged. "It's amazing how one bad choice can snowball into something you can't stop until it ends horribly. But it's over and I survived. Rennie is relatively untouched by it although she does go to play therapy once a month."

"What happened, Elise? Obviously it was her father, right?"

Swallowing hard, she nodded. She kept her voice low, mindful of Rennie asleep upstairs. "I'm not the only one with a story like this. I'm not a special snowflake. My ex-husband was an abusive, mentally-ill junkie. Thank God he was in jail for most of my pregnancy with Rennie."

"Was that who called today? Because if so, I'm totally free to show a man what it feels like to be pounded on by someone bigger than he is."

Unable to resist, she traced her finger over his lips. "Thanks, but no, it wasn't him. He's dead. It was his mother trying to bully me. It's her pattern." She shrugged. It wasn't a mystery that she hadn't met Ken's parents until after she and Ken had eloped to Vegas. Once she'd met them, she knew she wouldn't have married him if she'd been exposed to them for any time at all prior to the wedding.

"Can't you block her number?"

"No. The phone is for them to call Rennie once a month. It's better than them having my home number or knowing where we live. Anyway, she's vile and horrid and I hate her more than I ever hated her son. Thankfully, she lives in New York and we don't."

"Some people are assholes."

"Yes."

"We should make out."

She looked up, surprised, and then she laughed, launching herself into his lap.

11

Brody's car was in his driveway as she moved to the front door. He'd received a package, and for some reason, they'd left it on her doorstep.

She knocked and heard the stereo on the other side of the door and what distinctly sounded like a call to come in.

She set the package down on his kitchen counter and headed toward where she heard sounds.

What greeted her was the sight of Brody, standing in his doorway, back against the doorjamb, stroking his cock. His eyes were closed, his head back. At first she blushed from head to toe, but then he groaned and she gulped, probably making a sound of her own, and those big brown eyes opened as he started and relaxed once he saw it was her.

She should have turned around and left, she should have at least looked away, but she stayed rooted to the spot. "I'm sorry. I uh, I heard the stereo and thought you said come in. I got a package, or well it's your package and they left it on my porch and . . ."

Keeping his eyes on her, he went back to work. His fist held his cock tight as he pumped it up and down.

Her breath gusted from her. What a sight he made, totally nude, his hair wet from the shower, body so gorgeous he could have been in a skin mag right then. So beautiful, so totally in charge of his sexuality, it floored her.

Her nipples beaded and her pussy slicked. All she could do was watch as he jerked himself off, as he fisted his cock over and over. The head gleamed with pre-come and the muscles in his forearm were taut.

"I was showering and all I could think about was you. The way you make those soft sigh-moans when I put my mouth on your cunt."

The word was hard, not one she was used to. A word she'd always associated with a gender slur more than a body part. But the way he said it was not derogatory. The way he said it made her mentally play it over her tongue because it sounded evocative.

"It's such a pretty cunt, Elise. All those sweet, slippery folds, and you get so wet when I eat you. Your clit swells up and you get all breathy. I couldn't stop thinking about what it feels like when you come on my face, your sticky honey tastes so good. I was supposed to go back to work, but as I stood here in my bedroom and remembered the last time you were here and we fucked against this doorjamb, I had to touch my cock. I can't go back to work this way."

She knew what he meant. She had to pick Rennie up in half an hour, and if women could have blue balls, or blue clit she supposed, she'd have a raging case.

He kept fucking his fist as she watched, until she knew he was very close. She stepped to him and dropped to her knees, licking the head each time his hand moved down until he let go and she took over with her hands and mouth.

The sound he made then set off so much sexual pleasure and need within her, she had to arch a bit to get some friction against her clit from the seam of her jeans. Little frissons of delight skittered through her.

His hands in her hair tightened a bit as he came, filling her with his cock, with his taste, with satisfaction at making him feel this way. She kissed him until he'd softened, and then he helped her stand and took her mouth in a kiss so hard, so raw she felt like he'd pulled away two layers of skin.

"Good god. Where did you come from?"

"I'm the neighbor who just barges in."

He laughed and kissed her again. "Feel free to barge in anytime you want. Shit, I really have to go to work. Let me help you out." He reached down, but she stopped his hand.

"I have to go pick Rennie up. You can make it up to me, but I'm going to tell you something, so I hope it doesn't go to your head. Just seeing you there like that, seeing you with your cock in your hand, giving yourself pleasure and then finishing you? That was, *whoo*, *guh*, hot. I'm going to be, um, working that into my own self-pleasure routine."

"Oh man, you did not just tell me that you masturbate thinking of me, not right when I have to leave."

He pulled on pants and socks, grabbed a sweatshirt and yanked it over his head.

"Oh, I do. I've been . . . doing that since the first time I saw you over here. Before we'd even met."

They walked out together and he stopped her at his car. "Next time we're together I want to watch."

"Oh."

He grinned and got into the driver's seat. "I'll see you soon. And then I'll see you with your fingers buried in your cunt and watch you, see what you like."

Her face heated as she smiled. "You already know what I like."

"Man can always learn more."

Brody had thought of her and that scene for the rest of the day. He wasn't able to see her that night or for the next few because their schedules were off. Thanksgiving was coming and he'd been dealing with that. With employee schedules and shop hours and making sure Erin didn't have a freaking heart attack doing all the planning. It would be the first time she hosted it with Ben and Todd, and they were expecting a full house. Even Todd's father, whom he'd been estranged from for some time, had agreed to come. That had been a huge deal for Todd and, because of that, for Erin too.

Brody pulled up into his driveway a week after that incredible afternoon, and as always, his gaze moved to the house across the street and he caught sight of her through the front window. Hugging a man. Whiskey, Tango, Foxtrot?

Before he knew what he was doing, he was striding across the street just to see what the hell was going on.

She answered the door, happy and slightly harried, and he sent her a raised brow. "Busy?"

She cocked her head at him. "Hey, Brody. Wanna come in?"

"Sure." He walked in, smiling as he heard Rennie singing at the top of her lungs. "I noticed you had company. Am I interrupting?"

"What is up your butt?" she asked, her voice low.

"Look, I know you're not wearing my frat pin or whatever." He mimicked what she'd said that first day. "But we agreed not to see other people."

Her puzzled look dissolved into a grin, followed by laughter. "You're jealous?"

"Am not."

She only laughed harder. "Daddy? Mama? Come on out here, I want you to meet my neighbor and our very good friend."

"Christ." Her dad. He'd just thrown a jealous tantrum over her father. *Great.*

She just nodded, tears from her laughter leaking down her face. "I have to deal with Raven all the time; you got jealous of my father."

Rennie's singing had stopped and she came thundering downstairs with her grandparents in tow.

The woman at Rennie's left was very clearly Elise's mother. Taller by four inches or so, a little bit rounder and softer, but the same piercing blue eyes, the same pale blonde hair. Even the same cheekbones.

"Wow, I'd say someone has some pretty dominant genes. I can see where you and Rennie get your good looks."

"You didn't say he was so charming in that introduction." The woman swept forward, holding a hand out to Brody. "I'm Martine DuLac. It's a pleasure to meet you. Rennie has been telling us all about you."

"All good things, I hope."

The father made one of those Gallic sounds that said everything and yet nothing at all. He even gave the shrug.

"This is my father, Paul." Elise smiled to the man who'd approached her and kissed the top of her head. Where Elise and her mother were elegant beauties, this man was broad and dark. Green eyes took Brody in from head to toe and back again. He even had those professor eyebrows that only seemed acceptable on men like Paul DuLac.

"It's nice to meet you, sir." Brody offered his hand and the other man took it.

"You staying for dinner? My father has been cooking all day. Roast chicken. He's a really good cook."

"Since I was going to nuke something or call for takeout, I'll accept that invitation." He looked to her parents. "That is, if you don't mind."

Martine began to assure him they were more than happy, Rennie hooted her approval, and Paul continued to check him out.

"Can I help set the table or anything?"

Paul pointed at Brody. "You and I will have some wine. Rennie is going to go wash up, and the ladies will go into the kitchen and pretend they're the ones who cooked dinner, while the men have wine and talk about worldly, manly things. When, in reality, I do most of the cooking and they know I'm going to be grilling you." Paul shooed his wife and daughter from the room and turned to grab a bottle of wine and two glasses.

Elise said something in French to her father, and he snorted at her before turning her around and giving her a gentle push from the room. Brody laughed and nodded at her. He could hold his own, and in truth, he liked that her father wanted to know who the hell he was.

"My granddaughter talks about you all the time. You see them both a lot?" Paul handed Brody a glass and sat across from him.

"I see them both a few times a week. I'm glad Rennie likes me. I happen to think your granddaughter is an exceptional person."

"Like her mother."

Brody nodded. "Yes, sir. Exactly like her mother. Strong, intelligent, funny, pretty, talented too."

"Enough with the 'sir,' already." Paul waved a hand. "Paul is fine. So what are your intentions toward my girls?"

He wasn't going to ask for her hand or anything, so why did he want Elise's father to like him and approve of him? He'd never met the father of any woman he'd seen before. It was odd. "Elise is my friend. I feel protective of her and I enjoy her company. I would not harm either one of them, not ever."

"Is this romantic then? This entanglement?"

He laughed. "It's not an entanglement, but sure, it's romantic. I'm not going to treat her wrong, Paul. Elise is special, but she can hold her own. Anyone can see that. What brings you and the missus out west?"

"Nicely done. Let me just say that while my wife is very cultured and knows about forks and serving plates and other nonsense, I grew up scrapping in the streets of the ghetto I was raised in. Don't hurt my girls. I made a big mistake with that piece of trash Elise married before, but it nearly got her killed and she's paying for it even today. Martine and I are here because Elise is our only living child and Rennie is our grandbaby. We're older, we have the ability to move, and that's what we're doing even if my daughter throws a fit. She needs support of family. We're family, eh? This is what family does. And it's cold in New York. Not so much here. We like the green. We like being where our girls are. Know anyone selling a house?" And just like that, he became friendly now that his message had been delivered. Brody liked the dude.

Elise poked her head in and smiled at Brody. "Time to eat. Daddy, stop harassing Brody. Rennie, girl, wash those hands!" Brody couldn't get the words about her almost being killed out of his head. What the fuck? Had she used with the ex? No, there was no way she could have continued her career in such intense focus and with that much success if she was on the pipe. Abuse sounded more likely. Good thing that asshole was dead, or Brody would feel the need to pay him a visit.

Elise had to admit she liked seeing him at her table. It wasn't the first time he'd eaten with them or anything. But she liked it when he was in her life. She felt safe with him around, even loved the way he was with Rennie. Not fatherly, but he enjoyed her, that was clear. He listened to her stories and songs, laughed at her knock-knock jokes and even showed up from time to time at the park when her soccer team practiced.

He also looked hot. Smoking, ridiculously drool-worthy hot. She wasn't sure how he did it, but he simply emanated sexy effortlessly. Shorts and T-shirt, sexy. Jeans and a turtleneck? *Holy crap* sexy.

Her father looked smug, which meant he must have been pleased with whatever Brody's responses had been. The two of them were a lot alike, big, powerful, but they listened more than they spoke, which was a very good personality trait.

"Rennie, you need to chew or you're going to choke." Brody grinned at her. "It's good stuff, I know. But it looks like your grandfather made enough that you can take a breath every once in a while and chew. My Heimlich is rusty."

A discussion then broke out about soccer and school and other things of huge importance in Rennie's life, including her BFF Nina. Elise's parents soaked their granddaughter in, and even though she felt bad that they were moving across the country, leaving behind their life in New York, she was thrilled she'd have them around again.

"I should have made a cake. I didn't know we'd have such handsome company." Her mother blushed prettily at Brody, and Elise wisely withheld her amused snort.

"Oh, I'm sure I wouldn't have had room for it anyway. The chicken and potatoes and the greens and bread were more than enough."

"I was asking Brody if he knew anyone selling a house. He said he didn't, but he knew a real estate agent, so I'll be calling him to-morrow." Her father sent her a smug smile that told her Brody was on their side.

"If you insist. Brody knows everyone, so you're in good hands if he refers you."

Brody laughed. "Is that a compliment or an insult?"

She touched his arm, liking how warm and solid he was. "A compliment. I save my insults for when we're alone."

He stood and helped her clear the table while her parents put Rennie to bed.

"You look happy. They seem really nice. Rennie clearly adores them and that's reciprocated."

She wiped the counter down and turned the dishwasher on. "Let's walk you back to your place."

He took her hand, and she called up the stairs that she'd be back in a few minutes.

"Winter is near," she said, looking up at the clear night sky.

"It will be. But I expect compared to New York, you'll feel cheated. We get the big snow thing every few years, but mostly it's mild here year-round. Are you happy they're moving here?"

"I feel"—she paused, looking for words—"conflicted. Guilty. I want them here. I miss them. It's been so hard without them around, and I know Rennie is better off with them in her life regularly."

He motioned her toward the chairs on his porch and she sat. He followed her into the two-seater and put his arm around her shoulders.

"Unburden yourself, Elise. I'm not going to judge you."

She blinked back tears and rested her head on his shoulder. "I want them here. So much that I'm not going to put up too much a fight when they sell their house and leave their community to come out here because I can't be there."

"Why can't you be there?"

"The Sorensons are there. All their influence. And my past is there. I don't want that looking over Rennie's shoulder her whole life. Seattle is a fresh start for us both. She's doing so well here. Heck, I am too. I have friends, I have a business. I have a life, and it's been a long time since I have. So I'm selfish to want them here, but I do."

"Why is that selfish? And your former in-laws sound horrible."

"It's selfish because their home is in New York. My father's job is there, my mother's students and her connections are there. Their friends. And Ken's parents are textbook fucked up. They are vile, horrible, evil people."

He laughed and kissed the top of her head. "I think that's the first time I've heard you say the F word. They must be horrible. Are you all right? Safe?"

She nodded. "Yeah. For the first time in years I'm safe and things are hopeful and normal and happy. It's a blessing being here. My kid might just make it into adulthood without having to go to therapy four times a week."

"Wow, your shoulders must be so strong for you to take all that weight."

"You don't know me, Brody. You don't know what I've done." She stood and pulled at the hand he'd been holding until he let go. "You don't. Don't think I'm noble. I'm not noble." She was a fraud.

"Wait. Don't go away mad." He stood, and she put a hand out to hold him off. "Whatever it is, baby, it can't be as bad as you think."

"You don't know."

"So tell me. *Tell* me and let me help you." He stood and she stepped back.

"I have to go. I'll see you soon." Damn it, she couldn't keep the sob from her voice, and he took a step toward her. She was down on the sidewalk, moving quickly. She would fall apart if he tried to comfort her just then.

"Please don't go now. You're hurting, I hate that. Let me help you."

"Please. I can't. I *can't.*" She turned and ran back to her house and stood in her front hall, shaking, trying to get herself back together before her parents or Rennie saw her.

No one knew what she was capable of. Ken did, but he was dead and she wasn't sorry. She wasn't sorry and she knew she should be. What sort of person wasn't sorry that she'd killed someone?

12

"I'll pick Rennie up from school today. She and I have some shopping to do."

Elise's mother had not only made do with her new life in Seattle, she appeared to be thriving. In the weeks following Thanksgiving, she and Paul had found a house, sold their old place and planned to move in over the Christmas holidays after the deal on the new house closed.

Rennie was thrilled to have her grandparents around once again, and the night before they'd all attended Rennie's first-grade winter musical at school, where Martine had accompanied the children on the piano.

Things were very good.

Elise's only niggling worry was the distance that had developed between her and Brody. Maybe she was imagining it, but she hadn't seen much of him since that night on his porch. First there was Thanksgiving, where they'd both been busy with familial commitments, and then afterward she'd been helping with her parents' house hunting, dealing with her own preparations for her school's winter showcase and one Rennie-type school thing after the other. They'd spoken here and there, he'd called her, she'd called him. But they hadn't been together since before Thanksgiving, and she wondered if he'd grown tired of her or, worse, had thought badly of her after her breakdown on his porch.

"Okay, thanks. I'll be home for dinner. I just want to work on this last bit for the showcase. It's stupid to dance myself. I'm the teacher; it's about them."

Her mother just put a hand on her hip. "You're not just any teacher. Let's be honest. You're a star. You're what these girls want to be. Of course they want to see you dance. Every time you show them something, they all stop and stare at you like you're magic. I suppose you are, *bebe*. My star." She hugged Elise and kissed both cheeks. "Shine. They'll shine too, but do your two minutes and enjoy it. I'm off. I'll see you tonight."

"Make sure Rennie doesn't have homework. I know it's right before break, but she might have something."

"Does it look like I fell off the mother truck yesterday? Darling, Matthias was a master at homework avoidance and he made it through school. Too bad I couldn't train him to be a master of heroin avoidance, eh?"

That familiar pain flared. "Or I could have not brought Ken into his world."

Martine shook her head. "Elise, are you so silly you think Matthias never did drugs before Ken? Remember, darling, he'd been to rehab once already by the time you started dating Ken. Matthias, as beautiful a soul as he was, did not die because of you, or Ken, or even me or Daddy. He died because he never did have any concept of moderation. It made you want to look at him the moment he walked into a room. But it made him cheat on girlfriends and shoplift and drive too fast and shoot up heroin until it killed him. Here's the present I want to give you for Christmas, Elise. I want you to be responsible for what is yours and to let go of everyone else's failings. Eh? I'm trying it too. We can work on it together."

"I love you, Mama." Elise allowed herself some tears, some comfort. "I'm so glad you're here. Thank you for being here."

"I love you too. We wouldn't be anywhere else. You know as well as anyone that home is where your loved ones are. Daddy and I don't have any strings tying us to New York anymore. We like it here and that's that. Now, get to work while your daughter and I go spend money."

She stretched and warmed up and then put the music on. Some years prior she'd been in a production of *Carmina Burana* with the Boston Symphony. The interlude was short enough, not overly difficult, but it certainly showcased many different skills most of the advanced students should have mastered and be polishing.

As usual, she lost herself in the dance, fell into the music and the steps. Quick and slow, fouettés, pirouettes, jetés, it all flowed through her, these things she'd been doing over and over like a ritual since childhood.

When she finished, totally elated, knees a bit sore but feeling good, he was there in the doorway. She'd missed him more than she'd allowed herself to think about. Talking on the phone and waving hello here and there wasn't the same as being alone with him.

"I can never quite put into words, after I see you dance, just how beautiful it is. How beautiful you are. The stuff you do blows me away."

"Today I'm feeling distinctly not bad for an old woman." She looked up into his face, liking the curve of his lips. It was still there, that whatever they had between them. "I've missed you." It cost her a bit of pride to say it, but Brody was worth it.

He moved to her, pulling her into a hug. "Me too. I need to kiss you" was all she heard before his lips brushed against hers softly and then more boldly as she reached up to twine her arms around his neck, arching her body against his.

"Mmm. That's nice," she murmured as he kissed along her shoulder.

"Tell me you don't have to go anywhere."

"I have a little while before I need to go home. Wait here." She grabbed her keys and ran down the stairs to lock up. She didn't have any more classes that day, but she didn't want anyone else walking in.

Her hands shook as the need for him began to take over, making her rush to get back to him.

Brody wasn't sure what had happened. He'd headed to her studio after not touching her for three weeks. He needed to see her, to talk to her alone. The phone calls had been all their busy schedules had allowed, but he needed more and he could admit it. After that night where she'd revealed so much of herself on his porch, he'd been overwhelmed by how much she made him feel like protecting and taking care of her. He felt a lot more for her than he'd ever planned to, and he needed some distance to work it through. As he'd rolled out of bed that morning, he knew he'd been a dumbass for not seeking her out. Knew he needed her in his life and accepted it.

He needed her companionship. Missed the spot she filled in his life. He wanted to take a walk down to the Market or something, maybe grab a drink or a coffee, then he'd come to the top of those steps to find her dancing.

The look on her face when she'd stopped, so much joy. And the joy hadn't fallen away when she caught sight of him, easing a knot he'd been carrying since that night on his porch. Suddenly he wanted her then, hard and fast.

When she got back from locking the door, he pulled her to him as they stood at the top of the stairs leading down to the door. The kiss was a wild recipe of tongues and teeth, of sighs and entreaty as hands shoved and pulled at clothing to remove it or, in his case, get it out of the way so he could get to her best parts. Each bit of her exposed to his touch as he removed clothing called to him. Called for a taste, a kiss, a caress. And so he did.

Dropping to his knees, yanking at her bottom half, he thanked heaven above she was wearing leggings rather than tights. He made quick work of them, pulling them off over the ridiculously hot and yet totally complicated toe shoes whose removal would waste time. Time he'd prefer to spend inside her.

She grabbed the railing, holding fast to keep from falling over faint at how good his mouth felt, hot and wet, against her inner thigh.

"Here. I want you here."

As if she'd argue. But he still had his jeans on, they were only unzipped. His shirt was off, and she looked down as his mouth found another place she liked too. The firebird marking his back looked extra sexy as she looked from this angle, with his head, those thick, dark curls of his, bent over, his mouth on her pussy like a starving man's.

She tumbled into orgasm quicker than she'd expected to, but she wasn't about to argue with her body. There was only so much masturbating one could engage in with parents and a small child under her roof. Not that her fingers or any toy felt this good.

"There now," he murmured, petting her thighs, "the edge is off. On your knees facing away from me, gorgeous. On this step here."

He patted the step and she moved to obey, even as her muscles felt like warm goo. Happily, she noted the removal of his jeans before she turned around and braced her hands on the top step.

The sound of the condom wrapper tearing open made her gasp with joy, and they laughed together at her response. "I know, I want it too. It's all I've been thinking about for so long." She rested her forehead against her arm for just a moment until she felt the slippery pressure of his cock at her entrance, pushing to get inside.

A gasping moan trickled from her as she arched her back and he slid into her fully.

So good, so fucking good he nearly lost his mind with it. He wanted to rut on her, cover her with his body, his scent, until all she felt, saw, smelled, was him. Her body fit around him so tight and inferno-hot, pleasure clawed at his gut, pulled him into her body, and he never wanted to leave.

Sex with Elise wasn't just fun, it was the most intensely pleasurable experience he'd ever had. Every time he touched her, he wanted her again, until need made him blind. Not having her for three weeks had nearly driven him insane.

But what got to him so deeply right then was the sense of home he felt when he was with her. The empty or sharp spots inside him were soothed as well as excited just because she existed. No one had that kind of effect on him but her. He'd missed it, missed her. And thank God she'd missed him too.

He thrust into her, hard and fast, her little puffs of breath echoing through the narrow area they were in. He found her spine so alluring, each bump and dip of her vertebrae covered in that pale, satiny soft skin. Leaning down, he kissed the line of her back, tasting sweetness and exertion, the salt of her skin.

Her moan vibrated through her bones and flesh, into him, exciting him further. Her belly trembled beneath the fingers he stroked across it as he moved down to her clit. Her cunt gripped him tight when he stroked over it softly.

"I don't know if I can," she said.

He licked over her shoulder blade. "You can, gorgeous, and you will. Just let go and come again for me."

A broken sob escaped her as she came around him. He clenched his jaw, gritting his teeth, trying to hold out, but she felt so damned good he couldn't stop, and her orgasm brought his own as he pressed in deep and held himself there.

When he came back from the small bathroom adjacent to her office, she'd put herself to rights, having exchanged the toe shoes for a pair of sneakers.

He sat next to her on the top stair. "Those shoes are wicked pretty, but what a pain."

She laughed. "Toe shoes? All of us have fallen or lost balance when a shoe came undone. Makes you careful."

He nodded. "Makes sense. It just impedes me in getting you naked enough to fuck when you're wearing them with tights."

"I'll keep that in mind. How have you been?"

He wavered a moment, wondering if he should just fess up that he'd needed some space, but decided he'd only hurt her. Besides, he'd come through it feeling even stronger about her and their connection, so it wasn't necessary to say anything.

"Crazy busy. We've been down one of our full-time artists and then Raven decided it was too cold to stick around until the end of the year and went to Florida. So the shop has been insane. I'll be able to buy nicer presents though."

Her lips wore a very brief smirk. "She just left you in the lurch like that?"

"I've known Raven for about fifteen years now. She is who she is. You can't make her anything else." He shrugged.

She didn't look convinced.

"What?"

She shook her head. "Oh, no way. She's important to you, clearly an ex of some sort on some level. This is a no-win for me."

"I want you to be honest with me." He drew his knuckles down her throat and through the hollow at the base. He liked the way her breath hitched and her pulse jumped. "It's easy to misunderstand her. Many people do and she does have poor interpersonal skills. She's abrasive. I'm not going to be offended by anything you say."

"I'm not you and I don't have anyone like Raven in my life now. But I did at one point and I found it exhausting to love him. My brother is a lot, *was* a lot like Raven. And people used to let him get away with it because he was"—she paused, licking her lips—"special. There was no one like Matthias. He was, when he was in a good way, so much fun to be with. He'd be gone for like four months without a word. He'd miss important events and never apologize. But out of the blue he'd show up with some seashell he found in Bali and carried back just to show me the pink and to tell me a story about the sunset. The color of the sky was the same pink. He gave it to me so I could have a piece of the joy he felt when he saw that sunset."

She paused, looking off into the space ahead of her. Something deep stirred in her face, and he put an arm around her shoulders, craving more from her. Wanting her to share.

"He was five years older than me, so I idolized him when I was growing up. He was vibrant and so much fun. If he was in a good way and focused on others, he would do anything for the people he loved. But over time, good Matthias was around less and less. I suppose, deep down inside, Raven pushes my buttons for more than one reason. I don't like seeing her be careless with you in a way that it impacts your business."

"And the other reason?"

She licked her lips. "Even the most well-adjusted woman on the planet would be weirded out by the constant inclusion of the ex-girlfriend of the man she's seeing. It's petty, I admit it."

"I'm sorry about your brother. I can't deny the similarities. She's got a lot of talent and she just floats around, never trying too hard. But I'm not her brother. Behavior like hers from Erin or Adrian would be really hard to endure and not be hurt by." He kissed her forehead. "As for her being my ex. It's complicated. Do you have time for the story?"

"I want to hear it, but I need to get home for dinner. I promised Rennie, and she's been shopping with my mother, which is frightening, but at least it's not my credit card. Hey, would you like to come? It's chili day at my house. I started it in the slow cooker so I can come home and it'll make me feel all domestic and accomplished."

He laughed.

"If not, maybe you can come over later for a glass of wine?"

"Can I tell you something?"

"Of course."

She let him pull her to standing as he took her bag, and they headed downstairs as she turned things off and locked up.

"Yes, I'd like to come to dinner. I haven't hung out with Rennie in a while, so I imagine there are many new developments I need to be apprised of."

She grinned. "I like that you see how fabulous my kid is. I'm totally biased, but it makes me happy."

He stopped, cupping her cheek briefly. "I've never met anyone like you. I like that you compliment me with genuine things. Sometimes there can be so much artifice between people. You don't want to compliment too much or too intimately because you don't want to tip your hand with the other person and it's a power struggle or whatever. It's ridiculous and complicated and tiring. But with you, there isn't any of that. I like you, Elise. You're genuine and you're an amazing mother, and that's another thing I like about you. I love to watch you with your kid. She's not an accessory or an afterthought. You work hard to balance things so that it's about her. I admire that."

"That's a wonderful thing to say. All of it. Thanks."

"I'm parked in the same lot you are. Let's go and I'll be over at your place for dinner shortly. Maybe you can duck over to my place for the wine after Rennie goes to bed. Your parents are still staying with you, right?"

"Yes, they are, and I might just take you up on that."

13

He'd come to dinner with flowers for all three females. Her mother had flirted and laughed, and Rennie just rolled her eyes and started telling Brody about her life since she saw him last.

Elise's mother liked him, that was easy to see, and he treated Martine with respect and listened to her stories in the same patient, interested fashion he'd listened to Rennie's.

"Do you notice your daughter and your mother both seem to have a heart for your Brody?" her father said as they cleared up the dining room.

"He's a nice guy. They're both spoiled that way with you already. You set the bar awfully high."

"*Pffft.*" He tried to look tough, but she saw his smile when he ducked his head to put away a bowl.

Her mother came into the room. "Elise, Rennie is going to watch a movie with me and your father. We will have popcorn and soda, no caffeine of course. Why don't you go on over to Brody's house for a glass of wine and a quiet conversation?"

"Are you psychic or did he hit you up for babysitting services?"

Her mother laughed. "Darling, you're young. Why wouldn't you want a quiet hour or two with him? You'd planned to ask? Because Daddy and I would like you to know we are here. We've been begging you to go out and have fun. It's not a chore to be with Irene. It's one of our favorite things in the world."

"Thank you." She hugged them both. "I won't be out late."

"Be out until whenever you want. If you stay over, though, just let us know so we know to get breakfast ready for Irene in the morning."

She blushed. "I'm not spending the night. Mama, I made a promise to myself I wouldn't do that around her until I'm sure that man will be part of our lives long-term. I spend the night in the same house she does. I don't bring a parade of men through her life. She needs stability."

"The offer is there when you realize that boy in there will be with you, how you said, long-term. Now, go."

"Momma! Gran said you're going to Brody's for adult conversation and we're going to watch *Beauty and the Beast* and eat popcorn and drink soda and have ice cream!" Rennie hopped around the living room. "I brought blankets down and pillows so we can all snuggle up on the couch. I haven't never watched this with them, only you. So they'll love it."

She leaned down and hugged Rennie, kissing her several times across her cheeks and nose. "You be good for them, okay? I'll just be across the street and I'll be back in a few hours."

"Don't worry, Pops and I will be sure everything is cleaned up afterward," Rennie stage-whispered. Martine's aversion to washing dishes was well known, and amusing to the members of her family.

"Gotcha. I love you, Noodle."

"I love you too, Momma."

"Oh man, that chili was totally amazing." Brody patted his belly as he led her into his house. He took her coat and hung it on a peg in the foyer, and she toed her shoes off.

"Let me get the fire on so your feet don't get cold."

"Thank you. But your floors are really warm."

"Radiant heat. Awesome isn't it? A few years ago I finally got the energy to get rid of the ugly-ass carpet up here. So of course Adrian decides I need radiant heat, because he'd recently gotten it at his place."

Warmth from the fireplace crept toward her and she snuggled into the couch.

"So it was his present to me. Little shit. A present is luggage or a pair of gloves, not radiant-heat floors."

"He loves you and he had it in his means to give it to you, so he did. And I bet you let him know how much it meant."

He stood and turned, cocking his head. "You're scary some-times."

"Meh. I'm not so much. I've seen the way you are with them. Where's my wine?"

"Any preferences?" He moved toward the kitchen. "I've got a cabernet here and beer in the fridge, if you'd rather go that way. I can also make a mean martini, if you'd prefer that."

"Looks good *and* can make a martini. I'd love a glass of wine, thank you. I have no idea why you're wasting your time with an old woman with a kid when with talents like that you could be out with your pick of any tight-bodied twenty-two-year-old."

"Ha. You're not old, you're younger than I am. I've had my share of twenty-two-year-olds, but frankly, at my age I feel positively lecherous around anyone younger than twenty-six or -seven. And have you looked in a mirror?"

He brought her a glass of wine and settled in next to her on the couch.

"You're anything but a waste of my time." He kissed her knuckles before taking a sip from his glass. "So . . . Raven. I met Raven fourteen years ago. I was twenty-five and she the aforementioned twenty-two."

Elise snorted and he flashed a grin.

"I had all this responsibility in my life. I'd had it for a long time, really. Even before my parents died I took care of Erin and Adrian. They were both finally out of high school and working on this band thing. Things were good. I was tattooing and building a following. She was, well, she's not much different now than she was then.

"Where I had all this stuff anchoring me—family, a job, a community—Raven didn't. She was a free spirit and I couldn't get enough. She was everything I couldn't be. She floated around, doing whatever she wanted, whenever she wanted, and she wanted me. Which I found very attractive."

Elise just listened. Sometimes you needed to get it all out, even if she was sitting there listening to the story of how he fell in love with another woman.

"She and Erin became close as well, but Adrian never really trusted her. To this day there's distance between them. I fell and I fell hard. She told me not to. She told me that she wasn't into long-term exclusive relationships. And when it came to it, she cheated. Well, not really cheated; she fucked someone else and didn't hide it. To her, hiding it would have made it cheating."

Elise knew part of his attraction must have been that he thought he could be the one to change Raven. The more she told him it wasn't possible, the more attractive she'd have seemed to his twenty-five-year-old self. Also, she *really* hated Raven at that point.

Brody chuckled. "The look on your face makes me feel avenged. So you can probably guess I didn't end it. I kept at it for a few years on and off. It broke me, or I let it break me. Whatever. But when Adele was killed, she came and ran my shop for months. She refused to let me pay her anything but straight commission. She handled everything up here. She stepped in during the hardest time of my life and she gave me exactly what I needed. She watered my plants, she took care of my fish, she dealt with my mail and anything else I needed while I was gone or traveling back and forth. She did it all without me having to ask. Afterward, she sat with me and Erin both, many a night, listening to us pour out our pain. She stayed here for fifteen months all told, from the date of the murder until months after Erin had settled back in here, in Seattle. Everything was chaos, everything felt so hard just to deal with. And Raven made it so that all I had to do was support Erin."

"That's a wonderful gift." And it was, Elise couldn't deny it.

"So she's just, well she's just Raven. She's not perfect. She's not even likeable half the time. But she stood up for me and my loved ones when we needed it most. She's been an amazing friend to Erin through all she's gone through. She's special to me, but I don't make the mistake of not knowing exactly what she is and what she's capable of. She's not selfish, not really."

"She's at the center of her own universe and that's how it is." You can't hate those people, but you can try to keep them out of your life. She couldn't hate Raven, not after that story, but Elise didn't like her, and she didn't trust her either.

"But you're not her." He laughed at her reaction. "No, what I meant is, you're empathetic. You take care of people—not to your extreme detriment, but you go the last mile for people and you don't do it on your schedule."

"I cut my brother from my life, Brody. I didn't have him over for barbecues or even through my front door for about six months before he died, and even before that things were strained. I'm not Raven, but I'm not you either. I don't go the last mile. I have limits and it makes me selfish. I can accept that. Like I said, I'm not noble."

"You take on a lot. You carry a lot of guilt. Raven didn't steal from me, didn't put my loved ones in danger. Was he bad? At the end?"

"Yes. He'd burned his bridges, so no one would have hired him even if his voice hadn't been shot. I hated to hear his voice on the phone when I answered. Hated to see him waiting outside my building. He was a millstone and I resented that."

"Who wouldn't? Come on, Elise! Who wouldn't hate that?"

"If he took a shower and ate a meal with me, I gave him money. I know, I enabled him. Another mistake in a long line, I'm sure. But Jesus, he looked horrible and he was *sick*. He was so angry all the time. He said things, hurtful things you only know when you're close to someone. He heard things from my husband and used them to hurt me.

"And then he'd get clean for a while and be his old self. Silly and shallow in most ways, but he had a good heart. He was so good with Rennie when she was a baby. But he always fell back into drugs. I had to keep him out of my life. Out of Rennie's life. He ran with my ex, who had been in and out of jail, so that was always there between us. He stole from me. He shot up in my house! With my baby around. I couldn't do it. Having a junkie in your life is hell. You live in a place of fear all the time. Dread. What will he say or do? Will this ringing phone be the police or my parents tell-ing me he's dead? Will I be relieved when I hear it?"

"So it's your fault he overdosed? After being a hard-core addict for years? At some point, you have to let go. You have Rennie to think of."

"Ugh, you don't need to know more. It's all a cliché anyway. Just turn on *Intervention* on cable and there we are. High-functioning children, artistic, achievers, and one of them ends up shooting up junk and blowing men for twenty dollars."

"While the other is an international ballet sensation who has danced some of the most challenging and sought-after roles."

"Right. Why are we talking about my brother again? You were just trying to help me not think Raven was the kind of girl who'd fuck you again because she was lonely and didn't understand the promise you made to me. Not because she wanted to break us up or anything, but because she wanted to have sex."

Raven *had* come on to him at Thanksgiving, and no, she hadn't understood his promise to Elise. Part of him had been very sad that she'd wanted him to break a promise to anyone else. He'd said no, and Raven would be out of Seattle for a while, but Elise Sorenson was a very smart lady. A smart lady with a guilt-trip the size of Rhode Island. "This is very heavy."

She laughed, but bitterness edged the sound. "Yeah. Maybe it's easier with a woman who just shows up when she wants sex."

"Heavy in a *good* way. Raven is my friend in that way you like your eccentric aunt. But you and I are friends on a different level. More intimate. I'm too old to want easy and I'm glad you shared all that. But I think you take on a lot of things you can't possibly own. What were you like as a kid?"

"I liked everything orderly, but it rarely was. My parents are old-school in some ways, but decidedly modern in others. We had a lot of arts education when I grew up. We traveled. We went to museums in every city we visited. I started ballet classes when I was three. I went to very good schools. I got good grades. I rarely got into trouble because I probably would have been more upset than my parents if I had disappointed them. I loved school. I loved music and art and poetry and dancing. We were raised to understand learning came from all directions, and I loved that. We were sheltered in some ways. We never felt any type of want; though we did have to work for things, we lived well. Matty didn't start getting into real trouble until he went to college. He had to work really hard, and for a boy who'd been good at everything he ever tried, that was really difficult to accept."

He took her wineglass and refilled it. "Why did you really stop dancing?"

"I'd been wavering on quitting for a while. The divorce had been complicated. Rennie was getting older and it was harder to work around my touring schedule. Then I got hurt. My leg was broken in two places, the femur was shattered. I can't dance the way I have to. I don't have the strength or endurance I did before. So it was time. And while I miss the stage, I don't regret my choice."

"Still, must have been hard to deal with. The injury and knowing you had to stop doing something you loved so much. I have all this back pain I didn't have before. I have to take more time away from doing tats so I don't get all bunched up. I hate that. Makes me feel old."

"And yet, I've driven by your shop when Rennie and I go to Woodland Park Zoo and it's always packed. You're in demand. I searched for you on the Internet, I've seen all the articles. Talk about a kid who was good at everything he tried. How many times do you think the word 'genius' has been applied to your work?"

He burst out laughing. "Enough that it makes me happier when

I'm having a shitty day. I'm lucky. I'm good at something I love to do. It's something special to have that."

"Yeah. I won't dance *Giselle* again, or *Swan Lake*, but I can still dance and I do every day. My studio is growing so well, I'm thrilled. I took a chance and it's been wonderful. If I had to do something like run an athletic club or teach dance theory at a local college, I don't know if I'd be as at ease with my choice."

"I'm glad you didn't have to go that way, then. What are your plans for next Friday? Your mother informed me that you needed to get out more with friends and that they were quite happy to sit with Rennie while I made that happen. We do pool, barbecue and beer at the tavern. I thought I could see just how good a pool player you really were."

"Like a date?"

"Yeah, why not? I mean, about ten people will be around, but everyone knows we're sleeping together, and Adrian said I make cow eyes at you, so it's not like people would be surprised. Plus, everyone likes you, and I like you."

"Okay then. I'll talk with my mother to work something out."

"I think we have time for some smooching at the very least." He grinned, putting his wineglass down.

She placed hers next to his and clambered up into his lap. "Probably just a bit."

14

"Hey there!" Erin called out as Elise opened her front door the following Friday. "Ready to play pool?"

Elise smiled at the sight of her new friend. The woman was like rainbow sherbet or a sundae with sprinkles. Today her hair was a fairly normal shade, brunette, but with streaks of pink here and there.

"Were you lying in wait over there? Looking through Brody's windows to see when I got home?" She opened the door wider and motioned her inside.

"Totally. I think the boys got a little jealous that I was more interested in when you got home than them." Erin laughed and hugged her.

"I haven't been on a date in a very, very long time," she told Erin as they started to walk across the street to Brody's house. "I know it's not a romantic candlelit event or anything. It's a group thing with beer and pool. God." She stopped and grabbed Erin's hand. Erin squeezed. "What am I doing? I don't know what I'm doing. I should go home. I'm not young. I'm not hip. I'm thinking this is a date, but he doesn't!"

Erin hugged her when they stopped at the mailbox. "Listen here, of course you're nervous. You're taking all these new steps in your life. You can do this. This is life and you're meant to live it. You're starting over. I know, Elise, I *know* what that's like. I came back to Seattle and I was a mess. Empty. Brody and Adrian stuck by me when I was a zombie."

Elise knew it had to have been hard. It turned her cold just thinking about not having Rennie, imagining the hell of watching a child die.

"I admire you so much for who you are. You have two wonderful men who love you so much. It's so clear to anyone who looks at you that you're so strong."

"I made it through and you can too. Scratch that, you *are* making it through. Just let it happen. You're fine. You look gorgeous and effortless as usual. Everyone likes you, including and most especially Brody. He's a genuine person, a man who cares about the people in his life. You're in his life. We all know you two are together, no matter what you two call it. Of course this is a date. I think you and I need a girls-only evening. When your parents go back to get their stuff next week, let's get together, okay? I'll come over, we can make dinner and hang out. Maybe paint some nails and do hair with Rennie and then you and I can talk. I'll tell you my story, you tell me yours. Deal?"

Could she? What would that be like? For so long she didn't have close friends because of Ken. She was embarrassed by him, by what her life had turned into, so she just did her thing, and those friendships with the other dancers in the company only went so deep. The allure of having a friend she could share it all with was a heady thing. She already had such intimacy with Brody, but even at that, she hadn't told him everything. She hadn't wanted him to be disgusted with her or her past.

"That sounds so good. Thanks, you know? For being . . ." Elise swallowed hard.

"Your friend. And you're mine."

"Are you hogging Elise, Erin?" Brody called out from his front porch. "Should I be worried?"

Erin laughed and kissed Elise's cheek. "She's pretty hot, but she seems to like you better."

"If you both change your minds, can we watch?" Ben asked, coming out on the porch to join Brody.

"Ew. That's my sister, dude." Brody wrinkled his nose at Ben, who laughed.

"Well, then don't look. She's not *my* sister."

"Don't make me hurt you," Brody said, whacking Ben's arm.

"Pervs, the whole lot of them." Erin grinned, looking over her shoulder at the men on the porch before turning back to Elise. "You okay now?" Erin asked quietly.

"Yeah. Thanks for the pep talk, Coach."

"Let's roll, ladies. We've got a table, a few pitchers and some wings waiting for us." Ben took one of Erin's hands, Todd the other.

Brody let them go ahead, strolling slowly up to Elise until he reached her, pulling her in for a kiss. "Hey you. You look pretty."

"Thank you. Rennie reminded me that you like my hair down."

He laughed, putting an arm around her shoulders before they began to walk the several blocks toward the tavern. It was one of the big draws of this neighborhood that everything was within walking distance. The air was chilly, but they were all bundled up, and Brody knew that having grown up in Albany, Elise knew how to deal with the cold.

"Excited for the showcase?"

She looked up and smiled. "I am. I think they're ready. It's pretty much out of my hands at this point. They're in charge of themselves. Hopefully they'll do well. If not, I'll have to deal with high-strung dancers and their parents come morning."

Her mother had invited him to the after party she and Paul had planned, and he'd accepted. He liked being included in that part of her world. Wanted to be there for her big night as well. It was a surprise party, but he'd nearly mentioned it twice, so he reminded himself to shut up.

The tavern wasn't fancy. At first glance one might even call it a dive. But it was a family-owned place, the food was great and the beer was cheap. The pool tables were kept in excellent condition, and all was right with the world when he walked in and saw their group already assembled and ready to go.

And it wasn't like he was going to complain each time Elise blew the chalk from the cue or when she bent to take a shot. True to her word earlier that year, she was an excellent pool player, cleaning the floor with Ben, Adrian and Arvin.

"How hot is that?" Todd murmured as they watched Erin, Maggie and Elise play against Adrian.

"Yeah. I can't complain. That's a whole lot of very pretty, very capable woman there." Arvin grabbed a wing as he settled in at the table.

They watched as Elise won again and it was Brody's turn to play.

Elise's skin broke out in gooseflesh every time he walked behind her, taking care to get extra close. He brushed against her, bringing the line of his cock against her ass or thigh each time he moved around the table.

"If you think you can distract me with sex, you're totally right," she murmured as he leaned in beside her to take his shot. And missed.

She grinned and he gave her a hard kiss. "You did that on purpose."

"Totally. But I wasn't lying."

He laughed and she let Todd win because she wanted to sit down, drink a beer and eat some wings.

Brody's body next to hers in the booth was warm and reassuring, even as he set off hormonal earthquakes within her every time he touched her.

"I'm glad you could come out tonight." He leaned back and she rested her head against his shoulder. She was utterly relaxed, enjoying herself with her friends, having a moment with the man she liked; all was well in the world.

"I am too."

"How long has it been?" He played with her hair, sifting it through his fingers, making her feel like a pampered cat. He smelled good, familiar and warm, and totally sexy. She wanted to lick him. A lot. So she gave in and let herself nuzzle his neck, breathing in the way he was, letting that scent lodge in her senses until she shivered.

"You're distracting me," he said, amused.

"Sorry," she said, totally not. "How long has it been since I dated? Played pool?"

"Dated. Somehow, I have a hard time imagining you playing pool on a date before me."

She laughed. "Am I that much of a fuddy-duddy?"

"Fuddy-duddy? Wow, I haven't heard that one since first grade." He squeezed her to let her know he was teasing. "You're not a fuddy-duddy. I just meant I knew you were married and then were on the road and dancing."

"I happen to like the word 'fuddy-duddy,' thank you very much." She winked at Adrian. "Three years? Yeah, and then it was a few dates. Dinner, the theater, nothing as fun as pool." She shrugged.

"How long were you with your ex?"

"I was twenty-three when we met, and we were married by the

time I was twenty-four. I divorced him when I was twenty-seven, a few months after Rennie was born. It had been a done deal for about a year before that anyway. I'd kicked him out about two months into my pregnancy and then he did jail time. Blah, blah, blah."

"He sounds like a total tool," Adrian said.

"He was. But he gave me Rennie, and for that, I'm glad for him. Anyway, I'm out of the dating habit. I have no idea. Am I doing it right?"

Brody leaned toward her and kissed her nose. "You're rocking it. And Elise, tell me true, have you ever not done things right in your life? I bet you were good at everything growing up."

"I did well in school. I was a good dancer. Oh, it's my turn." She scrambled over him and out of the booth before he could say more.

"Dude, how long as it been since *you've* had a date?" Adrian leaned back and watched Brody, an amused smile on his face.

"What? *I'm* here with a beautiful woman. How am I failing again? Oh, please do inform me, since you're here with your steady girlfriend of five years. Oh wait, you're here alone, rock-boy. How you gonna school me with a record like that?"

"Talk's cheap, old man. Have you not noticed how she gets uncomfortable with any mention of how perfect she is? She was snuggled up to you, sending all the right signals, and you made the comment about her being perfect and she scampered off. Not very smooth."

Brody snorted at his brother, partly because he wanted to but partly because Adrian, damn him, was right, and had seen something Brody himself had seen but hadn't quite put together the same way Adrian had.

"We all have our wounds, Brody. Now you know what hers are about and you can avoid them, or at least poke at them in private."

Elise hadn't had such a wonderful time with other adults in

ages. Rennie came first, and she didn't resent that or wish it away. But it meant she didn't date much and she didn't have much time or energy for nights playing pool and laughing with friends.

She liked it.

She liked it as much as she liked the weight of Brody's arm around her shoulders. She liked the sound of quiet laughter and talk as they all headed back home.

Keeping her voice low, she said, "Ben, Todd and Erin are a bit tipsy. You need to offer them a place to crash when you get home. I'll go back to my place. I don't want them to feel like they have to drive right now."

Brody stopped and embraced her. "Smart woman but so dumb in some ways. Yes, I noticed, and yes, I will offer them, and Adrian, a place to hang out. But you are *not* going back home. It's eleven and everyone is asleep at your house. We're going to play Rock Band on the Wii."

"I wanted to have hot, noisy, wild sex for hours," she breathed against his mouth, and he groaned.

"That's not fair. We can, by the way, have as much sex as you desire. I have a door on my bedroom. They're all adults and know what a closed door means. If they knock, I'll kill them."

"Get a room," Erin called out softly, and Brody let her go and they continued to walk.

"I can't play Rock Band and have sex with you. I'm not that much of a multitasker."

"Like I need to play on the Wii when you're there willing to fuck me. Video games are what men invented to fill the sex void. Any man who'd choose video games over sex deserves to live in his mother's basement with his mint-condition, in-box *Star Wars* figurines and his real doll."

She burst out laughing.

But when they got back, there wasn't time for sneaking off, because the video game challenge was tossed out and it would have felt weird telling them all to play while she and Brody went off to have sex. It would have been good, but weird, and these were his siblings, people more like his kids than his brother and sister.

"I can't believe they're still here," he said on her doorstep an hour and a half later.

"They like to be with you. How awesome is that? I hope Rennie still wants to hang with me when she's this age. You should be proud, Brody. You give them a safe, happy space and they want to be in it. This is a good thing." She craned her neck to kiss him quickly. "Well, it's a sucky thing for our plans of wild, noisy sex, but it means you did your job right. That's something special. You three are something special. I'll just masturbate and think of you."

"You're really gonna get it when I get you naked again."

She laughed. "Oh, I do hope so."

"I want to be with you New Year's Eve. You're coming to Erin's tomorrow?"

That was lovely in its suddenness. Like he couldn't stand the thought of not being with her. It was nice. "In the afternoon, yes. Then we'll come back here, put a turkey on to roast, watch movies and feast. I've never been away from Rennie on New Year's Eve. We have a ritual of sorts, sort of a good-luck talisman for the next year. Rennie will stay awake until midnight and then conk out, only to be terribly cranky the next day when she insists on getting up to watch the Rose Parade and eat pancakes. Not very glamorous."

"Am I invited? It doesn't sound glamorous, but it does sound wonderful. I'd not expect you to be away from Rennie on New Year's Eve."

She warmed. He got to her. "Yeah, of course. My mother and daughter have a crush on you, my father doesn't hate you, and I happen to like you too. But I won't be offended if you have other plans."

"I'll be here. I'll bring dessert and some champagne."

"Yes to dessert, but my father is sort of a champagne snob. He's already bought the bottles we'll drink. Drove all over the area until he found just the right wine shop. You're welcome for breakfast the next day too. There aren't any spare bedrooms at my house though."

"I can make it across the street and back for the Rose Parade and pancakes." He tipped her chin up. "I can't think of a better way to spend my New Year's Eve." He kissed her softly. She wanted more but liked that he didn't push with her parents inside the house. Yes, she was an adult, but some things died hard.

"How about we all head over to Erin's together tomorrow afternoon? I know the best places to find a parking spot."

"You sure? You've never been in a car with my parents before. It's, well, you may need a Xanax before the day is done."

He laughed. "Looking forward to that. I imagine your dad will sit up front with me and you ladies in back."

"Or, if we take my van, you can sit in the back with my mom, and my dad will be up front. No matter what, he'll be up front and they'll need to be separated. Just wait. Boy, you're never going to want to see me again after that."

"I highly doubt that, Elise. I like seeing you. A lot."

That made her tingly inside. "Night." She unlocked her front door.

"Night. See you tomorrow." He gave her another quick kiss and stood back, waiting until she'd closed and locked the door before he headed back to his place.

15

That lovely midnight smooch brought the next year into Elise's life not with a boom, but in a sweet, gentle rush of wonderful. Brody was part of her life in a way she'd not expected after that first time at her studio.

Her showcase had gone very well. The surprise party afterward had been lovely, made her feel connected and celebrated. She was now working in an adjunct capacity with the Northwest Ballet Company. They'd asked her to come on as staff, but as they were based in Portland, she hadn't wanted to move. Still, it was a prestigious offer and she'd been quite happy to work something out with them.

She'd tried, and failed, to get together with Erin to talk for about a month but they were finally going to make dinner and have martinis that evening. After her last class she and Rennie headed over to Elise's parents' house for a few minutes and then home.

"I feel like I'm sneaking you away from my brother," Erin said as the three of them settled in to eat.

"Brody's like Mom's and my best friend. He's so gigantic and he likes to play catch and also he comes to my tea parties. There's loads of kids in my class whose dads won't play tea party with 'em and Brody's just our neighbor and Mom's special guy."

Elise widened her eyes and studiously avoided Erin's gaze or she'd start laughing. Or die of embarrassment. Or both. "He is our best friend and we all three know how special he is." *Mom?* What happened to the very sweet *Momma* Elise had loved for the last six years. Oh God, seven years. Rennie was about to turn seven the following weekend. Before she knew it, Rennie would be graduating from high school and going off to college and having her own life. It was a thought that simultaneously filled her with giddy anticipation and terror.

"And, he's very nice to look at. I heard Mom tell him that yesterday. He did look very nice. He had one of those hats, the kind you pull down on your head. I told him he should wear a cowboy hat. He looked sort of scared when I said so though."

Erin laughed. "I totally know what I'm getting him for his birthday." She looked back to Rennie. "Speaking of birthdays, are you ready for yours?"

Rennie took a big gulp of milk, eyes wide at what she was about to reveal to Erin. "We ordered the cake today. It has princesses on it."

"Princesses playing soccer," Elise added with a wink. "The father of one of my students runs a bakery in Ballard. He's making it to her specifications."

"Pretty awesome, kid! I can't wait to have a piece. This is going to be a very fun party."

"I'm super glad you're coming, Erin. I wish Adrian could be there too."

"I know he does as well. But he's on tour and can't get back here until next month."

Elise appreciated how kind all three Brown siblings were to them. Rennie needed stability, and she had it in Seattle. Now that Elise's parents were there as well, Rennie had the kind of community and connection any child would thrive with.

"He sent me a present, but Mom won't let me open it until my birthday. He's in Australia. I want to go there and see kangaroos and stuff. Do you think he's going to see any?"

Elise let the sound of the other two talking wash over her. This was home.

It was another three hours before Elise finally heard Rennie's soft little snuffle, the signal that she'd finally achieved sleep.

"We're trying for a baby," Erin said when Elise joined her on the couch.

Elise smiled, genuinely happy for her friend. "I figured it was that, or you were already pregnant, when you said you didn't want a glass of wine."

"You're very easy to talk to, you know? I feel a connection to you. Mother-to-mother maybe? You listen. It's rare that people actually listen. They talk."

"Thank you. Really. I haven't had a close friend in years, and now, between you and Brody, I've got two. I imagine it's a scary step for you to take. Maybe guilt too."

"I imagine you read or heard most of the details about what happened when Adele was killed. I loved being a mother. It was challenging and exhausting, but every time I even thought of her, my heart would soar. Nothing else is like it."

Elise nodded.

"So now I want that again. But the situation is complicated. And complicated is, of course, a total understatement when you're married and live with your boyfriend too. Or our nonlegal husband or whatever the heck you call the third person in your relationship who you love. Part of Ben's family isn't speaking to him still. Things are very shaky with Todd's dad and brother. And I'm afraid."

Erin sighed out a long breath and Elise just squeezed her friend's hand.

"Afraid of losing another child. Afraid that if it happened I wouldn't survive it. I'm getting closer to forty; it won't be the same as it was in my early twenties. I worry about the pregnancy. I worry about *getting* pregnant to begin with. And . . ." Her eyes teared up and Elise watched her search for the words, so she gave them to Erin herself.

"Of loving a new child and betraying Adele." Elise figured that had to be the hardest thing of all.

Erin nodded, tears falling, and Elise hugged her.

"It's okay to cry. It's okay to be scared. I think you're so brave to have made it through all you have. And to be happy. That's the best part. You have two men who love you so much. Who cares what you call Ben? He's yours. You're his. You all have each other and that's what's important. As for the other stuff, I'm sure you've spoken with an attorney on what to do and all the legal ramifications for Ben. You're not an operating-inside-the-box person, Erin. You'll forge a path with this baby, like you've forged your own path all the years leading up to now."

They sat there for a few minutes, Elise hugging Erin as she cried and then got herself back together. "I'm glad I told you that."

"I'll be here when you do get pregnant. Here to listen and to happily watch you be a mother again. I'm your friend. And, let's be honest, it'll take the pressure off me to give Rennie a baby sister or brother, because she can focus all her baby love on yours."

"She's going to be a great friend to the baby. I'm glad my kid will have you both around."

"The questions Rennie's going to ask me are going to be *wonder-*

ful. I'm sending her to you for a few. I should send her into the de-
livery room with you. Best. Birth. Control. Ever."

Erin laughed.

And Elise began.

"When I was twenty-three, I met Ken at a cocktail party. He
was everything I wasn't. Bold and larger than life. He was a painter
of some repute and in demand. He set his sights on me. You have
no idea how flattering that was.

"It went very fast between us and we eloped to Vegas four
months later. And then I met his family and it was totally clear
why he hadn't introduced me to them. Things were all right for a
while, but what had been a tendency to drink too much became a
much bigger problem. Within a few years he'd become a full-blown
crack addict. Worse, it was my brother who used with him. They
fueled each other's recklessness. Ken went to rehab and cleaned up.
I thought he really had changed. We reconciled, I got pregnant.
And he slipped back into using and I'd had enough. He harassed
me, called me, begged me to take him back, threatened to kill me,
and then his parents started calling, telling me they'd take the
baby. They refused to believe he was using again."

Just thinking about that time made her skin clammy. Her life
had been on the razor's edge that summer going into the winter, as
she got bigger and bigger, as Ken's life spun more and more out of
control. But it had been being pregnant that had kept up her re-
solve to keep away from Ken.

"I filed for divorce and that was a horrible, ugly mess. But I won.
He couldn't have any unsupervised visits with Rennie and he had to
pass drug tests to be allowed to see her at all. His parents got visitation, but never without me. Thank God she was an infant then."

She focused on Erin, really looked at her, and paused. "Honey,
are you all right?"

"I'm fine. It's just, you know, the terror when your child is being threatened. I have been there. It's not a good place."

"It wasn't, no. In spite of that, things were good. I traveled the world and continued to do what I loved. My life was for dancing and for Rennie. I didn't have time for anything else.

"In the meantime, my brother and Ken dragged each other down. Both of them overdosed a few times, until Matty couldn't survive anymore. After that Ken went on a binge and did eighteen months for breaking into my house, and I moved into a building with a doorman."

Elise got up and poured herself a glass of wine. She'd never told this story before. Her parents knew because they'd been there, but she'd only spoken to the police with the details. Her hands shook slightly from the adrenaline and emotion of the story and of the telling.

Erin cleared her throat. "You don't have to talk about it anymore. I know how hard it is to tell it. But I have to say, I'm glad I did it. I'm glad I shared it."

"It's . . . gah! Two months after he got out of prison, he broke into my building, killed the doorman and stole the master key. He got into my apartment and held me there for three hours. He beat me, threatened to kill me, raped me. The only thing that kept me from giving up was that Rennie was due home and I was sure he'd kill us all. So I managed to move enough to grab a nearby umbrella from the stand in the foyer and I hit him with it. I was . . . It was stupid, I don't know why I didn't try for something else, but he was blocking my way and I couldn't stand. It surprised him. He moved to backhand me, but the gun fell from his pocket, along with his rig—the gear he used to shoot cocaine with and his pipe for smoking it, all that lovely stuff. He was a junkie, so he grabbed for the rig, forgetting the gun. But I didn't. I went for it. I didn't think, I just pointed and shot. I hit him in the head, a total fluke. About a minute later the cops burst in and they took me to the hospital and Ken to the morgue."

"Oh dear god." Erin rubbed her hands quickly up and down her arms.

"I wasn't charged with anything. He'd beaten me so badly it was pretty clear it had been self-defense. He broke my leg in three places. My right leg. He knew what he was doing."

"Ended your career."

Elise nodded. "Then over the next year and a half, his parents dragged me through the courts, trying to take Rennie. Threatening to harm my parents professionally and financially. They're stupid rich. And they blame me for their son's death. Technically they're correct. I am to blame. It took eighteen months total to deal with the break-in, my recovery, the court bullshit and leaving the NBT permanently. The day after I learned I'd not only won full custody but limited their contact with her to once a month via phone, I packed our new minivan with our clothes and some food, a moving truck came to our apartment to pick up the last boxes of things we wanted to keep, and we came here."

"And look at you now. I admire you. I know what it's like to have to go through all this legal stuff. It's draining and frustrating. I can't even imagine what a custody battle must have been like."

"Not much to admire really. My child has a dead parent and the other one is a murderer. I'm the reason she had to have play therapy for a few years. She had very little exposure to him over her life, but she did have exposure to his parents. I wanted her to have a relationship with them, and it ended up upsetting her. I caused it. I can't erase my mistakes or I'd be erasing her. But they're my mistakes, no way to deny it."

"You're not a murderer. You reacted to protect yourself and your kid. You're a damned good mother. Your parents love her and they'll be around for her. We're all here for her. For you."

Rather than cry, she managed a nod of thanks. "Now you know my story."

"And you know mine. And, I have to say, we are two strong chicks." Erin smiled. "We're survivors, Elise. Two fucking thumbs up for surviving."

"Amen, sister."

"You should share this with Brody. When you're ready, of course. He cares about you."

Elise nodded. "I know. I'm just . . . ashamed. Ashamed that I've made so many mistakes. It's vain, I know. But I don't want him to think less of me."

"Why would he? It's a horrible thing, but you're not at fault here. You didn't do any of this. You *reacted* to a host of things to survive. To save your kid. You did the right thing, Elise."

"I have failed a lot of people. I'm not enough, never enough. Couldn't save my brother and I murdered the father of my child. I dance well and, all things considered, I'm a good enough mother. But I'm a fucking washed-up failure at most of life, Erin. You're a survivor. You're strong and capable. I spend too much time reacting and pushing away my anger and resentment. I'm not good. I'm not strong. I'm just hanging on because Rennie needs it."

"Shut up. Seriously, girl, shut the fuck up. Hanging on? Coming out here and starting your life over. Doing it in a way that enables you to be with your kid while still doing what you love, that's not 'just hanging on.' Can you really not see how strong you are? How successful and accomplished? How hard you work to make a better life for yourself and Rennie?"

"I just don't see it that way. But thanks for saying it anyway."

16

Erin had grown very close to Elise over the last eight months, and hearing that story at long last was illuminating. She knew there was tragedy, but the whole of it was huge. Brody had lucked out with this woman. She'd be a real partner when they both just finally admitted they were in love with each other.

Her brother was beyond smitten. In fact, she'd seen him smitten dozens of times. Brody was always smitten with women. He loved them, treated them well, had sex with them, and moved on in a few months.

But Erin had never seen him look at anyone the way he looked at Elise. The way he gentled around her. He came alive when he spoke of her or to her. And he adored Rennie. Her brother was quite convinced falling in love meant being *responsible* for someone else. And in a way, he was right. But it was that you *wanted* to be, not that you *had* to be.

And in the end, that's why she wanted to have a baby with Ben and Todd. She wanted to have family with them on a whole new level. She wanted to anchor herself with people she cared about.

She unlocked her front door and put her coat in the closet and her bag on the table. Moments later she heard the groan and she ran hot, knowing just exactly what that sound meant. She undressed quickly and quietly, then headed up to the master bedroom and stopped at the entrance.

On the bed, Ben and Todd rolled, the sheets tangled through legs, as mouths clashed and bodies thrust against each other. Her heart sped. Both men were so strong and big. She knew the feel of those hands on her skin, of those tongues against her own and in other places too. Knew the taste of each, his own unique flavor.

Individually they were enough to make her weak in the knees; together, they brought her to them. She stood still and quiet, holding in a gasp of pleasure at the sight of Todd grabbing Ben's hair, yanking him closer. Ben moaned, deep and taut. Erin barely managed to keep rooted to the spot and to not start masturbating as she watched.

The kiss broke and the hand in Ben's hair shoved his head down. Down to Todd's cock. God, how beautiful were they there? She swallowed hard, watching as Ben grabbed Todd's cock, harder than she ever did, angling it to his mouth and sucking it inside.

"Fuck, fuck, fuck, fuck," Todd whispered harshly as Erin dragged in breath. "That's it, suck me harder, take more of me."

Todd was a naturally dominant man—sexually too. Normally he and Ben both topped Erin, but watching Todd top Ben was on her list of very favorite things in the world. Men touched each other differently, with more surety, with more edge and strength. She loved to watch them together.

The light in the room was low, but the bedside lamps were both on, casting a golden glow against all that hard, male skin as Ben's mouth moved up and down on Todd's cock. Each deep suck he gave tugged within Erin; her clit bloomed, the scent of her own arousal met her nose, and that's when Ben's eyes opened and he met her gaze.

He licked the head after pulling off, and Erin caught her bottom lip between her teeth, still not moving.

Todd's eyes remained closed. "You going to join us, beautiful, or do you plan to watch like a perv in the doorway?"

She grinned and moved into the room. "You knew I was here the whole time?"

"You yelled that you were home when you came in. We might be horny, but we're not deaf." Todd reached up and grabbed her, pulling her down to the bed, and she found herself wedged between two very aroused men. *Score.*

"Ben, get back to my cock."

Ben pressed a kiss on her lips, and then on her hip, before he settled between Todd's thighs and began to suck him off again.

Erin couldn't take her eyes from it. So Todd sat up. "His mouth feels so good," Todd whispered in her ear. She turned her head and he kissed her, hard, possessive. The way he always kissed her, like she was as necessary to him as breathing.

His hands slid around her waist, pulling her close. She swallowed a deep groan, broke the kiss and looked down to watch him flex his hips, fucking into Ben's mouth.

Erin moved so that she was behind Todd, pressing her breasts to his back as she dragged her nails down his chest, over his nipples, bringing a hiss from him. He leaned his head back onto her shoulder.

"I'm gonna blow. Take it all," Todd said, his body leaning against hers while his hands held Ben's head, fingers sifting through his hair.

She let all her breath out as Todd's body totally relaxed and Ben sat up, that smile of his on his face as he looked toward them.

"C'mere, you. I'm dying to get inside you."

She kissed Todd's shoulder and went to Ben, into his arms, the heat of his skin enveloping her.

"I see we share common goals." Sliding her body against his, loving the friction, she kissed him, tasting Todd when she swiped her tongue along the seam of his lips and then inside.

He sucked her tongue and then broke off to kiss her jawline, down her neck and to her nipples, tugging hard on each ring there, just the way she liked it.

"Let me taste her before you fuck her." Todd rolled toward them.

"Greedy bastard. You just came," Ben teased.

"When it comes to eating Erin's cunt, I'm most definitely greedy. I'm just going to make her come and then you can fuck her."

Before Ben could argue, Todd pressed her thighs up and then out, exposing her totally, before falling on her, devouring her.

One of her hands held Ben to her and her other held Todd. "Oh, yes. That's sooooo good." Pleasure sparked through her from nipples to clit.

Todd wasted no time; he drove her up hard and fast, his mouth on her punishing in the press to bring climax. The edge of Ben's teeth scraped against her nipples just right. She drowned in them, until all those sparks united and exploded.

She cried out, her back bowed, and climax rushed through her; and before she stopped coming, Ben had moved Todd out of the way. He knelt and brought her up where he needed her, his cock pressing against her entrance as he slid home in one thrust.

"Damn, nothing feels as good as this," Ben moaned as he began to fuck into her body.

Todd rolled to his knees, kissed Ben and turned his attention to her nipples. The man had a serious thing for her nipples and the jewelry she wore in her piercings. Many of the rings and bars were those he'd given her.

"Mmm, been thinking about these all day long. Had to rub one out earlier, and then of course Ben helped me just now. But now my day is complete, now that you're home too." He tongued around the rings bearing heavy beads. Beads he'd added that morning because it had pleased him to know they'd make her horny all day long. Pleased him to know he'd be easing all that pent-up desire when she came home. The man was fabulously diabolical that way.

She laughed. "We had sex before I went to the café this morning; it's not as if you haven't had it in weeks."

He gave her nipple a sharp bite, just on the right side of the pleasure/pain divide. "There's never enough of you."

Smiling, she turned her attention to Ben.

Ben's eyes took her in as he found her gaze and latched on. "Missed you today."

So wonderfully sweet and sexy, her Ben. He took care of her, made sure she had enough sleep, made sure she took her vitamins and didn't run herself down. Took care of Todd in much the same way. Todd loved being loved by her and by Ben as well. They'd been best friends long before she came along and they still were. Only she was there too.

"Missed you too. But you came in for coffee, so that made my day."

"*That* made your day?" He thrust hard and deep. "Not this?"

She moaned as she rolled her hips, needing more from him. She was so wet from Todd's mouth on her and her orgasm, the friction of their two bodies was delicious.

"*That* makes my entire life."

Todd stopped a moment and kissed her. "That was nice." He turned back to Ben. "Harder, make her tits jiggle." He watched them move, the beads clacking against the metal of the rings. "So. Fucking. Hot."

"Yesss," Ben ground out, pressing as deep as he could while he came. Erin loved that, the way it felt as all that energy they'd been building up shot straight into her body, as his became heavier and the muscles looser.

"I keep hearing that trying to get your wife knocked up can be a chore sometimes. But I gotta say, not so much at this point."

Erin laughed, content to lie there, snuggled between them, the scent of sex in the air, her skin warm and tingly.

"We'll see what you both feel like if I'm not pregnant within six months."

"Erin, I'd have sex with you four times a day, every day, if we didn't have jobs and didn't need to leave the house. I fuck you every chance I get. Ben fucks you every chance he gets. I'm sure if I get too tired, he can take over while I get Erin's beautiful pussy detox."

Ben snorted. "Sometimes you have to take one for the team."

"Did you have a good time with Elise tonight?" Todd asked.

"We had dinner and hung out with Rennie. But after we wrestled Rennie down—and I remembered what it was like to be responsible for getting a little person with her own agenda into bed and had a wee panic attack—Elise and I settled in for a chat. For several hours. I told her about Adele and she told me her story. She's a good woman, I'm glad she's a friend. Strong to have survived."

"You gonna tell Brody?" Ben asked. He and Brody were tight, so she understood why he asked.

"Not unless it's necessary. I don't think it will be. It's her story, her choice to share it, or not. I think she will. It's not a poor reflection on her, what happened. I can see she feels the weight of it anyway. She and Brody don't look it on the outside, but they're so much alike, it's scary. She loves my brother, even if she can't admit it to herself. But she's afraid, I think. Afraid he'll judge her or that she'll be too much of a burden on him. I do hope she'll share with him now that she trusts him. Once she tells him, she'll see he wants more of her, from her."

"He's been in love with her for a while now." Ben kissed her shoulder. "I'm glad you could share your own story with someone. I'm glad you have another friend. I like Elise."

"She's a good addition to the family. Eventually it'll be glaringly obvious and they'll admit it." Todd idly slid a fingertip along her nipple. "Some people are just clueless and stubborn." He referred to how long it took him to realize he was made for Erin, and she laughed.

"Let's hope it won't take *them* ten years, huh?"

17

"Come by the shop and take me to lunch today."

Elise looked at her phone a moment and then put it back to her ear. "Am I your sugar momma now?" She didn't have classes on Wednesdays and Rennie was in school until after three. An afternoon with Brody Brown sounded pretty awesome.

Brody laughed. "You know I have a sweet tooth. I haven't seen you for three whole days. You haven't been to the shop yet. I'm hungry. We can combine these things for maximum efficiency."

How dumb was it that her heart sped when he said he'd missed her? They had such busy lives and she hadn't seen him since Valentine's Day, when he'd shown up at her door with flowers for her and for Rennie, telling Rennie he'd never forget his two favorite women. After Rennie had gone to bed, he'd made love to Elise for hours, leaving long after midnight.

Three days without Brody sucked. And she was wary of that. Wary of her need for him. But it was there and he filled it. And she liked that he filled it.

"All right, handsome. I'll be there in about forty-five minutes. Are we storming the café to bother Erin or heading somewhere else?"

"I'm dying for a slice of pie. How about Zeek's? Since you've been with me, I eat so good I rarely get takeout anymore."

She was with him? Like *with him* with him? That made her smile. She was such a fifteen-year-old girl sometimes, but there was no one to see her slide back to teenaged girldom, so she wallowed in it just the same. "I'm having ice cream too then. I'll just have to work it off later. You coming over tonight?"

"If that's an invitation to dinner and sex? What do you think? I'll see you in forty-five." He hung up and she grinned as she went back to loading the dishwasher.

Brody heard her; above the general din of chatter and the buzz of the needles, he heard that petal-soft voice.

He stood, moving through the shop, caught in the pull he always felt when she was near. She wore her hair down, and it shimmered against the bright red of her sweater. Even in faded jeans and flats she looked like she was royalty or something. So elegant and pretty. That he'd touched and kissed every part of her, that he'd been beside her as she laughed, that she trusted him enough to give herself so freely, just floored him.

She was speaking with Arvin as he approached, and when her eyes met his, that smile deepened, changed into something intimate and innately sensual.

"Hi there. I'm here to sweep you away to lunch. But you should show me around first."

He took her hand and kissed it. "You look pretty."

"Thanks." Arvin winked and Brody rolled his eyes.

"Not you, douche bag. Scrounge your compliments from your gorgeous and totally-too-good-for-you wife."

Admittedly, he was sort of nervous to show her the shop. He wanted her to be impressed. Hoped she would be.

"Are these pictures of tattoos you've done here?" she asked when he led her past the front where clients waited. The wall held photographs of various tattoos.

He nodded. "Yes. We have to do a 'best of' wall at this point. All the stuff we've done is in the book up front. *Books.*" He laughed. "This place has been mine so long we've got seven binders' worth of pictures."

She looked close at his stuff, smiling. "You have every right to be proud of what you've built here. You're really good, Brody. I've obviously seen your work on Erin and Ben, but this is absolutely amazing. So much talent. I'm in awe."

"Hi, Elise." Raven approached and put her arms around Brody's waist. It wasn't unusual, Raven was physically affectionate with most of her friends. At the same time, it made him uncomfortable, it felt forced and for an audience. She knew he was seeing Elise. Knew because he'd told her that several times.

Elise's gaze went to those arms, even as Brody removed them and stepped closer. Then her eyes moved back to Raven's face. Her back straightened, and her eyes, just warm and sweet moments before, went hard. "Raven." Even her tone had gone hard. Which was sort of odd. Except for the call he'd overheard with her ex-in-laws, she was nearly always nice to people.

Though Elise and Raven didn't have the friendship each had with Erin, he'd expected them to at least like each other. The tension between them didn't shine much light on that particular hope. Worse, he got the distinct feeling Raven wanted it that way.

"Where are we headed then?" Raven asked, inviting herself along.

"Elise is getting the tour and then she and I are headed out to lunch." He steered Elise around Raven and hoped Raven didn't say anything else.

"See you later," Elise said, but it wasn't with the same warmth she had with other people.

"This is my office." He flipped on the light and showed her the small space where he slept many a night. Luckily now he just did his weekly scheduling and the books in there.

She walked ahead of him. "Look at you guys!" She homed in on a picture of Adrian and Erin when they'd signed their first record contract. Brody stood between them, grinning like a fool. He loved that picture. How much youthful hope they'd all displayed then.

"Seems like only yesterday." He shut and locked the door. "On the desk, legs wide. I need to fuck you right now."

"I knew I should have worn a skirt," she said, toeing her shoes off and stripping from her jeans and panties quickly. Damn, how disarming was it that she'd just moved to obey like that? That she wanted him as much as he wanted her? "But I'm not wearing a bra."

As if he wasn't already hard enough.

One-handed, he reached for her, his hand palming the back of her neck to hold her the way he wanted, the way he needed to, to taste her lips. The other hand unbuttoned and unzipped his jeans, freeing his cock.

"Are you wet, baby?" He kissed her pretty nipples after shoving the sweater up.

"Yes. Please, inside me, please."

He drew his knuckles through her cunt, so wet and hot he had to close his eyes to get control. Control that slipped from him like sand every time she got near. "Christ, you're on fire."

"Since you called me earlier. I . . ." She grabbed his cock and guided it to her gate, letting that finish her sentence.

One movement of his hips and he slipped into her body as he

exhaled. So good. Her body around his was so good. They'd taken the appropriate steps and he never wanted to fuck her with a condom again.

He braced his hands next to her on the desktop and she braced her feet on the chair arms as he began to fuck her in earnest. The sounds on the other side of the door floated away; the scent of his shop, so familiar after so long, floated away. All he heard was flesh slapping flesh, sighs and gasps, all he smelled was the sweetness of her shampoo and the tang of her arousal.

She arched her back, wanting more, wanting him deeper. She was having sex at his job. On his desk while anyone could hear.

"What's that smile for?" He nipped her neck.

"What's not to smile about? I'm here with you, you're doing that thing you do when you hit that spot inside me and everything feels electric. Of course I'm smiling."

"You deserve to come for that compliment."

"I totally agree."

He laughed. "Lean back a bit."

She did and realized how clean the top of his desk was. "Did you clear off your desk or is it always this way?"

His fingertips squeezed her clit and her whole system came to attention.

"Busted. I cleared it off after I spoke to you. I've imagined this since the first time we were together. No, since before that. I'm going to like doing my books when I can have this memory in my head. We'll probably need to do it a lot so I can keep the memory fresh. It's for my business after all."

Surprised laughter danced from her lips. "I'm so easy you knew you'd have me on my back with my legs open ten minutes after I walked through the door? Oh crap, that's nice." She moved to get more friction against his hand, his cock filling her.

He loomed above her, impressively male. Big and ferocious as he took what he wanted and gave it to her too.

He knew just what she liked and orgasm was lightning-quick and hard as it flashed through her. She bit her bottom lip to keep from crying out.

"Should have made you wait, that felt so good around me." He licked his fingers and she moaned quietly, licking her lips in anticipation before he swooped down to kiss her. Her taste lay on his mouth, mixed with his as he kissed her as hard as he fucked her.

She drowned in him, but she no longer tried to swim against it. She let herself go, trusting him to keep her anchored.

"So good. So hot and wet and made for me," he panted as his thrusts increased in speed and intensity.

She was helpless against it when he said stuff like that. It wasn't something that could go in a greeting card, but it was so sexy and raw it always struck deep.

He groaned as his muscles froze under her hands. His cock moved within her, filling her as he came.

And then his lips were on hers and it was . . . different than it had been. So intense and tender she felt it in her toes, and in her heart. She tumbled like a rock in a fast-moving river, disoriented, owned by the intensity of the current, of the moment when he rushed into her heart and soul.

18

Brody knew it had been different too.

Since that day, he'd been unable to get it out of his head. Each time he saw her, he felt a deeper draw to her. It had gone from a few days a week to every day, even if it was just for five minutes. He needed her and he gave in to that need.

Right then, he watched her with the kids, setting up the balloons for the games they planned to play. Her face was lit with a big smile and he realized, not for the first time, that she was a whiz with kids.

Three of the group had birthdays in the same week, Arvin, Maggie and Adrian. They always celebrated in some way, but this year, since the weather had been so nice for late winter, they'd blocked off the street at both ends and set up barbecues, tables and games, and it had turned into a big neighborhood event.

"Your girlfriend is like model-perfect." Raven approached and handed him a soda.

"Is that why you're always needling her?" Adrian asked.

"I don't needle her. I don't anything her. I say hello, I try to talk to her, but she's always offended." She shrugged.

Adrian glared at Raven, who exhaled hard. "Just how you like it. You really need to buy a clue. It's not always everyone else. It's you. You cruise around through life, bulldozing over people and calling it being *free-spirited*. It's not free-spirited, it's fucking selfish bullshit, and apparently I'm the only one who will call you on it. But here I am, calling you on it because I like Elise a whole hell of a lot. She's strong and kind, and no, she's not as hard as you are, so you think it's fun to play with her like a fucking cat plays with a mouse. She's stronger than you think, but I don't like you messing with her for sport. You had your chance with Brody. He's with Elise now. Don't fuck it up because you couldn't appreciate what you had. You're jealous. Happens to everyone. Get over it."

Brody didn't know what to say. This was the most Adrian had said about how he felt about Raven in several years, and Brody hadn't realized it went that deep. While he'd noticed the tension between Raven and Elise, he hadn't realized Raven had been fucking with her. More than her usual behavior, which admittedly Brody was used to, so he didn't think much on it. Adrian wouldn't have made the comment if it hadn't been an issue. Damn it. He'd need to be extra watchful for it now.

"Is that what I've done?" Raven asked Brody.

He took his eyes from Elise, really not wanting to engage in this years-old dead-horse discussion, but it had to be done.

"You and I are square. I accept what you are. But I'm not going to let you hurt Elise. You fuck with her and I'll step in. Don't make me do that. She means something to me. A lot. *Fuck.* Pretty much everything, so don't make me choose."

Raven physically jerked back, pausing before speaking. "You've changed since she came around. Like a domesticated animal or something. You used to be free. And now? Not. You look to her every time you answer a question, like you can't speak for yourself."

"I am different, yes, in a good way. And fuck you on the looking-at-her-before-speaking thing. You've barely been around us as a couple, how the hell would you know?"

"I guess I don't think I want to like her. I don't want to be jealous of the way you look at her. Because you looked at me like that and I never appreciated it."

His anger wisped away at the sadness in her tone. Raven was a lost soul. He'd never be her lover again, but he still cared about her. Despite her flaws, she'd helped him when he'd needed it most. He'd never forget that. He smiled, wishing deep down that she'd get her shit together and let herself be loved. She'd been wrong on one thing, though it wasn't necessary to point it out. He'd never looked at her the way he looked at Elise. He knew Elise was different from anyone else in his life. Special in a way no woman had ever been before.

"There's no reason not to like her. She's pretty awesome, actually. But you're still my friend, and that's not going to change unless *you* change it."

He looked back up and saw a man in a suit approach Elise, hand her an envelope and walk away. Alarmed at the drastic change of body language and the look on her face as she opened the envelope, Brody began walking toward her, but it seemed to take forever as people kept stopping him for something or other.

Her face paled and she crumpled the sheaf of papers to her chest. Concerned, he moved toward Elise, now ignoring anyone who tried to stop him.

Her mother approached, but Elise shook her head, instead calling Rennie's name. Rennie, caught up in some game with her friends, didn't want to leave. Elise sharpened her voice in a way he'd never heard her use with her daughter. Apparently she didn't very often, because Rennie came over immediately.

Elise hugged Rennie tight, fighting the panic and the tears. Not again! She'd gotten complacent. They would not take her baby, damn it. She scanned the crowd, looking for Brody, needing the reassurance of his presence, and discovered him standing right next to her. Comfort and safety rushed through her, allowing her to swim past the panic and get hold of herself.

"What's going on?" he asked her quietly when he bussed her cheek.

"Mom, can I please go back and play? I'm winning!"

She couldn't seem to stop her hands shaking, so she held tight to those damnable papers and took a deep breath. "Don't leave my sight. Don't leave with *anyone* but me, Pops or Gran. Understand? If anyone you don't know approaches you, I want you to get away from them and tell me immediately."

Rennie's eyes widened. "Are you all right, Momma?"

Christ, what a horrible mother she was, scaring her child this way. She forced the tears away and brushed some potato chips from the front of Rennie's hoodie, the touch reassuring them both. "I'm fine, Noodle. I'm sorry I scared you. Go on and play."

"I'll go over near her, to keep an eye. You *will* tell Daddy what is going on. Right this instant." Her mother gave her the glare of immediate compliance and headed over to cheer the kids on and keep an eye on Rennie.

She couldn't help it, she grabbed Brody's arm and squeezed. Needing to feel him there.

"Tell me what the hell has you looking like you're about to freak the fuck out," he ordered in a low but commanding voice, his gaze roving over her face.

"I can't right now."

She knew she looked bad, but she couldn't seem to stop shaking.

Her teeth had begun to chatter, so she clenched her jaws. She didn't want to run to him with her problems. He was her friend, they had sex, but she didn't want to be a burden or a responsibility to this man who'd shouldered more responsibility by the time he was thirty than most had. She couldn't bear the thought of him seeing her as yet another thing he had to fix or deal with.

He took her arm and guided her, gently but firmly, toward her front porch. She wasn't getting away from him when he was that intent, and it began to push her buttons. "You'll tell me what has you looking like you're about to pass out."

"Let. Go." She dug her heels in, starting to sweat, her heart racing.

He turned to look at her and his face fell from angry to sorrowful in the span of seconds. "Holy crap. What did he do to you? *I'm sorry*. I just wanted to take you away from the crowd so I could hear you and talk to you. I didn't mean to scare you."

"I know you didn't. You just pushed some buttons." She swallowed hard and groaned aloud when her father came stalking over, looking like midnight and doom.

Of course Brody, seeing his fellow caveman in her father, smiled somewhat grimly and the two exchanged a look of understanding. Crap, they were going to double-team her.

"I'm fine. Both of you, I'm all right, and this is already catching attention, so can we just drop it?"

"No." Paul crossed his arms and glared, and to Brody's surprise, Elise glared right back.

"Elise, we just want to help. It's clear you're upset." Brody slid a hand up and down her spine and she relaxed a bit.

"You can't. Okay? You can't. No one can right now. I need to go and watch Rennie."

Her father stepped in her way, taking care not to grab her. Christ, what the hell had gone on to make her so fearful? Just imagining it made Brody sick with rage. Any man who'd harm a woman was a coward; any man who'd harm this woman made Brody want to pound him.

"Your mother is right there with her. Is Rennie in danger somehow? We can't help if we don't know the details. Don't do this, *bebe*. Don't shut people out. You don't have to shoulder everything on your own. You're my daughter. I . . . I didn't protect you before. I didn't protect Matthias. Let me help."

Anguish marked her normally pretty features. "This isn't about Matty. He was a drug addict; he made his own disastrous path to hell. It's not about you either. *Fuck. Fuck!*"

Brody had rarely heard her say anything worse than a mild curse. She shook, and sweat sheened on her forehead. Something was really wrong, and he wanted nothing more than to make it okay.

"Daddy, I'm hanging on here by my fingernails. I *can't* do this right now." Her voice broke and Paul hugged her briefly.

He spoke very softly, and Brody's heart ached even as anger coursed through him for her and at her. Why the hell wasn't she hugging *him*? Why was she holding back?

She stepped back and worked to get herself together. Brody didn't leave her side. "Just don't let anyone take Rennie anywhere. Keep an eye. Anyone but our friends comes here and I want to know it."

Brody traced a fingertip down her temple. "No one will harm her. I swear to you."

She looked up at him, tears swimming in her eyes, and he hurt with her, for her.

"It's them, isn't it? Those fucking Sorensons." Paul snagged her attention again, and she looked back to her father.

A sigh came from her lips so deep Brody felt the exhaustion seep from her,. "Yes. They want to take her. They're trying to take her from me."

Take her? Take Rennie from Elise? Over his dead body.

Paul took her forearms and put his forehead to hers. "It won't happen. *Bebe*, it's going to be fine. You won't do this on your own."

Damn right she wouldn't.

"Mom! Are you sick?" Rennie came bounding up and Brody caught her, bringing her into a hug. She wrapped herself around him like a monkey and stayed, so he kept holding her. Liking the weight of her. Irene Sorenson had worked her way into his heart, and he wasn't going to let anyone take her anywhere.

Elise looked up at her daughter, faking a pretty good calm face. "I think I ate too much junk, Noodle. I'm all right. Pops was just giving me a hug to make me feel better."

Elise's entire face lit every time she looked at her daughter. Obviously from what she'd said to her father, this had something to do with custody. Brody knew Elise, knew she adored her child and was dedicated to her, as much as Rennie adored her mother right back. This must be killing her. Hell, it was killing *him* and Rennie wasn't even his.

Rennie, still perched in Brody's arms, looked toward her mother. "I think Brody needs to give you a hug too. That always makes you happy. Your cheeks turn pink."

Just like they were right then. Brody didn't bother hiding a smile, and Paul shook his head, grinning at his granddaughter.

"Come with me. I see your gran over there near the ice cream. Have you had any yet?" Paul asked Rennie.

"Only *one* scoop. That's not hardly nothing. I'm a growing girl and all."

"*Isn't* hardly *anything*. And no more ice cream. Don't give me that look, Irene. You puke when you eat too much. You know my stand on vomit," Elise said and shuddered.

"We don't invite the pukey sick in!" Rennie took Brody's cheeks between her hands and smooched him noisily, and he couldn't seem to remember a time when he didn't love this little girl. She hugged his neck one more time and scrambled down and into her mother's waiting arms.

"We don't, because Momma is a vomit-phobe," Elise spoke into Rennie's hair as she held her.

"Rennie, we need a goalie!" Nina hollered from the street.

Rennie's head, which had been resting on her mother's shoulder, shot up, her eyes bright. "Gotta run, guys. The team needs me."

Elise sat on the bottom porch step, her eyes still on her daughter.

"I'm going to be expecting all the details later on," Paul said, a grim look on his face. "There's *no* way this is going to happen. Those Sorensons need a wake-up call. Think they can push my daughter and granddaughter around. Not happening. Not again." He kissed the top of her head before he stomped off toward where the kids played soccer.

Brody sat next to her, sliding an arm around her shoulders, and she leaned into him. "I'm giving you a pass because I can see how upset you are and I don't want you to lose it in front of Rennie. But don't think that means I don't expect to hear everything."

She heaved a breath. "I gotta tell you, Brody, I'm pretty done with being managed."

"Tough shit, Shorty. I'm not managing you, anyway. I'm asking you to share what is going on so I can help."

They kept their eyes forward, both of them watching the kids play, both scanning the faces of the people assembled.

" 'Shorty'?"

"You arguing that you're not?"

"If you weren't so abnormally large, I wouldn't be."

He snorted. "Thank you."

"I need to make a phone call. Will you . . ."

"What? Just ask me and it's yours." Christ, the moment words left him, he realized how very true that was. Everything inside him went still for a moment and then clicked into place.

"Will you just . . . Don't let anyone get near her."

"Of course." He turned her head, tipping it so he could see into her eyes. "Baby, you two are my girls. I'll protect you. I'll protect you both. Do you trust me?"

She nodded. "Yes. But I don't want to burden you with my shit." She leaned in and kissed him before taking one more look at Rennie and heading inside.

Her hands shook so hard she had to take a quick shot of tequila before she could dial the darned phone.

"Childers."

"Frank, thank God it's you. I'm sorry to bother you on a Saturday. It's Elise Sorenson and I've just been served with legal papers. The Sorensons are trying to take her again. I thought they couldn't! I thought this was done."

He sighed. "Damn those people. Honey, can you fax the papers to me?"

"Yes. I have a machine here at home."

"Okay. Get them to me and I'll look them over and call you tomorrow unless there's something really concerning. Try not to let this get to you. We'll make sure Irene is protected."

"How did they find out where I was?"

He sighed again. "I don't know, but it can't be that hard. You're running a school under your name. A little bit of investigative work and they'd know. They used investigators before."

"I hate them. How long will this be a threat?"

"We'll make sure they can't after this. Just fax me the papers so I can see them too. I imagine my office will be getting a copy of the filing, but they're not overly trustworthy."

"I'm faxing this right now," she said, looking out her front windows toward where Rennie played with her band of guardian angels. "Thank you so much. I'm sorry to bother you on your weekend. I didn't, well, I hope I didn't interrupt."

He laughed. Frank Childers was a very old family friend, she'd grown up thinking he was family because she saw him and his wife, Veronica, so much.

"Honey, you know you can call me anytime you need me. Now, try and relax. It might be wise to be sure the school knows not to release Irene to anyone but you and your folks."

She closed her eyes against that fear and thanked him again before hanging up.

By the time she went back outside, the shaking had stopped, but she'd read enough to figure out they were trying to declare Elise unfit and take sole custody. The papers filed charged a significant change in circumstances and appealed to the court, located in another county she noted, to intercede to grant them custody and stop Elise from seeing Rennie at all.

As she'd anticipated, her parents and Brody looked up expectantly when she approached the group.

"Mom! I blocked two goals. So Adrian let me have a bite of his ice cream. Just one bite and I stopped running around and rested and Adrian let me sit in his lap and he sang me and Nina a song. How awesome is that?"

Elise couldn't help but laugh. "Take a breath there. Sounds like an awesome time was had by all. Weren't we going to do some painting?" The best way to get through was to focus on something.

This was supposed to be fun. No reason to let them hurt her any more than they already had.

"Yay!" Nina and Rennie jumped up and down.

Maggie held up a bag. "I brought some old T-shirts from home. The kids can wear them while they paint."

"Good idea." Elise moved to the table and covered it in butcher paper while Maggie and Erin taped it down. One of the other mothers put out containers for paint.

Elise loved this kind of stuff. Ken's parents didn't do this with him. They never did it with Rennie either. They never let her run around, never took her to the park, never took her to a movie and let her have a blue Slushee just because. They didn't know her favorite color, they didn't know how she liked her eggs cooked, and they didn't know which pair of shoes was her current favorite.

Elise did.

Elise was her mother. Elise had taken care of Rennie without Ken's help since Rennie had been born, and there was no fucking way those assholes would steal her child out of spite. Irene was *hers*.

"You all right?" Erin asked quietly as they worked to set everything up.

"No. No, I'm not. But I have to be right now for Rennie."

Erin nodded. Elise appreciated Erin so much, so much she didn't know if words could ever capture it. Erin understood her in a way few others did. This on top of being a really fun person. They'd grown even closer since sharing their pasts. She had a best girlfriend for the first time in over a decade and it mattered.

"You know where I am if you need to talk. If you need anything. All you have to do is ask."

She hugged Erin briefly and began to squirt the paint into the containers as Maggie helped get the kids into the T-shirts. Once the painting began, the moms just stood back and tried to stay out of the way. Quietly, she gave Erin a very brief overview and asked if Todd or Ben could come over and check that her home security was in good order.

Erin excused herself and came back quickly. "Todd will be by tomorrow to look at everything."

Elise thanked her and felt marginally better.

She felt his approach before she saw him. His scent hit her nose as his body heat blanketed her side.

"You're going to have to hose Rennie down after this," Brody said, kissing her briefly. She allowed herself to lean in to his body and he hugged her tighter.

"She'll love it, even if the water is so cold her lips turn blue. My kid loves the water."

He grinned. "Did you know that Erin's building has a pool?"

"Oh my gosh, that just occurred to me." Erin turned to Elise. "We do have a pool. It's rarely used, but maintained really well. You two should come over and swim. That would be fun."

"Erin, your idea of fun puzzles me. You have two super-hot men to go home to and you think listening to Rennie screech and splash around is fun?"

Erin hugged her around where Brody hung on. "I'll need the practice. This morning there was a plus on the stick."

Elise hugged back, kissing Erin's cheek. "That's wonderful news."

"It really is."

"You two wanna fill me in?" Brody's look was patiently amused.

"Adrian needs to come over here too. But he's being flirted with, so I don't want to interrupt."

"You told *her*!" Brody pointed to Elise. "*She's* never made you chocolate chip pancakes, I bet." He sort of pouted, and Elise had no other choice but to cup his cheek. Good gracious, he was just so much to her. At that moment, she wanted to pour her heart out to him, wanted him to take care of things while she stayed in bed under the blankets. It sucked always to be the one to have to fix things.

Erin giggled. "She's cuter. Plus, you and Adrian are like a combo platter. I can't tell one first and not the other."

"Adrian!" Brody called out to his brother.

Adrian looked up from the conversation he'd been having with Martine and nodded in Brody's direction, but he continued to listen to Elise's mother, smiling and making Martine flutter her eyelashes.

"My mother is as bad as Rennie is with the flirting." Elise handed out new sheets of paper and took the others, using clothespins to hang the paintings to dry.

"You're an old hand at this," Brody said. "Then again, Rennie's quite the artist, so clearly it helps."

"I figured out pretty quickly that she loved to paint and draw, so we've perfected the process over the years. On days like this I can let her work outside. But normally I put out a painting tarp on the dining room floor and let her work there."

"You and I are going to talk later tonight," he whispered as he leaned in.

"Can't. My parents are hanging out, and tomorrow is a school day so everyone will be in bed early."

"You're going to tell me."

She sighed, thankful to see Adrian approach finally.

Brody kept an arm around Elise's waist, holding her in place. He liked her there with him and he liked everyone knowing it. Another part was that his protective instincts had gone into overdrive and he didn't trust anyone else to protect her as well as he could.

He also liked seeing how close she and Erin had become. Erin had told him Elise had shared her story. He was relieved she'd shared, but he couldn't help but wish it had been with him. Erin said she'd tell him if he asked, but that she thought Elise should tell him herself. He agreed with that, but at the same time he really wondered what had happened and if his basic impressions were true.

"Guys, you're going to be uncles again."

Brody's heart stopped for a moment when he'd really heard what she'd said. Then joy salted with a bit of sadness came over him as he moved with Adrian to hug their sister.

"When? When are you due? How long have you known? Are you okay?" Adrian said, sounding very much like the worrier he was. 'Course, Brody was worried too.

"I just found out before we got here. I'm not telling anyone else until I'm through the first trimester. I don't know when my due date is yet. I'll see my doctor this week and they'll have an approximate time. And I'm more than fine. I'm ridiculously happy. It's a good time in my life. Steady. Full of love. I have no complaints." Erin turned a bit. "Where are you going?"

Brody turned too, catching a red-faced Elise, who'd begun to slink away.

"Well, it's a private family moment. I didn't want to intrude."

Brody simply reached out with his open hand, and with a sigh from her, she took it and he drew her back to his side.

"You're a dumbass." Erin said to Elise. "You're family. I'd like you to be the godmother. Rennie can be like an honorary godassistant."

Elise hugged Erin. "I'd be so honored. Rennie is going to flip her lid when she finds out."

Elise was so grateful for her friends, Brody most of all, for keeping her laughing and entertained all day so she wouldn't dwell. But now that they'd cleaned up the area, it was clear to her she needed a long, hot bath and a big glass of wine.

But first to tell her parents after they got Rennie to bed. Brody had stuck around, hoping to corner her, but it had truly been so chaotic she wouldn't have had the opportunity to have tell him even if she'd wanted to. Rennie was more than tired, she was *over*tired and overstimulated, and she vibrated with that grumpy, hyper and suddenly weepy personality girls her age got after days like the one she'd just had. Elise was exhausted just dealing with it.

He'd finally kissed her and told her he'd be stopping in or calling very soon, and he ordered her to come to him if she needed anything. She liked that he was concerned, the allure of it, of un-burdening herself to a man like Brody, who would step in and fix it all for her, who was powerful. But at the same time, Ken had man-aged her for two years before she began to wise up. Even until the moment he died, he tried to control her, and now his damned par-ents were doing it in his stead. There was simply no way she'd be managed by anyone again.

"Holy cow," Elise said as she took the glass her father handed her way and collapsed on the couch. "She's out. Snoring and drool-ing already. I think today gets two thumbs up from Rennie."

They just stared at her until she sighed, took a big gulp of wine, and gave them all the details..

Her father shot to his feet and began a five-minute diatribe using all the best swear words in both English and French. Her mother narrowed her eyes at the mention of the Sorensons and their allegations that Elise was unfit. Unfit! The word agitated her, an-gered and insulted her. She was a good mother.

"Frank will contact me tomorrow and I'll know more."

"Is her passport up-to-date?" her father asked casually, but they all knew why he asked.

Elise nodded. She would run as far away as she could if the court awarded her child to those beasts. There's no way she'd put Rennie at their mercy so they could ice all the beauty, sweetness and spirit from her.

"Right or wrong, yes. It's up-to-date, as is mine."

Her mother leaned forward, her weight on her elbows. "The court isn't going to find for them. You know that. You're her mother and you're a damned good one at that. She's happy, well adjusted, doing well in school and has lots of friends. They're not going to rip her away from you. The Sorensons don't even know her. They've never tried."

"I *know* that in my head, but my heart isn't convinced. That's my baby and I can't let go of the fear in the back of my mind. I feel like throwing up."

"We'll make it through. This family will stick together and we'll overcome this challenge. We'll hear what Frank has to say and we'll know more then. Do you want us to stay over?" her mother asked.

"No, I'm good. I did talk to Todd today about getting a better security system here, and he's going to get me a quote later this week. But I'm afraid I'm not going to want her walking home with Nina until this is all taken care of."

"Daddy and I can show up on the two days a week she goes to Nina's and walk with them both."

"This makes me so mad! Nina lives a block from the school. Two first-graders walking one block with all those other kids out and crossing guards too, and I have to have her escorted."

"They've transferred all their energy to you for killing Ken. When he needed killing. If I could have killed him after you did, I'd have gladly done it." Her father had his mean face on and Elise felt better.

"Go home. I'm all right, Rennie doesn't need to know about any of this for the time being."

"If you're sure. If you two want to come stay with us for a while, we have the room."

"I appreciate the offer. Really. But I don't want them to disrupt her life any more than it has to be disrupted. I want her to have normal. It's why I came here."

Brody sighed as he caught sight of Erin standing in the doorway, smiling at him. "Figured you'd come over," she said. "Looked like Martine and Paul were going to hang on awhile." She led him inside and he took the beer Ben handed him.

He'd hung out at Elise's, but Rennie was a mess, tired and in the middle of a meltdown, so he finally gave in and left. He'd never seen her so wound up and grumpy. At first, the silence of his house had been a welcome thing, but after three minutes he missed Elise and Rennie both. Worried for them both. Suddenly, the house he loved and sought refuge in so often became dark and quiet. Too quiet. So he'd headed to Erin's, knowing everyone would still be up.

"Did she tell you?" he asked Erin, point-blank.

"Just briefly, not even all the details. She was really trying to hold it together this afternoon, Brody. If it makes you feel any better, Todd's going out there tomorrow to give her a quote on a better security system for the house."

"No, it doesn't make me feel better! I don't know what the fuckin' threat is! I thought she wasn't in danger. It was legal papers, I know that much. They had to do with Rennie and custody. What the fuck is going on that she needs better security?"

"That's really all I know too." Erin paused, pursing her lips. "Ya know, for a guy who says he's just hanging out with her as friends with benefits, you sure seem to be really concerned about her." Erin sipped her orange juice and watched him.

"She's my friend. Of course I'm concerned. I'd be just as concerned if it was Arvin or you or any of our friends." He began to pace.

"You're such a liar." Adrian shook his head from his place on the couch.

Now they were going to gang up. It's what they always did, a time-honored ritual. He wasn't usually the one being teamed up against though. "What?"

"You're in love with Elise Sorenson. Christ, it's obvious to anyone with eyes." Adrian shrugged. "You can bullshit yourself, but you can't lie to me or to Erin. We know you too well and this woman has your heart."

"I love her like I love all my friends. I don't deny she's special. I don't even deny that this supposedly casual thing is way more like a relationship than I'd envisioned, and I'll even give you that I don't mind that. I like it even. I like her and I like her kid and I like being with her. Okay? Is that what you wanted to hear?"

Erin sent him a challenging look. "You love her like you love Arvin? Really? You're full of dookie. You know, *you* raised us to be self-aware. What the fuck? You gonna puss out on this? You. Love. Her. Stop with all this crap about being with her and liking her. This isn't seventh grade. You don't like her, you love her. For Christ's sake, you eat her up with your eyes every time she walks into a room. You want to take care of her like you take care of me and Adrian. She's a wonderful person. Frankly, Elise is more than I could have ever wished for you. She's already part of us in a way not even Raven is. She's special, and to mess around with all this equivocation and crap is insulting to you both."

"I didn't come here to be attacked."

Adrian flipped him off and Brody rolled his eyes. *"Pffft.* Attacked? You big baby. Big, brawny dude like you and you think us refusing to buy your bullshit is being attacked? C'mere and I'll sock you in the junk; that's an attack. You came over here to get a reality check. We're handing it to you. Of all the people in your life, Erin and I are going to tell you the truth just the same way you've done for us."

"I'm leaving now. I'm going to go home and sleep. You." He pointed at Erin before stopping to hug her. "Take care of yourself and my niece or nephew."

"She's safe," Ben said, meaning Elise. Brody paused. "We put someone on the house. Just a cruise by every few hours. But I did get a gander at her house a few months ago; it has a decent security system, and unless professionals or ninjas go in to take Rennie, she's safe. After Ben and I are finished with it, she'll be safe from ninjas too."

Brody nodded. "Thanks."

Ben nodded back. He understood Brody and his fear. Understood what it was to care about someone and want to protect them. Brody appreciated that.

"You know I love you, Brody. You know I want the best for you. It's not a secret that I never thought that person was Raven. But I do think it's Elise, and I think you're a fool if you don't just admit it to yourself." Adrian hugged him.

"I love you too, dumbass." He sighed at his siblings, who looked at him with amusement.

19

She'd just hung up from her call with Frank about the papers she'd faxed over, when there was a knock at her door.

"I brought coffee and some Danish Erin had fresh this morning at the café." Brody walked in and headed for the table. She locked up and wandered back his way.

"Good morning."

"Rennie get to school okay this morning? She was strung out last night." He laughed at the memory. Which was easy for him to do.

"Yes. She was fine. Slept like a rock, as usual. Got up, ate a big breakfast, and then my parents showed up and we all walked her. She thought it was pretty cool to have an entourage."

"Thanks," he said when she pushed a plate to him for his Danish.

She sipped her coffee and smiled. "She made it with orange and dark chocolate."

"She knew what you liked and made it. Erin likes to take care of her people." He paused. "And so do I, so please stop this and tell me what happened. Both before and yesterday too."

"I don't want to burden you with this. With all my baggage."

"Stop it with that. It's total crap."

"My feelings are crap?"

"You're deliberately trying to pick a fight and I'm not going to let you. You're going to keep your pretty ass right there in that chair and tell me everything right now. How the hell can I fix things if you don't tell me?"

Elise knew he was trying to help, but damn if he wasn't pushing her buttons. She could feel it, recognize it, but she couldn't seem to not be annoyed.

"You can't fix this. I'm handling it."

"Handling it? For crap's sake! Why is telling me so bad? You told Erin."

"She didn't demand I fork over my past like a bag of chips." She stood. "I need to go to work. I have classes."

"In an hour. You can sit back down and tell me. I'm not leaving until you do. Stop being so pissy and tell me."

"This he-man thing does not work. In fact, I have to tell you, it just makes me want to refuse for refusal's sake. I'm trying to be honest here. Back off a minute."

"Fuck backing off. I backed off for months, waiting for you to tell me. And you haven't yet. Apparently you don't trust me enough to tell me."

"I trust you with everything I am. I let you into my life when I rarely let anyone in. I haven't dated since, well, in years. And before that, after the divorce, I never brought a single man into my house or her life. Never. I exposed the most personal part of me. I'm glad to know you appreciate it."

"*Now* you are succeeding in pulling me into this fight you want to pick so badly. You're not going to do this. You know how highly I think of your kid and of you too. I'm sick of this smoke-and-mirrors crap." His demeanor softened. "Tell me. I'm imagining far worse."

She relented. She took a deep breath and began to speak. "I'm a murderer."

He sat back down, looking curious, but not horrified or shocked, so she continued.

The time fell away as she told him the whole story, from the time she met Ken until she killed him in her apartment. When she finished and looked to him, he saw right to the heart of her and he didn't flinch.

"You're not a murderer."

"I killed him, Brody. And let me tell you, lest you think I'm noble again, I am not sorry. He stood between Rennie and safety and I did what I had to do, and I'd do it again. They know it, his parents; they hate me for it. That's why they want to take her from me."

His jaw tightened. "You killed him in self-defense, that's not murder. If he was around today, I'd kill him too. As for his parents, I gather they were a problem before now as well?"

"They filed endless motions to get custody, to make me stay in New York, to have me drug tested, to have her psychologically evaluated. I used to think they cared about Rennie on some level. Now, not so much. She's a possession they don't want to lose."

Brody's face was taut with anger, and she was relieved that he didn't think she was horrible. He didn't hate her, he wasn't repulsed. Part of her loosened at the discovery.

"You said your attorney called? What's going on with this newest motion?"

"They're trying to declare me unfit as a significant change in circumstances. They filed in the county where they have a vacation home. Frank, my attorney, advised me to get a local lawyer and they'd work to get the case transferred here. He doesn't think they have a case. Which is easy for other people to say so confidently, since they're not in any danger of losing their children."

Brody pushed from the chair and began to pace, and she steeled herself.

"Here's what we're going to do. You and Rennie will move in with me until this is all taken care of. I'll sleep in the guest room in the basement the whole time. We'll talk to Ben and Todd and get some extra security in addition to the new system they're going to install. By the way, I spoke to Todd before I got here and he said he was coming over tonight after you got home with Rennie."

"Whoa. Hold up there, Hoss, I don't need that."

"Fuck that noise, Elise. You do so need that. You need help and I'm going to give it to you." He gestured toward her bedroom. "Let's get you packed and we'll go to the school and tell Rennie it's like a sleepover."

How many times had other people taken over and she'd let them? Ken had controlled her that way; so had Matty, to a certain extent. She had to make her own choices, especially when it came to Rennie.

"I said no, Brody."

"And I said this is for your own good. You're coming home with me and I'm not taking no for an answer."

Everything inside her burst into flame. The fear of losing Rennie, the anger at having to deal with Ken's parents, and her fear that Brody wouldn't care, which warred with her fear that he would take over and she'd lose herself entirely—all swirled until it changed into the rage she seldom gave in to.

"I said *no*! What the heck do you think you're doing? No. *No. Nooooo!* I don't need another father. I have one, and he's bossy enough as it is. Get out. Go home. Go to work. Just get out."

"Shorty, I'm not leaving until you and I work out whatever the hell just pushed your buttons." He stood in the path to the front door, his arms crossed over his chest. It annoyed her that a shiver of pleasure at the way he looked slid up her spine. But it also scared her. She'd had her way blocked like that before, and although she knew he'd never harm her, her guts were as raw as her emotions.

"Get. Out. Of. My. Way."

Brody had never seen her this way before. Shrill. Angry and freaked the fuck out. Shame washed through him that he'd done anything to scare her. He relaxed his posture and stepped toward her. "Don't be scared of me. My god, I'd never harm you."

She fought tears. He heard it in her voice, saw it on her face. She looked so lost and so in pain. He ached to make it right, but what she said next nearly took him to his knees.

"It's not you. It's me, and I don't mean that in a clichéd way. I am fucked up and jagged inside. You don't need this, or me. Just go back to your life and pretend I'm just a neighbor."

He shook his head. "I never pegged you for a coward." She jerked back and he reached out. He'd meant to jar her out of her funk, not hurt her more. "I didn't . . . Fuck, I'm sorry."

She stepped around him and moved toward the door. "I'm going to leave now before this turns into a bigger fight." She grabbed her bag and headed toward the door. "Lock up when you go."

He called after her, even as she closed the door, but she kept walking. He didn't follow.

Brody slammed back into the café, softening when he saw his sister and remembered she was pregnant.

He poured the whole story out to her, and she made the appropriate noises and nodded her head.

"You finished?" she asked, taking away his cup. "Now, here's what I do know and what I'll tell you. You can't steamroll her, not over this. She had that before. Do you understand what I'm telling you?"

"I know she was abused, but I'm not some junkie loser who raped her. Fuck."

"Of course you aren't. If she really thought so, she wouldn't have let you near that little girl. But some wounds don't allow for rational thought. Sometimes people do things and the memory is so strong you can't filter it out."

"She told me I was pushing her buttons, but I thought she was just trying to push me into a fight. I want to help her."

"She probably *was* trying to goad you into a fight, but being honest too. It's hard to know what to take seriously and what to ignore. It's reading between the lines, but that's what you do sometimes with people you care about. Mostly, you want her to lean on you so you can fix it."

He sighed. "Yes. I guess so."

"Because you love her. You love her and you love that little girl. She's not just a woman you're seeing. She's not even your girlfriend. It's more than that, which is why the two of you clashed just now, because she knows more than most that you've taken care of other people for almost your whole life. And because she loves you too, she doesn't want to be a burden to you. Telling you that story was a whole different level of trust. She's trusting you to not reject her."

Scrubbing his hands over his face, he finally admitted it to himself. He did love her and he adored Rennie. He *wanted* to be responsible for them because they were his just like Adrian and Erin were his. Shit.

"She's just afraid. I know that feeling." She took Brody's hand and squeezed. "I really know that feeling, and it's so dark and lonely there. She's broken, like I was. I truly believe she loves you, because she's been putting you first. I know you don't see it that way, but she's been trying to keep you free from what she sees as her baggage."

"Fuck. Damn it, why can't it just have been her being pissy?"

Erin laughed. "I'm sure she can be just plain pissy too. She's a woman, after all. An artist, and you know how bad we can be." She winked. "But I think there's something more here. She's hurting and scared."

"So what should I do?"

She tugged his hair right above his ear. "You're such a good man. Be persistent but not pushy. You could tell her you love her, but whatever, you're being very pissy on that subject yourself."

"I didn't want a commitment. I didn't want to love anyone else. I don't have the room to."

She grinned. "But?"

"Okay so yes. Okay? Yes, I love her. Fuck. She'll be in classes all day and I have a full schedule too. Then Todd is coming over tonight, or going to her place, so I can't be alone with her."

"Call her. Leave her a voice mail and go to her tomorrow."

She knew he'd come at some point. He'd called and left her a voice message the evening before, full of kindness and strength. He wasn't angry with her, he just wanted to help. And would she let him? When she'd hung up, she ended up crying even more. Damn the man for being so sweet, but also so darned pushy.

But she wasn't really ready for the emotional impact of seeing him there, reflected in the mirror as she stretched at the barre.

"Wow, you're bendy." He grinned and her apprehension kicked back a bit. "Do you have time to talk?"

He knew she did. She had a two-hour break between classes on Tuesdays. "Let me lock up."

She'd hoped to be a bit calmer when she got back, but she wasn't. Instead she went to where he sat in one of the parents' waiting room chairs and sat across from him. "I'm sorry I was such a bitch yesterday. I just felt, gah, I don't know. Defensive."

He smiled and leaned to kiss her briefly. Enough to let her know he wasn't mad. "Everyone gets a bad day. I wasn't on my best behavior either. I can be sort of, um, high-handed when I'm worried about people. I'm sorry too. As for you? You had a lot on your mind. And I'm glad you shared it with me."

He nuzzled her in that sensitive hollow just below her ear, and she knew she was in way over her head with him. But she couldn't seem to want to stop herself.

"Would I be a total asshole if I told you how much I needed you right now?" he murmured against her neck.

"Only if you didn't make good on it." She let go long enough to drag him to her office, but he had other ideas.

"Here." He stopped in front of the mirrors. "I've wanted to fuck you here for months now." His grin reflected as she looked up. "Not that all the other places I've had you here haven't been pleasing."

His hands went to her shoulders. "Just watch yourself. Watch as I peel you open and devour what's beneath these clothes."

She began to say something, but all she managed was a soft sound, the longing threading through it.

"Hands on the barre. Wait, let me get this off first." He pulled her camisole up over her head and tossed it aside. Her nipples hardened in the air and then as his fingers rolled and pulled until she had to tighten her hold to keep standing.

"I love the feel of you under my hands. Of the sharpness of your nipples against my palm, of the swell of your breasts and the way they fit so perfectly."

He let go of said breasts and pushed her skirt, leggings and panties down. She stared at their reflection. Of him, fully dressed, sun-kissed skin, the darkness of his hair and those soft curls she wanted to feel sliding through her fingers. And her, naked and slight, pale hair and skin, blue eyes to his depth of brown/black. Opposites on the outside, but in many ways, she and Brody were similar. More similar than dissimilar as it happened.

Strong. They loved their families and would do anything for them. Stubborn. Scared of being a burden and of taking on any more. And yet, as she watched his reflection remove his clothes, she realized they'd both taken the other on.

He kissed her. Kissed her neck and her back, her shoulders and down her spine. His shirt flew to the side and she took his reflection in. Taut skin stretched over rippling muscles as he kneaded her thighs and calves. She groaned at how good it felt.

"Tip your pretty ass back. I want to eat you from behind." She did as she was told, and he moved her ankles wider so she was more opened up to his mouth.

In the mirror she watched his tongue stroke up and against her clit. She stood on her tiptoes to get higher, to give him more access, and he moaned against her, the sound carrying from clit to nipples.

She wanted to close her eyes, to luxuriate in the way his mouth felt from this angle, but she couldn't tear her gaze from him licking her. When he pulled back before she climaxed, a sound of keen disappointment broke from her lips.

"Shhh. I'm not finished, but it's hard to get all your best parts at this angle."

She put her heel up on the barre, leaving the other foot down, and he drew in a sharp breath.

"So beautiful and pink." He turned to face her, sitting flat so he was perfectly aligned with her pussy, and then he went back to work.

Her thighs trembled as the muscles burned. His mouth on her

was relentless as she caught her own eyes, heavy-lidded; her face was flushed, her hair tousled, lips glossy from where she'd licked them. Her nipples stood hard and dark. She held on to the barre with one hand and slid her other hand into his hair, her fingers gripping, holding him there as orgasm came, flashing through her and making her lock her knees to keep from falling.

He stood quickly, and she dropped to her knees to take him into her mouth. She loved his cock, loved the taste of it, the feel of his thigh muscles against her hands as she braced herself. He was so tightly controlled when she went down on him; she knew it was to keep from hurting her. But just then she needed his intensity.

When she rolled her eyes upward, she met his gaze. Wow. *She* did that to a man like him. It was wondrous that he'd be so enthralled with her, but she wasn't going to question it. Not then. She simply enjoyed it.

"Don't hold yourself back. I"—she swallowed hard—"know you want to fuck my mouth. You won't hurt me. Let me give that to you."

His breathing stuttered. "How can you be so sexy?" he whispered. And he gripped her hair. "Stop me if it's too much."

Her answer was a smile before licking her lips and letting him guide her back to his cock.

He nearly came when she told him to fuck her mouth. First because he'd wanted to forever, and second because she knew it. Oh, and last because hearing her say it from those lips that rarely said a bad word was beyond fucking hot.

Her hair in his hand was soft and cool as he thrust into her mouth while holding her in place. Her scent grew as she moaned around him, and he realized she was getting off on it as much as he was. Well, maybe not as much, but it was certainly turning her on.

"I love that mouth of yours almost as much as I love your cunt. I'd like to blow down that throat, but I'd rather come with my cock inside you."

He had to pull a bit on her hair because she seemed determined to keep going. Which only made him hotter, to see her hungry for him like that.

"I haven't fucked you against a wall yet." He looked around. "Over there in the corner."

Mirrors on both sides of them, he picked her up and she wrapped her legs around him.

She smiled, but as he slid her down his cock, she leaned back so they could both watch down her body and catch sight of his cock plunging into her, glistening with her honey.

Reflected over and over again there in the mirrors, it was better than any porn he'd ever seen, watching himself fuck her time and again, watching the creamy pale column of her throat and the jiggle of her breasts.

She watched as well, and he nearly had a stroke when she licked her fingers and slid them to her pussy and began to work her clit. She might have started out with less experience than he had, but she took her pleasure without shame and he loved that about her. Loved everything about her.

"That's the way. Is it hard and slippery?"

"Yes."

"Still wet from my mouth, I bet." He licked over one nipple and then the other, and her inner muscles contracted around him. "I love it when you come around my cock. Again." He licked and bit at her nipples and she hummed her satisfaction until her fingers moved faster and faster, her hips rolling to meet his strokes, and with a sharp gasp, she turned into a molten fist around him while she cried out and came.

He wasn't far behind, and within another two minutes, he laid his head on her chest and caught his breath after his own climax.

And then he carried her first to the small bathroom outside her office and then to her couch, where he put a blanket around them both and snuggled against her.

They'd talk in a bit. But for that moment, he wanted to simply breathe her in.

The sweat had cooled on their skin and she turned to look at him. "You're so warm. I use two down comforters and sleep in flannel and I'm still cold all the time. Very handy, you are."

"If you and Rennie came to stay with me . . ."

She put a hand over his mouth to stop him from saying anything else. "Okay, *this* is how we're going to proceed: you can't take over. Do you understand? It pushes my buttons. I can't deal with a man who tries to control me or take over. This is my kid we're talking about, and I would do anything for her."

He moved so quickly she barely registered it, but he came to his knees in front of her, the blanket sliding from her shoulders. "I would do anything for her too. And you. Damn it, let me in, baby. I'm dying out here with you scared and not letting me help. Even if you don't need the help, please."

Everything she'd built to keep from loving him was unthreading. She was coming undone and there was nothing to do but let it happen. He'd laid himself bare before her, opened up. He hadn't judged her. And she wanted to let him in. She wanted to let him in because she couldn't imagine her life without Brody Brown in it.

Her arms went around him, where they belonged, as she held on to someone she'd never expected. He wasn't supposed to be there in her life, but there he was and thank the heavens for it.

20

"I think I have an attorney your attorney can work with," he said quietly as she let him in the front door later the same evening. She'd been shaken very deeply by what they'd shared that day and hadn't had enough time to process it.

Pausing there in the quiet of her front hallway, he kissed her. Slow, gentle and totally sure of himself. That combination was as powerful to her as when he was all take-charge. That sureness of his sexual lure, of his connection to her, shook her even as it washed over her, making her happy. Even as he got bossy and tried to handle her, she was happy. Because he was there, touching her.

He smiled and went back in for another kiss. "I know." She looked up, confused. Knew what? Her head still reeled from the kiss and the way he affected her.

"I know how much this is." He motioned back and forth between them, indicating he felt some measure of what she did. "But also, I know you're chafing a bit at my presumption at doing a check on this lawyer. Listen, Shorty. I'm bossy. I can't help it. It's who I am and what I do. I'm pushy and I like to take over. But I'm going to work really hard not to do it too much, and you're going to try and accept me the way I am. Flaws and all. Because I'm good in bed, and I can carry heavy things and reach high shelves."

"You're ridiculously full of poop." She, of course, diminished her tough stance when she continued to keep her arms around his neck and cuddled close. "Good thing you're handy with your mouth."

He groaned softly, closing his eyes a moment. "Not fair. She won't be asleep for hours."

Elise laughed. "We're a package deal, Rennie and me. Get used to it. I have."

"Is that Brody?" Speak of the devil, Rennie came pounding down the stairs, and Elise's heart stuttered when he held his arms out and her baby jumped into them with a giggle. "You're here! I like when you're here. Are you having chili with us then? Aunt Erin sent over pie. I like her. I like pie too."

Aunt Erin? Elise smiled at the term. Erin *had* become somewhat like an aunt to Rennie come to think of it. She liked it. She didn't have any siblings left, but she did think of Erin as a sister quite often, and she was glad Rennie had that kind of connection with her too.

"I'm with you on both things. I love Erin and I love pie; the combination of the two is a very good thing. And I wouldn't miss chili for anything. Although it might be nicer if I'd been asked. That way I could say 'thank you' all pretty-like." Brody put Rennie down and grinned up at Elise.

He was something else. She smirked at him before her smile won over. "Excuse my terrible manners. I made plenty. Would you like to stay for dinner?"

He bowed and kissed her hand. "Thank you, I'd love to stay for dinner."

He checked over Rennie's math homework while she set the table, and she realized just how much Rennie loved him. She was a friendly kid; affectionate, yes, but her eyes twinkled when he was around. She saved all her best stories for him and she talked about him nonstop to her parents. Rennie cared what Brody thought, wanted him to be impressed with her schoolwork and her artwork. Brody was someone special to Rennie, and having special people was important.

At first Brody had held himself back a little, but Rennie had made it impossible for him not to open himself up. He listened to Rennie. Not the way some people listen to kids, which was with one ear open, thinking about whether or not to tape the new episode of their favorite television show. No, he focused on her, interacted with her.

She'd never expected Brody. Elise had never really considered finding a man who would come into their lives the way Brody had. She had always assumed she'd either never be serious with anyone again, or that it would be with a much different man.

Which would have been a shame, because Rennie didn't need a guy in a Mr. Rogers sweater. She needed a man like Brody who gave himself to people he cared about in a way that was unmistakable and made the other person feel special.

At the same time, he'd made it clear nearly a year before, when they'd started this affair, that he wasn't looking for anything permanent. They had something more than just a casual thing; there was a depth of feeling between them. She believed that, felt that. But it wasn't the road to marriage either. He'd made himself clear, and she knew thinking she could change someone was stupid. He was an adult; he knew what he wanted, and she respected it, even if she wanted him to want what she did.

She didn't have any plans to rip Rennie and Brody apart, though. She didn't want to. She wanted Brody in her life, and as she'd told him earlier, she and Rennie were a package deal. Elise just needed to be sure that Rennie didn't expect Brody to become her daddy, no matter how alluring that was to her and Elise as well.

Oh. My. Disorientation settled in as she realized the conclusion she'd just come to.

"You off woolgathering?" He put the business card on top of her cell phone, interrupting her panic attack. "I've done a lot of ink on his son. He's a top family law attorney here in town. I even had Ben check him out. I know, this is me being pushy, but I didn't want to rec him to you unless I knew he was the best. We can't risk Rennie on anything but the best."

Oh god. She loved him. She knew it when he walked into her studio earlier that day. Hell, she knew it when his was the first face she looked for when she got those legal papers. Knew when she'd sought refuge in his arms instead of kicking his ass out of her studio. His comment about Rennie just then capped it. Shit. Shit. Shit.

She had to respond even as her realization had sent her reeling. He was looking at her, worried. "I'll call him tomorrow. Thank you for the card and for the checking on him." One thing she knew: if she was going to love him, she had to just love him without fear of the end. It would happen, and she'd deal with the fact that she'd still have to see him every day. But it wasn't anywhere near over, so why not just be happy with him? She could be all adult and stuff, right? Stay friends with an ex when the time came? *Sure* she could.

"What are you thinking about?" He began to ladle chili into the bowls.

About how she was such a liar. She feared the end. But she'd love him anyway. You don't always choose who you love, sometimes it just happens. Brody, despite his general reluctance to be permanent with anyone, was a good choice. He was a good man. Honest. Hard-working. He cared about people and he'd been there for her every single time she'd needed him.

She managed a smile even though she was torn between weeping and laughing. "*You*. Thank you for being so good to us."

He smiled and kissed her quickly. "It's my pleasure. It makes me happy." He paused. "I care about you both. I want you to be happy and safe."

"Enough mushy stuff. I'm hungry." And she felt raw, exposed and vulnerable in a way she never had before.

He cocked his head, looking at her carefully. "You okay?"

Before she could answer him, someone knocked on the front door and she sighed, putting a bowl down in front of Rennie before starting toward her hallway.

Brody put a hand on her shoulder to stop her. "Why don't I get it?" Brody *sort* of asked, but his body was already heading toward the front door. Lucky for him she was just fine with him dealing with the Sorensons on her doorstep or anything of that nature.

The soft murmur, replaced by her father's booming voice, filled the house as they came in. Her mother had her arm linked with Brody's, and Elise realized once again that she and Rennie weren't the only women in the family who loved the man.

Her father kissed her cheeks and looked over her shoulder toward the slow cooker. "Smells good. You know how much I love chili." Her parents came in and made themselves at home, filling bowls and sitting at the table, chatting happily with Rennie.

Her family. Crazy-making but wonderful. And they were there for her. That's what counted the most.

After Rennie went to bed, Elise filled her parents in on the newest developments. They agreed to hang out for the guys coming over with Todd the following day to install the new security system. Brody looked tired, and she knew her parents weren't leaving anytime soon.

"You look tired. Why don't you go home and rest?" she suggested softly, following him into the kitchen.

"Because I want to be here with you."

She smiled, butterflies fluttering in her belly. "I want you here too, but you have dark circles under your eyes." She traced the curve of his cheeks and he closed his eyes, leaning into her touch. "And my parents aren't going anywhere. My father just got another glass of wine, which means he and my mother will break out the chessboard. I'll end up going to sleep before they leave. They're night owls."

His slumped shoulders admitted defeat. "You'll fill me in on whatever you hear when you talk to Bill? The attorney?" he clarified when she looked confused.

"Yes. Thanks again for that. I . . . Thank you for being here for me. For me and Rennie. We need our friends and you've been such a good one to us both."

He was the one blushing for a change. "There's nothing else I'd do. I'm here for you because that's what friends do. Tomorrow night, my house. I'll order pizza and we'll watch movies."

She nodded, swallowing past her urge to give him an out. He invited them, he wanted them there. She needed to stop questioning it.

"Sweet dreams. If you need me, I'm just a call away. Like if they go home soon and you need a cuddle. Or something." His eyes darkened and he sidled closer.

She laughed. "I will. I'll think of you when I'm using my special showerhead."

"I'll get you for that." He kissed her quickly. "See you tomorrow. Don't forget to set your system when I leave."

"Yes, sir."

"I know you're being sarcastic, but I like the sound of that anyway. We'll need to look into that a bit more when your mom and dad aren't in the other room. No whips, but definitely chains."

"You're a menace."

"I don't want to suffer alone in my cold bed."

"Your bed isn't cold. You have heated floors. Believe me, I'd much rather snuggle up to you than sleep alone."

He paused and kissed her. "Me too. I'll see you tomorrow."

He said good-bye to her parents and she walked him to the front door. "Night, Shorty. Dream of me."

She would.

21

Brody looked up to catch the sight of her walking through the shop's front door. He smiled, because how could he not? She caught his eye and motioned that she'd leave, but he shook his head and motioned her over. Puhleeze, as if he'd give up any opportunity to be with her.

Anyway, he'd been working on a half sleeve for the last three hours and he was near the end of it. More than that, the woman he was working on needed a break too. His client nodded enthusiastically when he suggested finishing for the day and having her return one last time.

Elise walked to him, straight to him, her gaze locked with his. He felt such a deep sense of belonging when he saw her. Instead of freaking or feeling suffocated, it rested him, soothed that spot inside that he hadn't known he needed to fill until she came into his life.

"I can come by another time. I figured you'd be busy but I was over at the café and wanted to stop in and say hello." She looked smart and confident with her hair up and wearing a pair of trousers and a wine-colored blouse. "I don't want to interrupt."

"Why don't you take a look at where we are?" he said to his client. She got up and stretched before heading to the mirror to check out the work he'd done. "You're not interrupting at all." Damn, she was fine to look at.

"I want you to give me a tattoo," she said without preamble.

"Hang on a sec. Sit right here and don't go anywhere." He gently helped her into his chair. "Be right back." He went to his client to speak to her about when to come in again so he could finish the last detail work. He knew he wore a smile, but he couldn't help it. Elise asking for him to mark her touched him, made him happy.

He returned, kissing her for good measure. "Stay in the chair. I'll sit here." He hopped up onto the table. "Of course I'll ink you. I'd be pissed if you went to anyone else." He wanted to mark that pretty skin himself. "But before we go there, what brings you here? Just the tat request?"

"I met with the lawyer. But I don't want to talk about that here and now. I wanted to stop by and thank Erin for some brownies she made for a bake sale at Rennie's school, and since I was next door, I thought I'd stop in and see you."

Man, he was a lovesick fool. She came to him to tell him about the meeting, to share with him. He liked that a lot. "You better have. I'd be really jealous if you played with my sister but not me." He grinned. "That sounds dirty." One of her eyebrows rose, and he only barely resisted the urge to lean toward her and kiss it. Christ, she wrecked him sometimes. "We can talk details about the meeting later on when we're alone. For now, back to the tattoo. Do you know what you want? Where you want it?"

"I want to start small. To see if it's something I can commit to first. I'd like to get a larger one, but not on my back because I want to look at it. This one would be a test."

"Nothing wrong with that. So you want a starter tattoo?" He laughed. "Okay, that's actually not a bad idea."

"I want something small here." She turned her wrist over. "It's going to sound really silly, but I want a bee, a bumblebee."

He kissed her wrist where she wanted the tattoo. "Rennie." He smiled up at her and he saw her face change, her eyes soften and well up with unshed tears. Guilt hit him; he'd wanted to comfort her, not upset her.

"I . . . It leaves me speechless when you get me the way you do. When you get Rennie. It's . . . Well, it means a lot. She's my most special thing, that you see it . . ." She shook her head, blinking away tears. "Thank you."

The knot of concern he'd had at her upset loosened, turned into more feeling for her. More love. "It leaves me speechless to get you that way too. But I'm glad I do and I think a bumblebee is perfect. You want it now?"

"I don't want to interrupt. I know you're like the big in-demand tattoo dude, so I don't assume I can just flounce in and demand you do it right now. You must be tired. I saw that tattoo you were doing on the lady here when I arrived. How long were you working on it?"

"You didn't flounce, although if you wanted to, that would be aces, since your boobs would jiggle and you know I like that." He said it low so only the two of them could hear, and she blushed, wearing a sweet smile with a hint of naughty. "You can be at the top of my client list, so be quiet about that. I can always squeeze you in at my house or after hours too. But that's not an issue right now. Lastly, the half sleeve I was working on earlier? That was three hours. It's going to be spectacular when it's finished."

"It's spectacular now and you know it. But spending three hours hunched over has to be tiring. I can do it another time when you're not tired."

He couldn't help the flush of pride that she'd liked his work. That she'd come to him for her first tattoo, trusted him to do it right. "Shorty, just looking at you energizes me. It really won't take me very long. Why don't you go and have something to eat at the café and I'll come over with a few designs. It shouldn't take but a few minutes. Do you need to run to get to Rennie? Or to get back to your students?"

"My students have a week off and Rennie is going to a playdate with my parents and Nina. They're going to paint pottery after school."

"It's good she has them here. I'm glad you have them here too. I'm also glad I have you to myself for a while. Now, head next door and I'll be over in a few."

He watched her leave; the graceful way she moved shot to all his best parts.

Next door at the café Erin owned and ran, Elise slid into a seat at the short coffee bar and ordered a decaf mocha. Erin slid a plate with a gorgeous blond brownie her way.

"Bless you. And curse you too. I've eaten so many of these I had to give Rennie a twenty to cover it for the bake sale." Elise took a bite and watched Erin make the drink. "I'm getting Brody to tattoo me," she blurted.

Erin's brows rose and her mouth curved into a sly grin. "Really now? Like today?"

"Yes. I just had this idea for a tattoo. But it was too big to be my first one. I'm a total wuss. I needed a training-level tattoo. So I thought about Rennie and what she's like and I decided I'd like a little bee. Right here on my wrist." She held it out for Erin to see.

"That's a fabulous idea! Oh, it's perfect for her, she's such a little bee. Brody's work is like beyond wow. What do you want the other tat to be? The non-training-wheels tattoo?"

"A swan. From *Swan Lake*? On my hip or just above it. Then again, if I get pregnant again or stretch too much, will it look yucky?"

Erin hitched up her shirt. "I've been pregnant once before and you can see here, on my sides there, the tattoo from my back trails up my sides and over my hips, and it still looks good. I just made sure to keep it hydrated with lotion and out of direct sunlight. Anyway, you're an athlete, Elise, you'll be fine if, or when, you and Brody have a baby together. I'm sure I'll stretch now, although I'm not in my early twenties like I was with Adele. And just in case you haven't noticed, Ben and Todd are huge. This baby is probably going to be gargantuan."

Sharp longing sliced through Elise. "Me and Brody having babies?" She knew her voice sounded funny. "I know he's not interested in a wife and kids and stuff. I mean in the future. Or if I just break down and do it myself. Maybe I'll borrow one of your dudes since you have so many."

Erin tipped her head back, laughing. Despite the grape-Kool-Aid-colored hair and the piercings and tats, Erin's beauty still remained very feminine.

"Elise, shut up. Brody loves you. Haven't you noticed it yet? Duh. And, just a clue here, you love him too. After this mess with the custody is over with, you both can stop pretending and get moving with the rest of your life, which includes marriage and babies."

She blinked at Erin several times, afraid to speak, afraid to believe her.

"Hey dude." Erin waved, and Brody came in, sitting next to Elise and spreading out a few pieces of paper with designs of bees on them.

"Coffee me up, sister," he said to Erin and then turned to Elise.

She saw the one she wanted right off and pointed. "This one. It's perfect." The bee was fat and fuzzy and Elise could imagine the throaty little buzz it would make. He'd done little broken lines behind it to indicate movement. Just a bit, a little loop-de-loop. It was Rennie.

He grinned and kissed her, hard and fast, leaving her struggling to breathe.

"That's the first one I did. My favorite too. Mmm, chocolate and brownie."

"Here. I added a bit of orange zest to yours." Erin slid a cup to him and he took a sip, sighing happily.

At first glance, she'd thought he was the dark and broody bad boy type. But underneath it, he was actually a man who was able to find joy in most things, be it riding his motorcycle on a sunny day or a little orange zest in his mocha. He wasn't a Pollyanna, but his basic personality setting seemed to be intense yet pretty happy.

"You ready?" He took her hand and kissed her wrist, sending shivers through her.

"As I'll ever be." She hopped off the chair and tossed some money on the counter and raised a brow right back at Erin, who pushed the money back toward her. "No. We've had this discussion before."

She'd been taken into the heart of the Brown family, and heavens-to-Betsy did it feel good. Safe. Protected. Still, she was totally going to pay for the coffee.

Brody laughed. "Erin, take the money. We're going to ink this pretty girl right now. I'll see you later."

He put an arm around her and steered her toward his shop. He bustled her to the back and had her sit before squirting stuff on her wrist and then transferring his drawing to just where he wanted it.

"You're very bossy. In some men, no, in most men, it would be annoying. Frankly, even in you it can be annoying. But I love to see you with your siblings. They love and respect you so much, you're all so close. It's good."

He looked up, grinning.

"You look like a pirate." Her voice had gone thick as his nearness and his beauty affected her.

"I do? And me without my parrot or eye patch."

She rolled her eyes. "It's the loot-and-pillage smile that worries me. Or, okay, I'm lying; not worried as much as curious."

"I'm totally going to loot and plunder." His eyes had gone hooded, dark.

"Only if you promise to pillage too."

He laughed. "You have my solemn promise. Now try to be still." He put her arm across his thigh. "Just relax. Think about being ravished and stuff."

The sound startled her when he turned the needle machine on, but she relaxed quickly, watching as he dipped it in the ink and then went back to her wrist. Pain, but not a massive amount, vibrated through her as he worked.

The light gleamed off the darkness of his hair. Hair she wanted to touch just then, but resisted because it was his place of work and all. After a few minutes she sort of fell into it, the buzzing, the metallic edge of pain as he worked and the needle hit her skin, the sounds around them, the scents—it all hummed through her and she realized just why people did this. It felt good, like a ritual.

It didn't take him very long. He wiped her wrist off and sat back. "What do you think?"

It was perfect. Just the right size. Nothing flashy or gaudy. A little mark of importance for Rennie.

"Oh." She looked at it, loving it. He'd only used black with a tiny bit of gray so the bee's stripes weren't yellow and black, but black with thin gray bands like those bees who happily buzzed away in her garden. "It's perfect. I love that you didn't use yellow. I hadn't even thought of it but . . . I love it. Thank you."

"I'm glad. We're on for dinner tonight, yes?"

She nodded. "I'm stopping by the deli on the way home because I don't want to cook."

He put some sort of goop on the tattoo, a thin layer of gel, and taped a bandage over it. "First things first. Leave the bandage on for two hours. When you take it off, wash it with a mild soap and dry it. Pat it dry, don't rub at it. Then put this on it." He handed her a tube. "That's made specifically for tattoo aftercare. This should heal up pretty quickly. Take care of it. Keep it out of direct sunlight for long periods of time. I know how much you like long baths, but if you take one, keep the wrist out of it. Don't pick at the scab or the skin either. I'm going to give you a paper that'll detail what you need to do and I'll be there to make sure you're fine."

"Ew. I promise not to pick scabs. Like, ever." She curled her lip. "Holy crap, I had no idea it was this involved."

He shook his head. "It's all common sense stuff. I'll be your personal tattoo doctor."

"I like the sound of that." She lasered her eyes on him. "Now, you're going to charge me for this tattoo. The regular price. Oh, okay if you wanted to give me a discount because we get naked, I won't say no. But no freebies."

"It's my shop and I'll charge if I want, what I want. That was the most fun I've had doing a tattoo in a really long time. It was my pleasure to give you your first and I'm thrilled that you like it so much. I eat at your house at least four nights a week. You never charge me for groceries."

"No, but you leave groceries in my pantry. Don't think I don't notice. And don't think I miss the twenty that shows up on the counter or tucked in my purse. I don't charge for dinner, but that's not even applicable here and you know it."

She put a hand on her hip and met his narrowed eyes with her own. He snorted. "I'm not charging you. Period."

"Fine," she said lightly. "I'll just have someone else do the other tattoo I want."

He caught up to her in two steps. He grabbed his jacket and told Arvin he was gone for the day.

"You're not leaving early just for me. This is your business!"

"You would argue that the sky was blue." His arm about her shoulders steered her outside as people called their good-byes.

"Are you saying I'm stubborn? For no reason other than I'm just refusing to expect free tattoos from you?"

"I'm saying you're argumentative. And no one else is going to tattoo you. I'm the best and you deserve the best. Now, tell me the tattoo you were thinking of."

She shoved money in his hand and he groaned.

"Now I feel much better. There will be no one at my house for another hour and a half," she called out over her shoulder as she walked to her car and got inside.

He grinned as he knocked on her front door. Grinned even harder as he heard her look out the viewer before her locks all started to disengage. Absolutely infuriating, but fascinating. Strong. Gorgeous. Smart and steadfast. He'd simply buy her groceries now. He was just as stubborn as she was.

"That grin doesn't bode well for me, I think." She opened the door, standing there in absolutely nothing. Sometimes she surprised him in all the best ways.

"No need to worry." He went inside and locked up behind himself, setting the alarm and following her to her bedroom. He sucked in a breath when he caught sight of her, settled on the bed. "All my thoughts of you, especially right now, are pretty fucking positive."

"Bring it." One of her eyebrows arched in challenge, but he barely registered it because, hello, naked.

He tossed himself on the bed, careful not to crush her. "Wow, I thought bad things were supposed to happen when you left work early to be with your girlfriend. I may have to leave early every day now."

Her hands paused a moment as she removed his shirt, but he'd said it deliberately. They'd moved to a new stage in their relationship and he wanted to say it out loud. Aside from a tiny bit of panic, he felt fine. Better than fine in fact.

He feasted on her mouth. She opened to him, her hands roaming all over his body, nails scoring his sides where they drove him to shivers of delight, his lower back as she urged him closer.

Not wanting to hurt her with his zipper against any soft parts, he pulled back and set to removing his jeans while her eyes remained locked on him as he moved.

"Hair down. Please."

She sat up enough to pull her hair free of the pins, and the room filled with the scent of her shampoo when her hair fell around her shoulders.

"You know, I do believe aside from you playing with your clit and making yourself come while I'm inside you, you haven't masturbated for my entertainment at all."

She laughed. "Brody, you know I adore you, but when I finger my clit"—she blushed when she said it, but she said it—"it's for my entertainment. I'm glad it works for you too, though."

"God how I love it when you blush that way."

She fell back to the pillows, her hands over her face while she shook with laughter.

Since she was busy, he brought her ankle to his mouth, pressing an openmouthed kiss in the hollow just behind it. Her laughter melted into a soft groan.

"Touch yourself." He kissed the other ankle and moved to kneel between her legs.

"Okay."

He knew without her telling him that he was the only person she'd done this for, and it meant something. Made a difference. She got inside him and settled there until he couldn't remember a time without her. Couldn't remember a moment in his life when he didn't think, *I've got to tell Elise about this,* when something happened during his day.

Erin had told him, when they were in Las Vegas for her wedding to Todd, that love often came as a total surprise. And she was right. There wasn't a moment Brody could think back on and identify as the time when like tipped into love. But he was there and it rocked him down to his foundations, and yet loving Elise was the most comforting and natural thing he'd ever felt.

Elise's eyes drifted closed as her hands slid down her torso. His body kept her legs open, and from his vantage point, the glistening, dark pink folds of her pussy beckoned to him, to his hands and mouth, to his cock. How beautiful she was there, laid out before him, offering him everything.

He watched as her hips undulated while she grasped her nipples and pulled. *Whoa*. That was fucking hot. He wanted to talk to her, tell her how hot she looked, but he didn't want to break in yet, wanted to let the moment be hers alone for a little while longer.

His fingers curled into her calves where he'd been holding her, and she moaned. His mouth watered to taste the velvety skin where thigh met body, wanted to slide across the wet of her cunt, up her belly, over her nipples and to her lips.

Magic. Elise Sorenson was magic. Rare. The most beautiful and elegant thing he'd ever possessed, had ever wanted. When he was a kid, his mother had some fragile porcelain figurine his father had given her when they were teenagers. Brody had never touched it, fearing he'd break it or harm it, but he'd watched it. Stood and looked at it, so regal and perfect. The lines so perfect no matter how the sun hit it, even on their totally normal suburban mantel.

Elise was all that desire for something fine and beautiful, but come to life, because she was that way inside too. Such a good mother, competent, no-nonsense, but also whimsical and silly. Sexy that, the way she took care of her kid. Made him wonder what it would be like, to be a family with them, to come home to his girls every night. In loving her, he was a better person.

Part of him went cold a moment at how far he'd gone with her without even realizing it. And then he relaxed, warmed, understood it had been happening every single day since she'd touched him, just before they loaded him into the ambulance almost a year ago. He only worried that she didn't feel as deeply. If she didn't, he'd wear her down until she did. He knew without a doubt that he loved her and wanted to be with her, and her child. He'd wait until after all this legal bullshit was squared away; he knew she'd need all her focus on that. Once that was taken care of, he'd be asking her to marry him.

He moaned softly when her fingers finally slid down and into her cunt, his breathing in sync with hers as they both dragged in a deep breath when she pressed two fingers up into her gate and then pulled them back out.

"I'm dying here, watching you," he said in a low voice. Her eyes opened slowly and focused on him. "This is so sexy. Like the hottest thing I've ever seen."

Her mouth curled up into a smile as she blushed again. But she didn't stop the hand on her pussy.

Elise had never been so turned on in her life. Doing this for him, showing him something so intimate that she'd never shared it with anyone before, thrilled and titillated her straight to her toes. Even though her eyes were closed, she felt his attention, knew his gaze caressed her body, her nipples, where she'd buried her hand between her thighs—his eyes would be dark and stormy as he watched.

She opened her eyes again, wanting to see those eyes, and his gaze met hers. A ripple of awareness passed between them, rolled through her with so much power it brought her to a very brief pause.

"Don't stop," he murmured.

So she didn't. Nor did she close her eyes. The way he looked at her then was so beautiful she couldn't tear her eyes away. Didn't want to, because it made her feel desired and loved.

Orgasm came, cell-deep, slow to expand through her body like honey. She wanted to curl into him and nap, letting him protect her while she did nothing but dream.

He swooped down and kissed her; barely reined hunger made him taste urgent and hot. His intensity woke her up, washed the languid away, replacing it with need. More. How much could she take? She wanted to have so much of him she overflowed.

"I just want you so much," she whispered against the skin of his chest, before biting.

He rolled, bringing her atop him. "Take me. I'm yours to take, Elise."

She pushed herself to sit, quickly positioning herself and sliding back onto his cock. Still for long moments, she simply let herself feel the thickness of him buried deep. And then she looked down at him, mussed up, a big, sexual man with an edge of darkness, and he reined it in for her.

His tattoos were so ridiculously sexy. She'd say something like he didn't know just how sexy, but as she began to ride him, rising up and coming down over his cock, she knew he did. "You know what's one of the most sexy things about you?"

He grinned up at her. "No, but I'm always ready to hear such things. Do tell."

She laughed. She often laughed during sex with him. She'd never laughed with a man in intimate moments before. But with him, the happiness always found a way out.

"You know how hot you are. You know the tall, dark and handsome thing with the tats and the nipple ring is like sugar water to hummingbirds." She pressed down hard and circled her hips, grinding herself into him.

He sucked in a breath. "I like that move a lot. You're saying I'm vain but you like it?"

Her nails dug into his sides, and he arched into it, she knew, loving that bit of pain to spice the pleasure.

"I'm saying you understand your sexual allure and you embrace it. You're a very sexual man. Add the bad-boy thing to that and you're like catnip for women."

He laughed. "I think that's the best compliment I've ever received."

They fell silent, the only sounds the birds out in the backyard and the slap of flesh meeting. Having him inside her felt so good she luxuriated in it, taking her time, teasing him up, higher and higher.

"I'm going to die," he croaked out, his fists in the blankets. She knew he wanted to take over and leaned down to kiss him.

"Don't die. I need you here to fuck me."

He cursed low, and those hands landed on her hips, his fingers digging in to guide her movement, to speed her up and bring her down a little harder. She loved it when he did this, lost his rein and guided her just where and how he wanted. Still she was surprised when another climax blasted through her body.

He must have been too, because he nearly snarled as she contracted around him. He began to thrust up as he pulled her down against him. His upper body tightened as his muscles worked, and then with a long groan, he came.

"I'm starving." His voice was muffled against her hair.

"I'll make you a sandwich. Meatloaf okay?"

He tipped her chin and kissed her. "Thank you. And you can tell me about what happened at the attorney's office. You think Rennie would like to go out to Chinese food tonight? I feel like taking out my two best girls."

He rolled from her bed, and she couldn't help but bury her face in the pillow he'd been on. She loved his smell. "I think she'd love it. You know how she feels about you." She got out of bed and he followed her into her bathroom. Rennie wasn't the only Sorenson who loved Brody Brown.

22

Elise fell into the rhythm of making him a sandwich. He'd helped her wash and dry the tattoo and had shown her just how much of the gel to put on. Such a big man, but always totally gentle with her.

"They're trying to drag me back to New York. To a different county than where we were before. This one is where a lot of vacation homes for the rich and famous are located, so Frank and my new attorney—yes the guy was really good—think the Sorensons want to get me where they have a better chance at taking Rennie."

She put the sandwich on the table and followed with a glass of orange juice.

He took a big bite of the sandwich and looked across to where she sat, eating an apple because we can't all be men who can inhale four thousand calories a day and still be slim. Not that she was bitter. Not at all.

"Who'd have thought meatloaf would be so awesome? This is so good. Thank you." He took a drink. "I hate these people. Just on principle, but also because they're trying to hurt you and Rennie."

"Bill will handle most of the motions, with Frank helping out in New York. They're filing a motion to dismiss. And also to keep the case here in Washington where I live and where Rennie lives. Apparently they filed more papers today as I was talking with them both. Frank was going to fax it all to Bill and they'll get back to me."

He took her hand across the table. "It's going to be fine. You're a wonderful mom. Rennie is happy and healthy and thriving. And so are you, Elise. You grow brighter every day, more vibrant and full of life. You're making your own way here, and it shows. What can I do to help?"

"Thank you for being here for me. That's the most important part."

"There's nowhere else I'd rather be. I'm also available for things like babysitting if you need to be somewhere and your parents need a break or can't do it."

"You really do care about Irene, don't you?"

Confusion washed over his features for a moment. "Of course I do. Isn't it obvious?"

"She's my kid, I obviously think she's fabulous, so it's easy to assume everyone else does. But not everyone else does, of course. I'm just grateful she has people who care about her in her life. I can't let this case get dragged back to New York, Brody. I can't take her back there. I can't go back there. I'm here where things are good and right. We're good here. I don't want to look back over my shoulder again. And they're making me. I hate them."

He finished his sandwich, pushing the plate and empty glass aside to take both her hands in his.

"If you have to go back to New York, I'll be with you. At your side. I promise. There's no looking over your shoulder now. Only the future and it's all good. I have to ask you, are you going to reply to these allegations with how upset Rennie gets after the calls with them?"

"I've tried too hard to be fair. Even after this mess. I wanted her to have some contact and connection to her father. Ken wasn't always the man I had to kill. I loved him once. He loved me, I truly believe he did. So I wanted to honor that and let Rennie have that, because there will come a time when I have to tell her the whole story and I don't want her to hate him or me. I've made so many mistakes. Failed so many times." She covered her face with her hands.

"There are many words that come to mind when I think of you. Failure isn't one of them."

She tore her hands from her eyes and looked at him. "I have failed at everything in my life but dancing. I saved Rennie from Ken and I'd do it again. But I killed her father. I took her away from her paternal grandparents, but it was necessary. They are bad and wrong and they don't even love her. How can they not love her?"

He shook his head and took one of her hands back, holding it between his. "I don't know. It's impossible for me to understand how anyone could resist Rennie. And you did what you had to do, Elise. It was self-defense. You're not a failure because your ex-husband was a crazy, fucked up junkie. That's his failure."

"I am a shitty daughter. I was a shitty sister. I was a shitty wife. I never really had any friends outside of the other dancers, and sometimes not even them, because the competition for roles . . ." She shrugged. "I am a total failure but for two things. First is my dancing. I've been good at it since I was four and I've achieved all I'd ever dreamed of and more as a dancer. Later, but far more important, is Rennie. I've made mistakes, yes, but I've been a good mother, the best I could under the circumstances even if I'm not perfect. I've *tried* to be better at things, but . . ." She licked her lips, not finishing the sentence..

He moved quickly, sitting in the chair beside hers. "Do you honestly think you're a failure? Because when I look at you, when I know you, Elise, I don't see it. No, don't interrupt for a moment." He put his finger against her lips. "I see how you are with your parents; you're not a shitty daughter. I see the little things you do for them both, the special tea for your dad's joints, the way you include your mother at your studio so she feels important, so you can share your love of dancing with her. What I see is not failure, but a family. They moved out here to be with you and Rennie because they genuinely want to be with you two. As for your brother . . . Tell me. You told me some, the highlights if you will. Tell me why you think you're a shitty sister."

"College was when it all seemed to get out of control for him. He was always looking for more. He gorged himself on everything, which is part of why he was such an amazing performer. He went to keggers and got into minor trouble. But my parents always made excuses for him; he was the favorite, you see. I don't blame them for it. He was, he was like a dragonfly, flitting through your life, iridescent and magical. You couldn't take your eyes from him. I knew he'd started using speed, but I didn't tell on him. I should have right at the very start. I didn't and he died."

"He was how much older than you when he started using speed?" He looked at his watch. "When is Rennie due back here?"

"Five. My parents are going to a lecture at the UW tonight and then out to dinner with the speaker. He's one of my dad's old colleagues."

Brody nodded. "Okay then, we've got a while." He stood and drew her into the living room, where they snuggled on the couch.

"He was five years older than me. He was twenty-one or twenty-two when it first started. He'd moved to the city. I knew, but I didn't say anything to my parents. And then I met Ken and it all went to hell."

"Before you expand on your failures as a wife, why don't you tell me what a typical day was like for you when you were seventeen. What was your schedule?"

She glared at him. "Got up at five to get into the city for dance classes in the morning. I'd finished up high school by the time I was sixteen. I graduated early. I always planned on taking college courses, but never got around to it. There was rehearsal for whatever production I was in at the time. More classes in the late afternoon. I ended up moving into an apartment in Manhattan because the commute got to be too much."

"You lived on your own at seventeen? In New York City?"

"You raised kids at that age! I shared an apartment in a relatively murder-free neighborhood with three other dancers. My grandmother had left a trust; it paid my share of the rent until I joined the company, and, well, I was still dirt poor for some time to come. Funny though, poor as I was, it was such a magical time. I was on my own and doing what I'd always wanted to do. And then I met Ken."

"On to your failure as a wife then."

"Ha ha, it's all a joke to you."

"Do you really think that, Elise? I'm making light, yes, but it's not a joke that you've endured and survived and been so successful and you see yourself as a failure. I want to understand because I don't see it."

"Ken was"—she licked her lips—"the life of every party. He was color spatters on a canvas, mad creation at two a.m. and then back to bed, where we'd make love until I had to rush out to class. What

I learned over the happy times into the not-so-happy times was that he had no off button. He never got enough. No matter what it was. And then the drugs with Matty.

"So I left him finally. I left him and he continued to get in trouble. I took him back when he kept clean. And that's when the condom broke and Rennie was conceived. You know the rest. He started using again. I kicked him out, changed the locks and eventually filed divorce papers. What a fucking idiot I was. I thought I could save him. I thought I could be the stability he needed to keep clean."

Brody listened to her, listened to how torn up she was at other people's failings. Knowing she considered herself a failure made him ache for her. He thought he'd be uncomfortable hearing about her ex, but he wasn't. Angry, yes; jealous, no.

"You can't do that for people. They have to do it themselves. Our dad was an alcoholic. He was found to be responsible, in part, for the accident that ended up killing both him and my mom."

"I know that now. I wasn't enough for him. A child on the way wasn't enough. Nothing was enough."

He turned to face her better. "You're not a failure for preventing other people from fucking up. You're not God and he didn't step in with your brother or Ken either. So if God didn't, why are you suddenly more powerful and responsible?"

"Do you feel responsible at all? For your parents?"

He swallowed hard. "Yeah. Sometimes. I was fuckin' glad to get out of that house. I loved my brother and sister and still checked in on them, but I was gone from the day-to-day hassle of my father. Not having to deal with the dread when he wasn't home in time for dinner, or the embarrassment when he got too drunk to walk . . . it freed me. And then I felt like a traitor when they died. My last words with him were angry. He was a good guy once, when I was young. Why couldn't I hold on to those memories instead of the bad ones?" He shrugged. "But it's not my fault. He drank too much, period. And nothing I could have said would have been enough to make him stop. It wasn't about me. Just like your brother's overdose wasn't your fault. Just like Ken wasn't your fault."

"Maybe it's me though. That I drive people to it."

He laughed and kissed her. "Shorty, I'm here, aren't I? Successful business, just like you. Nary a need for crack or hookers. I do like to have lots of sex with you, because, duh, look at you. But some people are driven to excess. It's not about anyone but themselves. Let go of all this guilt. You're not responsible for anyone but Rennie and yourself. Did you love your brother?"

"Yes. But I hated what he was like when he was tweaking. I resented him for not having the strength to stop. People kept saying he was sick, that he had a disease. I wanted to be understanding, but he left a bloody needle in my house! At some point I just sat up in bed and realized he'd never have a wife or kids or anything to sustain him and he was going to die. I think it was impossible to sustain him." She broke off, shaking her head. "I spend too much time thinking about what used to be."

Ah, there was something there. "And what about that? Do you want to be what you were?"

"No." She swallowed and wiped her eyes with the back of her hand. "After, when I was in the hospital and they'd, god, they used a rape kit, I was doped up, covered in blood, freaked that Ken had given me something. Worried about Rennie and my parents. My father had to be sedated, he was so upset. It was a mess. But my mother kept saying to hang on so I could be just like new, just like I'd been before. Even when it was plain I'd never be able to dance professionally again, people kept saying they wanted to see the old me. I danced. It's what I did, who I was from three to thirty. I achieved more than I'd ever imagined. And then I had Rennie. But the rest was filled with chaos. I don't want to look back. I don't want to go back. When I look into my mirror every day, I don't wish I was that woman. I like my life here. It's *normal.* Normal, and that's wonderful. Normal is a luxury."

He took her face in his hands. "You don't have to be anything but who you are right now. Let go of what was. I don't want you to be who you were before. I want you to be who you *are.*"

She simply crawled into his lap and curled into him. He kissed her shoulder and they sat, enjoying the moment.

Deep inside, Brody processed all the things she'd just told him. Loved her for her strength, loved her for her guilt, even as he made up his mind to make it stop. He liked normal too, when it included this woman.

23

"You're going to have to repeat that." Elise wondered if she'd heard Bill correctly when he recounted the allegations being made about her by the Sorensons.

"You heard me." Bill shook his head. "These people remind me why there are days I hate doing family law."

"Just be glad there's a whole country separating them from the rest of us. I *am* dating someone. Brody Brown. He lives across the street from me, and yes, Rennie is exposed to him. But he and I have been together for a year, this thing between us is stable. He's a good guy. He plays catch with her, he goes to the zoo and the aquarium with us. Everyone in our circle is a good person. They might have tattoos or they're musicians. They're all good people. That's not unfit!"

"Elise, I know you're not unfit. I know Brody through my son and I agree with your assessment of his character. I've looked over all the paperwork, I've read the reports, I've spoken with her teachers who tell me Irene is a great kid, happy, smart. They did say that

once a month she's easily upset for a few days. Around the fifteenth."

"It's *them*. They call her and she's a mess for a few days after.
They tell her she's going to come and see them, to ask me to
see them. They promise to take her to Europe and to let her ride
horses. They give her nightmares. She's afraid they'll take her. I've
never said anything negative about them to her, but they are a cancer in her life."

"Are you saying you want to move to end their contact with
Irene?"

"I've given it a lot of thought. Yes. They're not a positive influence on her at all. I try to put a positive spin on it, but it's been
nearly a year since we moved out here and it's only getting worse.
They've begun to ask her questions about me all the time, to encourage her to ask me to let them do things they're not allowed to
do. I sent a letter through Frank asking them to stop it. But they've
now taken to calling my parents and threatening them; they call
me too."

Bill sighed. "I tend to agree with your assessment about the
negative effects of contact with them. The question is, do you want
me to push for a dismissal and leaving status as is, or do you want me
to answer this change in circumstance with our own? Petition the
court to cease all contact with her. It'll be more costly, and we'll
most likely need some expert intervention here. Interviews, assess-
ments, that sort of thing. But you'd have them out of your life and
out of Rennie's life. If you choose to go this way, I'm fairly certain
we can move the case here."

"Can I have a few hours to think on it? It's the fifteenth and I've
got to get home to be ready for the call. Rennie's with Brody this
afternoon. He took her and her friend Nina to the park. He loves

my kid and she loves him. He's good for her. It's good for her to see men like him and my father. Steadfast men who don't hurt women or walk away from them."

"Look, I don't usually . . . If it were me, I'd think getting these people away from you once and for all, totally away, would be worth pursuing. And you'd have the added plus of using this attack on you to do it. Frank agrees, by the way."

She stood. "Thank you, Bill. I appreciate it. I'll leave a message on your voice mail later tonight which way I want you to go."

Brody hugged her when she got to the park. She looked around, wondering if someone with a camera was lurking. "Your mom and dad are at your place right now. They went to the deli, said they were making dinner. They said to tell you they were staying for dinner and then they'd go to the lecture. They want to be there when the Sorensons call."

"They worry, especially on the fifteenth. How's Rennie?"

"She's burst into tears twice, but mainly she's fine. My god, Shorty, these people are making her physically sick." He looked so concerned it sliced right to her heart. Made her love him even more, if such a thing were possible.

"*I know*. I'd hoped it would get better. I try to be upbeat. I have a picture of them in her room; I encourage her to send them things, pictures she draws, that sort of thing. But she took the picture down before Christmas and she won't send them anything."

"Hey girls, time to go!" he called out and they came running.

"Thank you for being here for her. For me."

"Nowhere else I'd rather be and that's a fact. I always sleep like a rock after hanging out with Rennie for any amount of time."

Rennie ran into her mother's arms and began chattering about her day, about Brody picking them up, how he'd scored them corn dogs and chips and had let them go really high on the swings.

They dropped Nina home and walked back to Elise's house. Rennie stayed between the two of them, holding on to their hands tightly. Brody looked worried but kept a smile on his face. Elise's parents had prepared a nice dinner and they all ate. Or Elise pretended to eat, but nausea killed her appetite. Rennie threw a tantrum over the lack of pickles and then cried more, worried she'd made her pops sad.

"It's nearly six, your other grandparents will be calling soon. Where do you want to take the call?" Elise asked as she pulled the cell from her bag.

"Pops, can I sit in your lap, please? That way if I feel lonely or sad, you're right there to hold on to."

Paul met his daughter's eyes first and then managed a big smile for Rennie. "I'm not going to turn down any excuse I get to snuggle with you. Come on into the front room then, so you can hear better." He took the phone from Elise and squeezed her hand briefly before taking Rennie into the other room.

Elise put her head down for a moment.

"It'll be over in ten minutes, Elise. Tell us what the lawyer said today." Her mother patted her hand.

So she did and watched both Brody and her mother get angry.

Brody shook his head. "*I'm* what makes you unfit? That's total crap. I'd never do anything to hurt you. Either one of you."

She took his hand, pressing it to her cheek. "Of course not. They had a stack of photographs, but Bill pointed out none of them were bad. They've been using investigators again, but it was shots of us playing at the park, working in the yard, out for dinner, all totally normal. Rennie was in almost every shot looking perky and happy, and well loved. Someone is always touching her or kissing her. The kid isn't wanting for attention, I'll say that." And then she told them what she'd decided.

Her mother nodded. "Okay. For what it's worth, I think it's the best choice. It's the big-picture choice. Each time she deals with them, it hurts her. Daddy and I have money set aside for her; if you need help with the legal fees, it's yours."

She smiled at her mother. "Thank you, but I don't want you to do that. She'll need the money for college and all that stuff. The studio is doing well. I have some savings too. I'm fine. It's your emotional support I need and appreciate so much. Rennie too." It was tearing her up, knowing Rennie was upset right then, knowing she couldn't stop it. But she was going to. She was going to stop the Sorensons from harming her kid once and for all.

Brody accepted the hug from Rennie and settled in to wait for Elise to come back downstairs. Her parents had left for the lecture, prompting another meltdown from Rennie. It was tearing Elise apart, watching this insanity and not being able to stop it. Seeing them both in such emotional turmoil tore at Brody. He loved them both and he wanted to make everything all right.

Still, despite all the insanity and uncertainty, Elise continued to grow and thrive, and so did Rennie. Elise came to him each day more satisfied with herself and her position. Her business was booming and she'd begun to turn a real profit.

And each day, Brody fell deeper in love with her. He couldn't be happier unless they were already living in the same house. But now that the Sorensons were alleging this crap about her being unfit and his presence being negative, he knew he'd been wise to hold back a bit. Elise needed to focus on this court crap, and then the way would be clear for both of them to move forward. He didn't want her to feel as if she had to choose.

It was a challenge to hold back and not take over. He wanted to make everything all right for them both. Wanted to fly back to New York and beat the ever-loving hell out of those two fuckheads and stop them from hurting his girls. He wanted to pay Elise's legal bills, wanted to yank the phone from Paul's hands and tell the Sorensons they would not be torturing Rennie anymore. He wanted Elise safe and happy. He wanted to take away the fear of losing Rennie. God knew he spent more than a few hours a day concerned that something would happen and they'd lose Rennie forever. He knew that would kill Elise.

So he'd continue to be supportive, continue to show them both how special they were, continue to listen and love them because they were his to cherish and they needed it as much as he needed to do it.

"How does this look?" Elise asked Erin, who sat on her bed and watched as Elise tried on a few different outfits for the court date the following day.

"You look fine. Pretty. Youthful. Responsible. The kind of woman who loves her kid. All the things you've tried on have been lovely.

"Momma?" Rennie wandered into the room and got up on the bed with Erin, who immediately hugged her.

"What's up, Noodle?"

"I like those shoes, but not with that skirt. Wear them with that blue skirt and the shirt in your hand." Rennie yawned. It was getting near her bedtime, but she'd been downstairs with Ben, Todd and Brody, playing on the Wii.

"You're right. That's what I'll wear. Thank you. Now go brush your teeth and wash your face before getting into pajamas." She bent to kiss Rennie's head.

"What's a cunt?"

Erin and Elise both froze a moment.

"What did you just say?"

"What's a cunt?"

"Where did you hear that word?" Elise's heart sped; if she'd heard them having sex or if one of the visitors to the house had said it, she worried what a judge might think.

"Mrs. Sorenson said you were one. It's on the voice mail."

"What? On the cell phone? You heard this?" Her hands shook with anger, but she tried to keep her voice calm.

"No, on the phone here. I checked to see if Nina called while we were at the grocery store, but it was *her*, Mrs. Sorenson, and she said that word."

"The way she used it is a bad word. I don't want to hear you repeat it. It's a bad word people use about women. It's also what some people call your vagina, which sometimes can be all right, but you're nowhere near the age for that."

"She's mad all the time, Momma. If they don't like me and you, why do they make me talk to them every month? I don't want to. I told the judge that already and no one listens to me."

Elise had only a fingernail's hold on her emotions. She sat on the bed and Rennie crawled into her lap, curling into her body. "I'm trying, honey. I'm trying my hardest. But until the court says otherwise, they have a right to talk to you every month. I'm sorry you had to hear that voice mail. From now on, we'll just have Momma check it, okay?" She hugged Rennie tight. "I love you so much."

"I love you too."

"I don't want you to worry, okay? When the attorneys talk to you, or the court people, I want you to tell them the truth. It's fine if you want to talk to the Sorensons, or know them. If that's what you feel, that's what you say. I love you no matter what. You can love more than one person, it doesn't meant you love me less."

"Like how you love Brody and me too?"

She looked at Erin, whose eyes were filled with unspent tears. And then back to Rennie. "Yes. And like how I love Pops and Gran. And Erin too. Your life can be full of people you love. It's okay with me if you love lots of people."

"I love the people who love me. Like you and Pops and Gran. Nina is my bestest friend and I love Miss Maggie and Auntie Erin too. Ben and Todd are nice, Uncle Adrian too. But Brody is my favorite after you, Pops and Gran."

Elise had to close her eyes a moment, and Erin broke in, tears in her voice but a smile on her face. "I love you too, Rennie, and so do all my guys. We're family. Sometimes family is made up of people you're related to like your mom and your grandparents, and sometimes it's made up of people you choose to make your family, like Brody and me."

"Can I wear my princess dress to bed?"

"Nicely done on the sympathy pull, Irene. But how about you sleep in pajamas? That dress isn't for sleeping in. Go on now. I'll be in to read you a story in a few."

"Adrian is reading me a story. He already called dibs on it."

"Okay then. But you still need to wash your face and brush your teeth."

Rennie ran off in the wake of kisses and hugs, and Elise headed out to the kitchen for the phone.

Brody sidled up to her and kissed her cheek. "What's going on? Rennie listened to the voice mail and ran back toward your room."

"Dunno. I need to listen to something."

Listen she did. Listen as her former mother-in-law called her a whore and a cunt. Listened as they threatened to end her, to take everything she'd ever loved. Her hands shook as she made sure to save before hanging up.

Brody, seeing her distress and not bothering to ask, picked the phone up and dialed back in, listening to the message. He'd checked her voice mail often enough he knew the code. Part of her liked that, even as his face darkened while he listened and then hung up.

"You need to send that to your lawyer. Now."

"Yes. I want to get Rennie to bed first and then I will. I can't fall apart right now. She can never see how much they affect me. I won't allow it."

"I'm sorry. I wish . . . I wish I could just poof them out of existence. She's wrong, you know. Vile and hateful and totally wrong. You're none of the things she said. Why would she be so stupid as to say all that? I don't understand it."

"They never seem to get that they'll be held responsible for the things they do and say. She knows I'm not only going to fight back, but that they opened the door with their petition and that must burn her buttons. They can't argue against a significant change in circumstances when they're the ones who brought it up. So now the door is open and she can't handle not being in control."

He sighed and held her for a moment. "Just hold on. You're going to win here."

"I hope so. It's a huge gamble. But she threw up after the last call. I can't have that."

"Nope. And you don't need to be called a rasher of names on your own voice mail."

"The awesome thing was that they were insisting they didn't know my home phone number. They complained about not having it in case of emergency, saying I held it back. Which I did of course, for this very reason. But this proves they have the number, so *pffft* to them."

She waited until Adrian finished the story before tucking Rennie in and turning out her light. Then she forwarded the voice mail to both her attorneys. She wouldn't allow them to break her. She needed to be whole for Rennie. Needed to be whole to run her business and live her life. They wouldn't steal it from her any longer.

The hearing the following day would be a preliminary one, but an important one. She visited with everyone for a while longer, but they all left by ten, including Brody. He wanted to stay, but she needed the time to get herself together, needed the space. And he'd been grumpy about it, but he'd gone after a kiss and a promise to see her the next afternoon.

As she lay in bed, listening to the sounds the house made as it settled, she realized Brody had been incredibly accommodating. He'd worked hard not to be pushy, and although he still was, he was trying. She appreciated that. Appreciated how much energy he put into being with her. He'd called her his girlfriend the month before, and it was true. She'd come a long way in the last year since she'd arrived in Seattle, and he was part of it.

If luck would just hold out a bit more and keep Rennie where she belonged.

24

"Hey, Brody." Raven plopped herself into his lap and put her arms around his neck.

He raised his brows at her. "Raven, what brings you to my lap?"

"I like it here. It's just the right size for me. You haven't played with me for a long time. I feel neglected."

"We just all went out to play pool last Friday. We played then."

"Not that kind of play. Anyway, you brought *her* and never took your eyes from her all night long. Like I wasn't even there."

"What's up with you, Raven? I mean, come on, I've been with Elise for a year now. Even before that, there was no romance between you and me for at least two years."

"*Pfft* romance. See, that's what I mean. Before she came along we didn't need romance. We had fucking. Do you remember fucking?"

He sighed and moved her so he could stand. "Cut the shit. You don't want me. Why the hell are you pulling this crap? We're friends and you're endangering that. We've been friends for longer than we were lovers. I have a lot of shit on my plate just now. Elise is dealing with some personal stuff and I need to be present for her and Rennie."

"Isn't it just like Little Miss Helpless to heap her crap on you, the big man who will fix her life for her. The Brody I knew would have steered clear of a woman like that. Is her pussy magic? What is so appealing about her? She's got a kid. You can't go out very often because she's got a kid! You don't go to shows anymore. You've turned into an old married man and your wife is like a freaking PTA president or something. Don't you miss exciting women?"

He sighed. "I've tried to make allowances for you. You're Raven, so you get a pass on a lot of shit other people would get called on. I love Elise Sorenson, got that? I love her and I love her kid. She's strong and smart; she doesn't *rely* on me at all. In fact, I beg her to let me do more all the time and she won't. We get into fights over it because she wants to be self-sufficient. She is exciting. Beautiful, willful and the best mother I know. You're being fucking petty right now and I don't like it."

"*Love?* Are you fucking kidding me? You can't love her, Brody. You love puppies and tacos. You love your family. You don't love a chick like her. As for exciting? Come on! She's a *ballerina*. She's past her pull-by date and she's loaded down with drama. Is that what attracts you? The drama? Now that Erin is happy and settled, you need to have a chick in your life with issues?"

"I've *had* a chick in my life with issues." He gave her a pointed look she chose to ignore. "Take a long, hard look at yourself. I'm so beyond tired right now, and I'm hard-pressed to understand what your issue is. *We aren't together*. We haven't been for years now. Long before Elise came into the picture. I love her. I didn't go into this thing expecting that; we both said we were too busy for it. But it happened anyway and I can't be anything but happy about that."

She launched herself at him, her lips landing on his, and for one moment he responded because he always had before. And then, just as quickly, he grabbed her by the waist and set her back from him.

"What the hell was that?" They were standing in his shop; the kiss had happened in full view of everyone.

"You're still interested. You kissed me back." She crossed her arms over her chest and looked satisfied. He looked at her, still seeing how pretty she was but feeling none of the spark he once had with her. Instead he felt sorry for her. Worse, wary of her.

"No. For a half second I didn't shove you off me, that's different. I wasn't expecting you to throw yourself at me. I told you, I'm not interested. And I'm not."

"You'd rather have her than me?" Brody could tell she was truly confused, and that annoyed him even more.

He shoved his hands through his hair, frustrated. "Are you high? Where is all this coming from? Before Elise you didn't want a relationship, and now what? You want to marry me and bear me children?"

She sneered. "Hell no! I don't want marriage or kids, and neither do you. Why weigh yourself down with either? You don't want that. Old people want that."

"I guess I'm old, because I want marriage and kids and I want them with Elise. It's a good kind of weight."

"You don't. You just think you do because Erin went off and did it. You need to be free. We can have what we had before. Don't you want that?"

He looked at her, wondering if she'd hit her head. "No. No, I don't want that. I didn't want it before Elise either. Raven, I don't want to hurt your feelings or anything, but we *never* loved each other. You never wanted anything serious with me. Fuck, you cheated on me when we were in a relationship, or I thought we were, and you never bothered to correct my assumption until I found out you were having sex with other people. So whatever, we broke it off and went very casual and that was fine for a while. But it's not now, because I'm in a relationship with someone. You have to stop with this stuff or I won't be able to be friends with you."

"That's the first step. She's going to emasculate you. Make you choose her over your friends."

"There's no choice. I love her. My friends should support me in this, they certainly shouldn't come on to me to try and drive a wedge into my relationship."

"If you just give us another try, I know we can make it. You looked at me like that once, why not again?"

"I never looked at you like that. I've never looked at anyone like that before now. She's special. Took me nearly forty years to find her, to appreciate love, but I have it now and I'm not going to question it. You and I had a fling and we're better as friends. Don't ruin that last part."

"His *friends* wouldn't pull this shit in the open where it'll get back to Elise." Adrian strolled up and then turned to Brody. "Hey, asshole, I've been sitting at the front watching this whole spectacle unfold along with all these customers and your employees, who happen to know your girlfriend. You don't think she's going to hear about this?"

"If she hears, it had better be what happened instead of what anyone's pervy brain makes up. Now, I have a tattoo to do, and then I'm going to go home so I can have dinner with my girlfriend and her daughter. Because I like to." He focused back on Raven. "And this better not come up again."

He motioned for Arvin to send back his next appointment, feeling frustrated and pissed off.

Raven touched his arm, but he stepped back. Her mouth firmed. "You're making a mistake. People like us aren't made for monogamy."

"No. People like *you* aren't. And that's fine, I'm not judging. But I'm also not you. Now, please, go before this turns even more ugly."

She stomped off, and his client sat down with eyebrows raised. A regular, so at least Brody didn't have to play get-to-know-you when he just wanted to see Elise, to know how she was. She'd be done with her call by that point but would have had to rush to her studio to teach her afternoon classes. He hadn't had time for a call and had barely glanced at her text that she was okay and would talk to him tonight about the details.

"She's going to try to fuck you over," Adrian said, making himself at home by sitting at Brody's workstation.

"No, she's not. It's over. Why are you here?" He turned back to his client and they spoke about what he wanted. Brody began to set up.

"Fine way to talk to your baby brother. I came in to have you touch something up. I could just go somewhere else where they deal with rock stars and are nice to them."

"No one in this town would touch my tats, smartass." He grinned up at his brother and then got to work.

"After that, I need to run out and grab something for Rennie. She's been out of sorts lately. I know she's picking up on everyone's anxiety." Adrian flipped through a magazine and chatted idly with Brody's client as he worked.

"You like her, don't you?" Brody kept his eyes on his work, but Adrian knew he was talking to him.

"Rennie or Elise? I like 'em both. Elise is wonderful. She's quick and clever and she's good for you. Aside from being beautiful, she's nice to be around. Soothing in a way. Rennie? How can you resist her? I'm looking forward to watching her grow up and being the uncle who spoils her."

"She's already spoiled," Brody said with a laugh, and then he looked up and met his brother's gaze. "I'm looking forward to watching her grow up too."

She bustled around the house, cleaning up the stuff Rennie had tossed on the couch when they'd come in. It was a way for Elise to keep her mind off her legal issues. She needed to wind down after the day she'd had.

Rennie had had dinner with her grandparents, who'd just dropped her home half an hour before. She'd taken a bath and done her home-work and now was finally asleep. Brody was supposed to have come over earlier, but there'd been a disaster at the shop and he had to stay to deal with it.

She tried to push back her agitation. He wasn't at her beck and call. He had a business to run and she understood that very well. If the pipes had busted at her studio, she'd be there dealing with it herself too, that's what you did. Anyway, just because she loved him didn't mean she wasn't stupidly aware of the rules they'd set out a year before. She was his girlfriend, she knew that, and she knew it meant way more than just sleeping together. It had made her happy, the way they'd been growing closer over the last months, knowing he cared about her that much. And she did know it; he was good to her and Rennie, there for her, and not just for sex.

But she also knew it wasn't a declaration of love.

She sat and then got up again. She should just go to bed. Drink a glass of wine, read a book and go to bed. Damn, she needed him. Needed his arms around her to reassure her, and that was so bad. It was like eating cookie dough. You know you shouldn't, but you can't help it. Cookie dough was a fine idea, though, she thought, heading for the freezer.

She didn't want to need him. She hadn't needed anyone a year ago, and that had suited her just fine. But he'd come into her life, and from the first moment she'd laid eyes on him she'd been fascinated. It had been so much more than sexual from the first, and it had grown until he was rooted in her life.

Bringing the dough, a spoon and the bottle of wine and a glass, she trundled into her bedroom and changed into pajamas before pouring a glass and feasting on cookie dough while watching reality shows.

Her phone rang, waking her up from her dough/wine nap, and she nearly spilled it as she scrambled to grab it and answer.

"Did I wake you?"

She smiled at the sound of his voice as she sat up. "It's okay. Is everything at the shop taken care of?"

"I'm right outside your front door. If I knocked, would you let me in?"

"On my way." She hung up the phone and hurried toward the door, but not before a quick check in the mirror showed her to be reasonably non-haggy.

He stood there, as promised, looking tired, but he smiled when she opened the door.

"You're just what I needed to make this day end on a high note. Much better than it's been the last several hours." He hugged her, surrounding her with his scent and heat, pulling the stress and fear from her until all that remained was the warmth of being held by him.

"Come in. Are you hungry?" She locked up and then led him into the house.

"I am. I'm sorry I'm so late. I know you had a rough day, I wanted to be here for you."

"Sit." She waved to a chair at the table and he sat with a long sigh. "Want a burrito? I made them for dinner for myself. Rennie went out to pizza with my parents, so there are plenty of leftovers." She put a beer in front of him and he took her hand, pulling her into his lap.

"Sorry, I needed more of this."

"I'm not complaining." She smiled into his neck.

"I missed you today. I wanted so much to be here with you earlier, to have dinner with you and Rennie and hear what happened at court today. Christ, the pipes were a mess. Erin's going to be pissed. Her kitchen, everything on the bottom shelves got wet. My back wall is fucked, the floor in the bathroom and the employee lounge was a disaster, but we got it cleaned up. The plumber said it looked like there'd been a long, slow leak and it finally just gave. The back wall where the pipes burst is going to have to be re-drywalled."

She hugged him and then got off his lap, bending and kissing him before going into the kitchen to make him something to eat. "So you stayed to be sure Erin's place got cleaned up because she had a doctor's appointment today. You're a good man, Brody. Erin's lucky to have you. I'm sorry. It sounds like a horrible mess. Will you have to close the shop?"

She bustled around the kitchen, microwaving the beans, heating the tortillas and putting everything together.

"Tomorrow, a friend of mine who's a contractor will come out to look at the wall to see what needs to be done, how long it'll take and how much it costs. Hopefully just tomorrow and the next day. I hate to disappoint clients, but I don't want to be open with all that dust and water around. So tell me how it went. Rennie's asleep?"

"Yes, my parents ran her ragged at the pizza place, so she was pretty much out by the time she got out of the bathtub." She put a plate in front of him and sat. "They're going to keep the case here in Washington."

He nodded as he began to eat.

"That's the first big hurdle. Now they're looking at their assertions that I'm unfit and my assertions that further contact with the Sorensons is detrimental to Rennie's mental and emotional state and that they should be allowed no visitation or contact at all unless or until Rennie asks for it. It was all preliminary. This stuff can take a while. But because of the visitations being so upsetting, Bill and Frank both believe the judge will hear things sooner. It'll all be back and forth between attorneys, and then there'll be another meeting with the judge where she goes over the findings and hears from experts if she wants to. Apparently this is very narrow, so it won't be a repeat of the trial I had in New York the first time. I just want it over."

He put his fork down and took her hand. "It'll be over soon. You'll finally be free of them and we can all move forward. I'm glad the first step worked out. Keeping the case away from some crony of your ex-father-in-law's will be a very good thing. I'm sorry I woke you. I just . . . I just didn't want to go to sleep without touching you."

She loved him so much right at that moment, loved him until she thought she might burst from it. And then loved him more. He was what she needed, what she wanted, and if she could just be with him and not spook him off with declarations of love, she could continue to love him. She wanted to tell him she loved him, wanted to tell him so much her heart ached.

After this whole legal mess was finally over, she'd sit down and figure out what to do, but for the time being, there wasn't a darned thing wrong with loving him and being with him.

"I'm glad you did. I ate cookie dough."

The confused look on his face morphed into understanding. "You ate cookie dough because you missed me?" He smiled so broadly the dimple usually shadowed by his mustache showed. "Erin used to eat cookie dough. By the log. She was the moodiest teenage girl to ever exist. I'm totally certain of it."

"Until Rennie. Gah, I cringe to think." She wished he could spend the night. Wished she could close her eyes with him there next to her and just fall away, knowing when she woke up he'd be there still. But with all the allegations that she was some sort of skank who paraded a group of bikers through her bedroom nightly while Rennie was forced to watch, she had to be careful. Besides, spending the night wasn't part of the deal between them.

"You look so tired. Why don't you go home and get some rest." She caressed his cheek and leaned in to kiss him.

"You look ten kinds of sexy in that tank top and those shorts. Now, if I could wake up to this every day, I'd never want to leave my house."

Maybe she wasn't the only one who liked the idea of a sleepover.

"I think I might be able to do something about you being tired and me being sexy." She stood and put the dish in the sink and his beer bottle in the recycling. "Come on back to my room."

Once inside, she closed and locked the door. "Get undressed and get on the bed, facedown. I'll be right with you." She lit some candles and headed into the bathroom for a few things.

When she returned, she paused in the doorway, content to just look at how beautiful and sexy he was, stretched out across her bed. The sight was ridiculously sexy. He was so big and his shoulders so broad, the tattoo on his back lent him an edge of danger. His body was toned and muscular. Every inch of the man was gorgeous. Having him there, in her bed, in her house on a night like this one made her happy. Content.

She crawled up on the bed, straddling his ass.

"Hey." He tried to turn around, but she pushed him back into place. "You can't sit on me totally naked and not let me look or touch. That's torture."

She poured almond oil into her hands and then rubbed them together to warm it before she touched the skin of his back. Her reward was a long, deep groan of pleasure from him as she began to work her fingers into his muscles.

"I'm supposed to be here comforting you."

She laughed softly. "I like to take care of you. It makes me happy. This *is* you comforting me."

His breathing slowed, deepened as she worked. This man had done so much for her, had taken care of her, had shown with body and mind that she was beautiful and capable. No one had ever made her feel the way he had. It scared her to her toes to imagine him not in her life.

"Damn that feels good. Are you a licensed masseuse too? Since you're a jack of all trades and all." His voice was muffled by the pillow.

"Jack of all trades, master of none." She laughed. "You'd better be good at massages so you can trade them with people when you dance. Man, you're so tight right here." She worked into the knot at his right shoulder.

"Between working all day and then dealing with the cleanup from the burst pipes, I guess I'm a mess. Good thing I have you to take care of me."

Yes, good thing. She bet that selfish bitch Raven didn't do this for him. Didn't make him something to eat when he got hungry, didn't worry about how tired he was. Okay, so maybe she was un-fair; Raven did seem to care about him, and Erin too, but it an-noyed Elise to see the woman around all the time. She was totally hostile and she touched Brody way more than Elise would have pre-ferred. Which would be *zero* touches, damn it.

"I'm here for that. Anytime."

The stress went out of him slowly as he relaxed heavier into her bed.

"It feels so good to be with you here. To be taken care of."

She scooted down to get to his lower back, ass and upper thighs. "You always do it for everyone else. Someone needs to take care of you for a change. Don't think I haven't noticed how you go around making life better for everyone else. You're a good man." *And I love you.*

"Mmm, god that's nice. And I'm just doing what needs to be done. If I don't, who will? Who'll do it right so the people I care about are okay? I can, I trust that."

Holy cats, was she gone for this man.

"Turn over."

He did, a lazy smile on his lips. "This is the best part."

She smiled back. "Are you suggesting sex? Mr. Brown, I'm really sure I'm not supposed to do that." She fluttered her lashes and he slid his hands up her thighs. "Don't you get tired of being laden down with other people's stuff?"

He locked his gaze with hers. "Some people. But other people?" He shrugged slightly. "Other people I like taking care of. I like knowing I'm the one making them safe or healthy or whatever. I guess it's a god complex, but there it is." He took her breasts in his hands. "Taking care of you and Rennie is in the latter group. Yes, I can see the worry on your face, hear it in your voice. You two are mine, I take care of what's mine."

"You don't feel suffocated by yet more people on your to-do list?"

"Did someone say something to upset you, Shorty? Have I hurt your feelings or made you feel bad?"

She shook her head. "No, not that. I just . . . I know when we started this thing we said it would be light and fun, and I'm realizing it's not so light and fun for you when I have legal crap and stuff. I just don't want to step on your toes or . . ."

She couldn't help but squeal when he rolled her over so suddenly. "Shorty, when we started this thing, we didn't know each other the way we do now. I like having you in my life. I like your kiddo in my life. I like taking care of you. I like knowing you're safe. I hate this legal shit because I know you're scared and I hate those people for trying to scare you and using Rennie to do it. It makes me crazy that I can't fix it for you both. Seeing you so worried hurts. I want you to be happy."

She would not cry. It was just hormones and emotion.

"Please touch me," she whispered around tears.

"Baby, please don't cry." He brushed his lips over her cheeks. "I'm here and all I ever want is to touch you."

"Then do. Please. I just want to feel you."

"If I have to," he joked before meeting her lips for a kiss. She wrapped her arms around his neck and held on as his soft kisses grew deeper.

She arched, writhing to get more of her on more of him. His skin was taut and very warm, slightly slick from the almond oil she'd used. The friction was delicious.

"Just for the record," he said before licking one nipple and then the other, "I always want to feel you. To taste you. Elise, I want to breathe you." He hovered over the dip of her belly, his breath hot against the super-sensitive skin there. His tongue slid over her hip bone and down the seam between thigh and body.

How could she not love him? There must be three dozen women walking around Seattle totally heartbroken that this man wasn't with them anymore. Maybe that was Raven's problem. *Hmpf. Too bad, goth girl. You snooze, you lose.*

His tongue against her clit brought her hips forward, unabashedly seeking more. It had been a week since he'd gone down on her. They'd had sex, but it had been quick and hard, which she'd needed. This was slow and decadent, and it felt so good she just soaked it in. He held her thighs open and flat against the mattress as he licked and nibbled, laved and flicked his tongue over her pussy.

She arched, stretching her muscles as the pleasure took over. His mouth on her was sure, and with good reason. He knew what worked, what she liked, what drove her to shiver and beg—and he did it. Over and over until she became a trembling mass of desperate woman.

Which she was as he teased his mouth down and back up again, his tongue sliding over her perineum, shocking her eyes open again. He moved one hand and teased his thumb over her back passage. That was so . . . she swallowed, experimenting with it . . . Forbidden. Dark. Taboo.

He sucked her clit between his lips, and her breath gusted from her mouth, right as he pressed his thumb just slightly inside.

Ribbons of light decorated her vision as she came, hard and swift. Her fingers tightened in his hair as she pulled him closer, even as she bit her lip to keep from crying out.

Brody kissed her belly again and lay on his side next to her. "Now you're nice and ready to be fucked. My favorite." She cracked an eye open and caught the light in his eyes as they raked over her body. "Let's try something new."

"Hope you don't want to try something acrobatic. I don't think I've got the stamina for that after what you just did to me."

He laughed. "That's a fine compliment. And no, Shorty, all you have to do is stay on your back, put one leg up and over my hip and the other can go between my thighs. I'll do all the work from there."

She scooted over, moving one leg up and the other between his thighs, and then he thrust, entering her easily because she was so wet.

"So good. I like it this way because you're so lovely to look at." His pace was leisurely.

"So far, I've had zero complaints about your prowess. There must be jealous women all over town because I'm hogging you. By the way, I have no plans to share anytime soon."

"Good. I like keeping my prowess right here between your thighs. God, your skin is so pretty by candlelight. Your body is so lovely, lithe, strong. Just exactly right."

"I ate a hell of a lot of cookie dough earlier. I'm surprised I don't have a pooch."

His fingertips danced down her belly and over her thighs. "Mmm hmm. Not looking so round here. Not to me. You eat pretty well, but you can when you exercise hours a day the way you do."

She laughed and ended up writhing because he hauled her even closer, getting deeper. "I went a little crazy when I was rehabbing for the leg. First I was immobile, which I rarely am, and you don't want to hear all this detail."

"I do. I like hearing about your life. But for now? You're so tight and hot. I love this, Elise. You and me, candlelight and quiet. I feel settled and very happy."

"You're going to make me cry again," she mumbled, trying to turn her face away from the intensity in his eyes. He made her crave those things she knew she couldn't have.

"Why? I don't understand." He continued to slowly and completely devastate her with those deep thrusts as he spoke.

"I'm just strung too tight."

"You're full of shit." His next thrust was harder. "I know you, Elise. Something is making you upset. Is it Raven?"

"Why are you talking about her while your dick is in me?" Horrified, she tried to move away, but he held her in place.

"You're right, sorry. This first. This always. Then we can talk."

"Now you're talking."

His strokes became more urgent, his eyes darkened, one curl fell over his forehead and sent a rush of tenderness through her. He'd come here, tired and overwhelmed by his day; he'd come to her, and that meant something.

"I think you're ready to come again. Show me."

She kept her eyes on his face as she moved her hand down, snaking it between their bodies until she found her clit, still slippery and sensitive. It wasn't necessary to move her hand at all, his thrusts moved her body instead, bringing the friction she needed.

She simply let it happen, let climax rise within and break over her with a slow inhale. The muscles on his neck corded as he went deeper and deeper, until he slammed home one last time with a low, nearly feral growl.

Brody gathered her to him, holding her tight, breathing her in. He hated to see her so upset. No other woman's tears had ever made him feel so frantic to fix whatever was wrong. Seeing her that way made him want to punch someone. He wasn't a violent man, but she brought out all his protective instincts in a way he'd never experienced other than in defense of Adrian or Erin.

"I'm glad you came over." He felt the curve of her smile as she pressed against his chest.

"Me too. It's going to suck to have to leave." He wanted to sleep with her every night.

She'd taken care of him from the moment he walked through

her door. Feeding him, listening to him vent, massaging him and understanding him. She got him, which felt like a gift. He didn't have to be anything with her. Just who he was and what he felt like at any given time. They all fit; he already considered her and Rennie family.

It had amused him, not that he'd ever say so out loud, to see her get so pissy when he brought Raven up. Jealous even. It also helped him to know Raven hadn't said anything to her. Not yet.

"Why Rennie? Why not Reenie?"

She lazily poked her head up and then let it rest on his biceps. "When she was an infant, my mom would come into the city to help during the week so I could go to rehearsal and get back into shape. Anyway, one of the costumers started calling her Baby Rennie and it stuck. My mother was not pleased"—she laughed—"but she's been Rennie ever since."

"Tell me about after the attack. You what? Ate a junior bag of Doritos and wept?" He liked teasing her.

"I should pinch you for that, but I'm so full of endorphins and afterglow I can't work up the energy. Eating is an issue for many, many dancers. Eating disorders are common, especially with the younger dancers. It's very harsh sometimes. The way a dancer might be critiqued. I've been told I was too fat more than once. But overall, my metabolism is fast, so as long as I'm active, I can keep tone. But being in bed and then on crutches was hard. I didn't have the discipline I had when I danced. I was depressed, so I ate and gained a bit of weight. I still carry it in my boobs and thighs. But the pressure isn't there for me in the same way it was before. So I joke and all, but I'll eat cookie dough anyway and not feel one bit guilty. Except for the raw eggs part. That's bad, I know it."

"Rebel."

"You know it. Your brother stopped by earlier and brought Rennie a present. He's very sweet to take the time, and she's crushing on him almost as hard as she crushes on you."

He laughed. "As long as I'm still in first place, I can accept that. I can't believe anyone would say you were fat. That's a mind fuck."

She shrugged. "It's the way it is. How you look is important. Your size is important because your partner has to pick you up. But I can't lie and say it's not part of what I hated and hate now with the girls I teach. There's a line, you have to be aware of it and deal with it. Some of these mothers are my best advocates when I'm trying to drive home the importance of good nutrition; others are big supporters of crap diets to keep their kids thin. I'm glad Rennie wants to paint instead."

"Good thing she'll have us around to keep her grounded." He smiled, thinking about what Rennie would be like as a teenager.

"I'll need a full contingent of adults to back me up with her. She's already a force of nature at seven." She snuggled into him again, warm and small and smelling so damned good. "I wish you didn't have to go either. You feel so good and warm here in my bed. By the way, when does summer start anyway? It's still cold."

"Welcome to Seattle, Shorty. We cruise into summer. Round about July it gets hot. We like it that way."

"If you were in my bed at night, I'd be fine. You're like a furnace."

"I can wake up before Rennie and get out of here before she comes downstairs."

"I wish you could. I know it doesn't matter if I am the slut they're trying to say I am, it doesn't make me unfit. But they're watching me. I know it's stupid, but I'm so afraid. Afraid they'll take her and something I did will give them a reason. My attorneys keep assuring me everything will be fine, but she's my baby."

He kissed her. "It's okay. We'll have plenty of time after this is all cleared up. I'm sorry you're afraid. But your attorneys are right. You have rights as her mother. They barely saw her when she was living right there, they're negative influences on her. Just a little while longer and you'll be free to live without looking over your shoulder."

The Sorensons were robbing him too. Taking away his time with her, with Rennie. He hated that Elise had to think twice about stupid, everyday things when she was such a good mom.

"I should go soon. If I fall asleep, I'll be out until the morning."

She sighed heavily and sat up, mesmerizing him with the fall of pale hair over her shoulders. "I know. You need the rest, you have a big day tomorrow." She traced under his eyes with the flick of her thumb and he leaned into the touch.

"We'll see each other though. In the evening. How about we go grab burgers and then go see the new kid flick, with the robot. I saw an ad on television."

She closed her eyes a moment and then licked her lips. "It means a lot to me, that you think of her the way you do. That you understand she and I are linked. It's important to me."

"Of course I do." He sat up too, facing her. "I love your kid to pieces."

"I know. But will you just be careful with her? She's very attached to you."

He kissed her. "I know she is. Do you think I'm not keeping her safe? When she's in my car, I use the booster seat. I don't think I let her play with knives or anything."

"No, no, not that. It's just, when you walk away, give her time."

She thought he was walking away? Anger flashed through him. "You think I'm gonna make your kid love me and dump you both? Is that what I'm giving off now?"

She backed up a bit, alarm on her features, but relaxed a tiny bit after a moment. "I-I don't. I just, I know you're not looking for two more people to take care of."

"I'm asking you here, is that what you think I am? What I'd do?"

"You *said* that's what you'd do." She punched the mattress before getting up and pulling her clothes on.

"When the hell did I say that?" He joined her, getting dressed quickly.

"When we first started sleeping together, you said you weren't looking for forever, that you were too busy! What else was I supposed to think? You said it yourself."

He hauled her close and she shuddered. "Fuck, fuck, I'm scaring you. I'm sorry. It's just, I'm *not* walking away from you. You or Rennie. It's important to me that you know it." She relaxed into him and he let go of his anxiety.

"I said a lot of things a year ago. But I didn't know you then. I know you now. I know you, Elise, and I know your daughter and I cherish you both. If you'll let me, I have no plans to stop."

"Oh." She blinked up at him.

"Just so we're clear."

She nodded and he couldn't help but grin.

25

Elise sat on a lounge chair and watched Rennie and Nina swimming with Brody and Adrian. Erin, now fully showing and happier every day, sat across the pool with Ben and Todd, laughing with everyone. It had been a lovely summer day. They'd come over to Erin's to swim and then they'd have a picnic on Erin's terrace afterward.

It had been wonderful until Raven showed up. Elise noticed the crowd was split between the Raven lovers and the Raven haters or distrusters. Adrian was firmly in the anti-Raven camp, and it didn't seem like Ben liked her much either. Over the last month or two, she'd noticed Brody having cooled toward her considerably. She'd left town, and Elise had been looking forward to a few months of peace, but she returned just a few weeks later.

And now she'd decided to take the seat next to Elise.

"How's it going?" Raven said after they'd both been silent for a few minutes.

"Good. You?"

"So everything with whatever personal shit Brody's all caught up in, that's all fine now?"

Elise whipped her head around for a moment, but then moved her gaze back to Rennie. "What the heck are you talking about?"

"Brody was going on and on about having to be *present* for you and the kid, so he couldn't go out with his friends and stuff. Stuck at your place or something." Raven shrugged.

Elise was struck dumb for several moments as she weighed what Raven had said. She knew it wasn't true, but deep down it had been a fear of hers, she could admit it to herself.

"What's your problem?" She took another quick look at Raven before looking out over Rennie again.

"I don't have any problems. I just call 'em like I see 'em."

Elise snorted. "What a crock of crap. You know what kind of people are fond of saying things like that? People who like to confuse blunt with mean and petty. So why don't we just cut the aforementioned crap and you tell me what your deal is."

"Oh, so fucking perfect, aren't you? You come here with your education and your money and you waltz right in using your kid to get attention. I know your game."

It was so absurd it cut through her fears about Brody and cleared her head. And left her fighting mad. It was time for a Come-to-Jesus with this bitch.

"My game? I don't have a game and I didn't *use* my kid for anything. Brody is with me for *me*. That's your deal. You managed to convince him he was better off with fleeting, no-strings relationships so he'd always be available to you when you got bored. Now he's not and you can't handle it. Brody wants me and not you, and even though you slept with all those people, you can't stand it that you can't have him."

"I can't have him? Really now?" Raven moved so that she leaned into Elise's vision.

Elise put an arm out and pushed her back. "I'm watching my child in the pool, don't get in my way."

"Don't you touch me. You're a fake and a phony. You play it up for sympathy."

Ben interrupted, approaching them. "What the hell is going on?"

Raven turned to him. "Little Miss Perfect is just full of shit. If she touches me again, it's on."

"Drama much? If I wanted to hit you, I'd have hit you." Elise rolled her eyes but kept her voice down.

"That's enough, Raven. If you upset Elise, I'm going to kick you out of here. Just chill."

"Just perfect. Then she'll have her way. This is bullshit. Why can't you people see through this act?"

Elise didn't bother responding; Raven had ramped up on her little tirade, and Elise had done the tirade thing enough over the course of her life. She wasn't going there again. It had caught Brody's attention, though still he kept with the kids. She appreciated that, even though she knew he was dying to come over and intervene.

Not so encumbered, Adrian climbed from the pool, inserting himself between them. "There are children here. Keep it down," he said to Raven.

"Oh sure, blame me. We used to have adult fun, now there are kids everywhere and we have to watch our mouths. *Boring*. By the way, Brody kissed me not too long ago. Don't think I can't have him if I want. I *have* had him. I'll have him again. You can't hold him, you have nothing to offer."

Raven stood up and headed for the door.

Elise turned to Adrian. "Please watch Rennie." She hurried away
as Brody called for her. "No. Stay here with the girls. Keep playing.
Let me handle this."

She caught up to Raven near the elevators. "Wait up. We're not
done."

"I don't have anything to say to you." In the light of the windows nearby, Raven was pretty, but she wore her anger like a gar-
ment. Elise felt sorry for her, wanted to see what Erin and Brody
saw in her, but that didn't mean she'd be taking any more crap.
Raven punched the elevator button repeatedly. Elise had her effec-
tively trapped. Good.

"*I have.* You don't love him. You just don't want anyone else to
have him. And that's selfish. If you cared about him, why wouldn't
you be happy he was happy? They still care about you, you know.
I'm not displacing you."

Raven jerked to a stop. "What the fuck are you talking about?"

Bingo. That was it. "Erin loves you. You're her friend. I'm not
taking that from you. She and I are friends, sure, but that doesn't
diminish what you have with her. And Brody still cares about you.
Make no mistake here, you can't have him. He's mine, and as long
as that's true, I'm holding on tight. But I wouldn't stop him from
being friends with you. I'm not trying to push you out. You're part
of their family."

Raven stared at her until the elevator opened up and she got on,
leaving without another word.

"Jeez," Elise mumbled before going back to the pool deck.

"Everything all right?" Adrian asked when she sat back down.

"I don't know. I'm sorry for making a scene."

"You didn't. She did. She was out of line, Elise. She shouldn't
have been like that at all, but especially in front of the kids. But
she's always been a spoiled bitch. Sometimes it's amusing, other times

not. She's not all bad, she's been good to Erin and Brody both. But there's something inside her that drives her to make bad choices." He shook his head, but all Elise could hear was that Brody had kissed Raven.

"I don't think she's all bad. Clearly Erin and Brody care about her, and that means something. But I'm no one's whipping boy and I won't bring my kid around her. That's a lot of negative emotion. Rennie has had enough negative outbursts in her life."

Adrian nodded. "That's totally fair. She didn't notice much, not that I saw. Brody kept her and Nina entertained."

She shrugged. While she was willing to try and see another side of Raven, while she'd actually *seen* part of that today in the hall near the elevators, she wouldn't expose Rennie to Raven again anytime soon. In fact, dealing with that kind of angry irrationalism made her stomach hurt. Reminded her an awful lot of what it had been like with Matty at times.

They all had their past wounds to get over. Raven was just as human as Elise was, she knew that. But she also knew she wasn't lining up to be abused again. Not ever.

"Are you all right?" Brody asked as they sat out on Erin's very large deck later on.

"I was just hungry. And agitated."

"Raven? I'm sorry. I didn't expect her to flip out. Ben said she got pretty mean. I don't know where this is coming from."

"You don't? Really? Because you've lived under a rock for the last umpteen years? You don't know why a woman you once dated would flip out on the one you were currently dating?"

"Okay. Okay, that's probably part of it. Although she's never been like this before."

"Did you kiss her?" she blurted.

He sighed. "Sort of."

She raised her brows. *"Sort of?* Which means what?"

He laughed and then stopped, putting his hands up in surrender. "Don't hurt me. We had this heated discussion at the shop. Like two months ago. She threw herself at me, literally like jumped into my arms—you can ask Adrian, he saw it—and kissed me. I extricated myself. For like two seconds I kissed her, but it was more automatic than an actual romantic kiss."

She frowned and narrowed her eyes at him. "I told her that even if she wanted you, she couldn't have you."

He grinned. "You're right."

"But she doesn't. Want you. I mean, gah, that sounds mean even when, hello, you did not tell me about this kiss and that sort of makes me mad. I think she's afraid of losing you and Erin. Of being displaced by me. I know it sounds very pop-psych, but she was halfway nice to me at the very beginning. The longer we've been together, the worse she's gotten. I don't need everyone to like me, but I don't want to have this drama. I have enough drama. In the future, I'm going to have to not attend any events with Rennie if Raven will be there."

"Come on, Elise, she's not going to hurt anyone. She's just upset. And totally out of line, yes, let me be clear. I'll talk to her."

"Why don't I line up to have my kid exposed to some random woman's crazy, hostile behavior? Is that a serious question? If so, you know where you can cram it. My kid had a father who would flip out on the drop of a dime for no apparent reason if it suited him. I won't have her around that sort of instability. *I* don't want to be around it either. I dealt with it enough for ten lifetimes and I won't do it again. She's something to you, but she's nothing to me and she doesn't want to be, so fine. But don't ever imagine that I'd put my child at risk, because I won't."

His jaw unclenched and he sighed again. "I'm sorry. I didn't think of it like that. I'm also sorry I didn't tell you about the kiss. You just had a lot on your plate and I didn't want to add to it with something that didn't mean anything. I'm not interested. You know I wouldn't . . . that I have no desire to be with anyone but you. Right?"

"I don't like that you didn't tell me. I don't like that it was used to hurt me. I want to understand why you and Erin care about her so much. I respect you both, so I'm clearly missing something when I deal with her and want to smack her upside her head. I'm not saying you can't be friends with her, I don't have that right, and frankly, I think that's what she expects me to do."

He laughed and kissed her. "You fit in just fine with us and we with you. You don't have to like her, and if you'd prefer I not hang around her outside work, I can do that. It's not unreasonable, and why wouldn't you have that right? I'd be pissed if some dude kissed you."

For some stupid reason, she liked hearing it. "You're an adult. You have to manage your own life. If I worried about every woman you came into contact with, I'd spend all my time worried. If you want to cheat, I can't stop it. I'm leaving that choice up to you." My, how mature she sounded. If he cheated on her, she'd be devastated. She'd also kick his ass. But she'd be devastated while she did it.

"You'd spend all your time worried? Am I that much of a flirt?"

"No, you're just very attractive on every level I can think of. Good-looking, you have a great job, a great house, you're funny and smart." She shrugged. "What woman doesn't like those things? You're in a tattoo shop; I've seen the way people look at you. So shhh. But I can't give over to worry. You're an honorable man, so I have to simply trust you to make the right choices. I learned a long time ago, the hard way, that you can't live anyone else's life for them. Ultimately, we're all responsible for our own lives and the choices we make, or don't."

"I make the choice to be with you every day. Can't say I've been sorry." He traced one eyebrow and she sighed softly. "You're a lot kinder than she gives you credit for. But . . . not a pushover either."

"Some people mistake kindness for gullibility or being a pushover. If she tries to kiss you again and I see it, I won't be as nice."

He leaned in to whisper in her ear. "It totally turns me on to see you jealous."

She turned, her mouth just shy of his. "Everything turns you on. You're fabulously easy that way."

"Ha."

"Indeed."

26

Brody knocked on her door while balancing two bags of food and some coffee. She opened, and the fear and stress on her face went straight to his gut.

"Hey. I figured some breakfast might be warranted." She let him in, and he moved past her parents to drop the bags on the table. And then he hugged her, tight. "It's going to be fine, baby. I promise you."

"Don't make promises you can't keep," she mumbled, and he marveled at how she bucked up, standing straight and smiling up at him. "Sorry. Got a bit maudlin. I'm glad to see you. Thanks for breakfast."

"Erin sent Ben over with it all. He sends his love and so does Erin. She also says you have to call her as soon as you hear anything." He looked around Elise to her parents and smiled. "Hey, you two. Have some food, please."

Martine kissed his cheek idly as she passed by. Paul nodded his head and looked back to Elise, worry on his face.

"Rennie get to school okay this morning?" Brody put milk and sugar in a coffee and handed it to Elise. "Eat or I'll tell Erin."

She laughed. "You'd toss me under the bus?"

"To get you to eat? You betcha."

She grabbed a bagel breakfast sandwich and took a bite. "Thank you. I'll thank Erin myself later. Yes, Rennie got to school fine. She doesn't really know what's going on, and I want it that way. It took her a week to get over the interview she had to do with the expert."

He wanted to see these people, to look into the eyes of the people who'd use a child the way they had. So he could punch them.

"You clean up nice." She smiled, looking up and down.

"Meh. This is one of Ben's suits."

"Meh? You look very handsome."

"So do you. I mean, you look beautiful. Responsible. That color is really pretty on you. Um, so although I know I look awesome in this monkey suit and all, I'd really like to go to court with you today. To be at your side. I won't even punch either one of the Sorensons." He drew a big X over his heart. "I promise."

She wasn't fast enough to hide the flash of surprise and the tears. Her father handed her a handkerchief and she mopped up.

"I didn't mean to upset you. I just . . . I just want to be there for you and for Rennie. You're my girls."

"I'm not. Upset, that is. I'm just very thankful right now. For you and my parents, for my friends. I could have done this alone, I'd have survived. But I'm glad I didn't have to. The Sorensons, they're not nice people. You don't have to expose yourself to that."

Her mother gave an undignified snort, but her parents moved to another part of the living room to give them some privacy.

"I can handle not nice. I'm not feeling so nice toward them myself. They're trying to make it out like I'm a bad guy. Like I don't care about you or Irene. When I do. You're safe with me. I want the judge to see that. Unless you think it's bad. You can't see any of my tats or anything."

She hugged him tight. "Even if you could, it wouldn't make you anything but what you are. A good man."

"Your man," he murmured against the silk of her hair.

"That too. If you're sure, then yes, I'd appreciate the friendly face and the backup in there."

Brody looked over her head, at her father, who sent him a nod of support. He'd do anything for her; he needed her to understand it, needed everyone to understand it. He couldn't wait until this damned stuff was over with, so they could move forward. He wanted to tell her he loved her, he wanted to sleep at her side every night. He wanted all this external stuff stowed away so he could spend the rest of his days loving Elise and Rennie.

"They're here already, inside the courtroom." Frank motioned to the doors and Elise nodded. She was not going to let them intimidate her. She was in the right. Rennie was hers and she wouldn't let them take her. Period. If they had to come all the way to Seattle to finally get it through their heads, so be it.

"We figured they would be. They've got a team of lawyers, but it doesn't matter, Elise. You're going to be fine." Bill smiled and she smiled back.

She would. She had realized, over the last year-plus that she'd been in Seattle, that she would be all right. She could handle it, had been handling it and would continue to do so. Brody was with her, at her side right then, supporting her. Her parents were there and she had right on her side. It would be enough. She had to hope it would be enough, because despite the lingering fear of losing her baby, she had to believe in justice too.

"This is Brody Brown. Brody, this is Bill Weston. You know his son of course, and Frank Childers. Brody is my, um . . ."

"I'm her boyfriend. Significant other, whatever you want to call it. But I'm hers and here to do whatever you need me to today." Brody shook hands with both men and then put his arm around her. Her parents greeted Frank, who'd only arrived late the evening before.

"Good. She'll need you today. Let's go in and get this taken care of."

They were already seated when Elise walked into the courtroom. Courtrooms had a particular smell, and it brought memories she'd rather have not experienced again. Still, she looked them both straight in the eye before sitting down. Fuck them, they had no right to do this to her or Rennie. She would not quail in fear. Or at the least, she'd keep her fear where they couldn't see it.

Brody's presence was as welcome as it had been a surprise. She needed him and he was there. It only made her love him more, and she made the decision that once all this court crap had been resolved, she would tell him how she felt.

He sat right behind her, his presence at her back making her feel safe and secure. He stood for her and her child, and she doubted he knew how alluring that was. Her father squeezed her shoulder and kissed her cheek before sitting next to Brody and putting his arm around Elise's mother as they all kept their eyes forward.

The rest of the morning was sort of lost in a series of surreal moments, like when Elise's ex-mother-in-law stood up and screamed that Elise was a murdering whore and the judge blinked at her before rapping her gavel and sternly ordering the attorneys to get her under control.

Elise had to admit she felt disconnected, as if she watched the proceedings happen to someone else. She answered some questions the judge asked, clarified things, kept her calm even when she heard her father mumble under his breath in French. Bone deep, she believed everything would be all right. Now that she sat there, she just knew it.

They took a recess and the judge said she'd call them back for a decision. Brody hugged her in the hallway. "You all right?"

"I am. I feel very, I don't know, settled? This is surreal, even though I've been across the aisle from them several times already. I just feel very calm. I was scared earlier, but now? Not so much. It simply has to end my way. There's no other way for the judge to see it."

He smiled and kissed her forehead. "That's the way to look at it. You did great in there. My god, how did you stand them for the years you were married to Ken?"

"Lots of wine." She stepped back, squeezing his hand. "I'll be right back."

Once in the bathroom, she did her business and touched up her hair and lipstick. That's when Bettina Sorenson walked in. Elise sighed and kept her hands busy so she wouldn't punch the old bitch out.

"You think you have that judge fooled, don't you?"

Elise looked her former mother-in-law up and down and moved toward the door, but the wraithlike woman blocked her way.

"Excuse me, I'd like to go out."

"I don't care what you'd like. You killed my son. I'm going to take your daughter. Over time I'll twist her until she hates you the way she should."

"You totally need a mustache to twirl when you say stuff like that. It's total cardboard villain. I wonder, do you ever hear yourself speak? You don't love Rennie at all, you just want to use her. Yes, I killed your son and you know why. I killed him, and while I feel bad for the Ken of those first years, I'd do it again. He was a threat to my child and I'd do anything to protect her. Now, get out of my way. I'm done here. I'm done letting you harass me and my family. I've tried to be nice. I've tried to encourage you and Rennie to have a relationship, but you view her as a tool with which to hurt me. Just having to speak to you on the phone makes her physically ill and you don't care. In fact, I think you like it."

"Good. I'm glad it breaks your heart, the way mine was broken when you killed *my* son."

"You never cared about Ken either. It's easy for you to pretend now, now that he's gone. But when he was alive you couldn't be bothered. I loved him more than you ever did. But I couldn't stop his descent single-handedly and you couldn't be wrenched away from your bridge club to help. And now he's dead. We're both at fault there, but at least I can accept that. I loved your son very much. Enough to make a child with him. I don't think you can say the same."

"Your love." Bettina snorted. "You're trash. Middle-class, foreign parents, an *artist*. He could have had any woman he wanted. I don't need to love that child. You want her; that's enough for me."

Rage rushed through Elise at that moment. "You are the most vile woman I've ever met. Keeping in mind that your son brought crack whores to my home, let me assure you I've met plenty of vile women. Get. Out. Of. My. Way."

"Or what?"

A toilet flushed, startling both of them. Bettina rushed out first, leaving Elise behind to catch her breath and try to keep her temper when all she wanted to do was slap the shit out of Bettina. As she left the bathroom, she noted the person coming out of the stall was the judge.

"Are you all right?" Brody asked, concern on his face as she returned to where they'd been waiting.

"Fine. Just had a run-in with Bettina in the bathroom." All she could hope was that the judge didn't think she was a cold-blooded killer. The argument in the bathroom had made her angry, yes, but it had also settled things inside her. She was right to be doing this; they didn't care about Rennie at all. Once she got it all straight in her head, she might talk about it, but now, that shared moment of eye contact with the judge was something she held tight.

Half an hour later, they were called back in.

"I've given this a lot of attention because a child's well-being is at stake. I never take the removal of custody or visitation lightly. A child surrounded by loving family is a child who has a leg up in life. Some serious allegations are being made against the mother by the paternal grandparents. I've looked over all the evidence and do not find myself compelled. In fact, this child, by all accounts, including the experts hired by the grandparents, is bright, well adjusted and happy. I do not find any significant change in circumstances that would warrant the removal of the child. As to the allegations the mother makes regarding contact with the paternal grandparents, while the child is well adjusted and happy, the only problems occur on and around the day of the month the grandparents make their visitation call. Given the reports in the file, I'm compelled to make the decision to halt any further contact of the child by the Sorensons. The child may decide on her own to seek out contact as she ages, but it's clear to me after a read of the material here, and after witnessing the behavior of the grandparents today, that this child would only benefit from their absence. Further, I am issuing a no-contact order with this finding. The Sorensons are ordered to refrain from contacting Elise Sorenson or the minor, Irene Anne Sorenson, in any way. Violation of said order will result in civil and criminal penalties." She banged the gavel and Elise stood, head held high, as the judge exited the courtroom.

The sound of dramatic weeping cut through the silence, but Elise felt nothing but release and joy as she walked out, surrounded by her family and friends.

Once they'd all driven back to her house, she took Brody's hand. "I need to go to Rennie. Pick her up from school." She needed to see her baby so much she had to force herself not to run down the street to the school. Brody smiled at her, a smile so beautiful she caught her breath. "Thank you. Thank you for being here for me and Rennie." She hugged him and he hugged her back, holding her body to his as he breathed in slow and sure. It calmed her even as things began to quiver low and deep in her belly.

"Will you come to me later? I know you need to see Rennie now, but can we see each other later today? I want to talk." He kissed her and she smiled.

"Am I in trouble?"

"The best kind."

"I like the sound of that. My parents are taking her out for library time after school today. I'm trying to pretend nothing special is happening. Will you be at the shop? I can come by later if that works for you."

"I'll be waiting for you. Can I take you and Rennie to dinner tonight? Red Mill burgers and onion rings with milkshakes? We can take it to the park, eat it there."

Dear god, he was something so special. She loved him so much and having this court stuff over and done brought it all into sharp focus. If her parents were standing right there, she'd have blurted it out just then.

Now she had to see her little girl and know everything was all right.

27

Brody watched her rush off, tears on her face, joy absolutely spilling from her. It made him smile, made the part she held inside him grow. For the first time in months, since he'd realized he loved her, he was free of the nagging fear that she'd lose Rennie and be devastated.

Whistling, he went into his house to change and then head over to the shop.

He grinned as he entered the shop. Everyone turned to him, expectant looks on their faces, and he realized he wasn't the only one who loved Elise. "Everything is fine. Elise won the case and even kept her former in-laws from having any contact with Rennie. She's over the moon. I'm pretty freaking jacked too."

"Hi."

It had been over a month since he'd seen Raven last. She'd headed out of town after the confrontation with Elise at Erin's place. Admittedly, things had been smoother without her around, but Brody had worried. He didn't have romantic feelings for her and she'd

tried to hurt Elise, which made him pissed off and defensive. But
he worried for Raven because, as Elise had very intuitively pointed
out, Raven was a wounded bird. Damn, he loved Elise even more
than he'd thought possible.

"Hey, Raven." He hugged her, happy when she didn't hang on
too long or make any inappropriate comments. "You here to work?"

"I'm here to apologize. Your Miss Perfect was right. I hate that."

He laughed. "She's right a lot, just so you know. She also seems
to think there's something worthy inside you somewhere."

Raven made a face. "It sucks that she's so nice."

"It's one of my favorite things about her. I love her, Raven. I
love her and her kid and I want her to marry me. That's what's going to happen, and if you can deal with it and make your peace
with it, you're welcome in our lives. If you can't, it's your choice,
but I'm going to have to choose Elise and Rennie. I care about you
and I don't want to not have you in my life, but it's time you grew
up and accepted reality."

She cocked her head and looked up at him. "I wish things had
been different. I blew it between us."

He shook his head. "You act like it was just yesterday. It was
years ago. We can still be friends, just like we were before, only
without the sex, Elise would frown on that."

"She might be able to take me. She's little and all perfect and
shit, but she's got a mean streak. I don't want to lose you. You're a
big part of my life. So I guess I can make nice with her and not flip
out in front of her kid too. That was out of line. I know it was."

"My kid too. I want to adopt her. And I want you in my life
too." He hugged her, kissing her cheek.

It got quiet, and when he looked around to see what had happened, everyone was looking toward the door, where Elise stood, a

horrified look on her face. She must have seen the last bit between him and Raven.

"Elise, wait!" he called out, but she turned, her movements jerky and uncoordinated as she tried to hurry away. That's when he knew for sure she loved him back. Seeing his normally ridiculously graceful Elise reduced to that sort of clumsiness shocked him even as he rejoiced.

Elise knew her face was red, knew her tears would smear her makeup, and yet she couldn't seem to care. She needed to be away, needed to wash away the shame and humiliation of coming to tell a man she loved him and walking in to see him tell another woman he wanted her in his life as he hugged her.

"Wait, damn you, Elise!" He ran up behind her and she braced for his touch. But he didn't touch her. Instead he ran in front of her and dropped to his knees, bringing her to a surprised halt.

"Damn *me?* You're joking right? Your hands are all over another woman and you dare to say that to me?" Tears thickened her voice; she knew she'd feel better if she kicked him extra hard. She stifled the desire though. For now.

"It wasn't at all what you think. I love you. Do you hear me? *I love you, Elise.* I was telling Raven that. She was apologizing for how she'd been. I was telling her I loved you and that I was glad she could be part of my life because she accepted that."

"You love me?" she squeaked, and he grinned in response.

"How can you not have known that before now? I love you. I love you. I've loved you since before the block party earlier this year. I wanted all this legal stuff out of the way before I told you. I knew you needed to keep your focus on Rennie."

She blinked as her world turned on its ear.

"Marry me."

"Marry?" The squeak again. "Why not just dating? You can sleep over now."

He laughed. "That's so not the response I imagined. First, can we—?"

"I love you too. I've loved you since New Year's when you kissed me at midnight, and I've wanted to tell you so many times but I didn't want to spoil our deal. I knew you didn't want love and forever and all that. I came here today to tell you that and to ask you to do the tattoo, the big one, mark the occasion."

He stood and pulled her to him. Her feet left the ground and she wrapped her legs around him, holding on tight as he kissed her silly.

"Okay, now that we've established how stupid we've both been in not just telling each other our feelings earlier, let's get back to marriage. I can't just date you. I've *been* dating you. I need to be married to the mother of my child. I know you and Rennie are a package deal. Marry me. I love that kid. I want to make a home with you and Rennie. I want forever and I want it with you."

The tears came freely now, but they were good tears.

"Yes. Yes, I want to marry you. But you know Rennie has a part in this too. She's my first priority and I want to be sure this is okay with her." She loved that he loved Rennie too, but this was important; his understanding that Rennie needed to be an active participant in this, this most important decision, was paramount.

"I made some reservations out at the coast for this weekend. I thought we could all go out there, play in the sand. It's a two-bedroom suite. The weather is supposed to be nice. What do you say?"

"I say I'm lucky." She held on, held on until she knew he wasn't going anywhere.

"And, um, I'd really like to adopt Rennie. Make her mine officially. If that's okay with you."

The tears started again as she threw her arms around his neck, tightening her legs. Her tears had morphed into sobs, and he worried until she began kissing his face and lips. "Are you for real? You want to be her dad?"

He laughed. "Good thing you're so light, because I'm not letting you go anytime soon. Yes, baby, yes, I love you and I love Rennie. I already love her like she was my own. I want us to be a family, I want her to know I think of her as my daughter. We all belong to each other, and I just thought it would be the best way to go about it. If you're uncomfortable, we can wait."

"I'm not uncomfortable. When I think of the things I want the most in the world, you're it. All of it. A best friend and partner for me and a dad for Rennie. I can't believe you're real."

He kissed her again and nipped her bottom lip. "I'm real and we'll be a family. Just like you two deserve and I've wanted for a very long time."

"I love you like cupcakes," she said, laughing.

"Wow, that's a lot of love. And as a plus, you can lick me anytime. Now, what do you want and where do you want me to do it?"

"That sounds dirty." She didn't even complain when he carried her back into his shop and people cheered.

"That can be arranged. The dirty part. But just now I mean the tat."

He sat her on the table.

"I was thinking a swan, you know, from *Swan Lake*?" She drew up her shirt. "Right here on my belly and side."

"Hm. Yes, that would be nice. Can I make a suggestion?"

"Of course."

"You're a phoenix. You've been down and have risen up, survived. You're beautiful and fierce and ethereal." He traced over the skin of her belly and side. "I have something I drew up." He reached over and pulled a sheet of paper from a drawer and opened it. It was amazing. Beautiful.

"Oh. Brody, this is . . . Wow. I'm blown away."

He smiled. "Good. I'm glad you like it. I'd put the head here." He touched her left side. "And trail the wings across and up your other side. It would be mostly red, with some black and gray. It'll take some time to get it all finished, but I think it'll be gorgeous."

So much better than a swan. "And it matches yours. I mean, the design is different, but . . ." She shrugged, blushing again.

"I hope you never stop blushing. It makes me so hot. And yeah, I thought the connection was nice. I got mine when I started raising Erin and Adrian."

"And mine will be about you too. And about Rennie and new steps. A new life you've been part of since nearly the first. I don't . . . I don't want me and Rennie to be yet another thing you have to take care of. I don't want to be a burden to you."

He kissed her in front of the whole shop and she didn't care one bit. "There's a difference between a burden and a responsibility. A family is a responsibility. You're my family. But you're not a burden. I love taking care of you, I love it. It makes me happy."

"Okay. Okay, I just wanted to be sure, because once we're married, you're not going anywhere."

"No kidding. Now, let's get moving." He looked at his watch. "It's nearly dinnertime and Rennie will be home. You go on back and I'll stop by Red Mill and grab everything."

"Why don't we just spread out a blanket on your back deck then? You know how much Rennie loves your tiki torches."

"Oh, *Rennie* loves them." One of his eyebrows rose and she hugged him.

"Okay so *I* love the tiki torches. Sue me. Or don't, I'm pretty done with courts."

"How much time do we have before Rennie is back?"

She sighed happily. He was hers. For real. "Not enough time for sex."

He cursed. "Okay, tonight then." He kissed her again and her toes curled. "Here." He handed her a key. "To my house. Let yourselves in if I'm not back. I'm going to stop and get champagne too. We have a lot to celebrate."

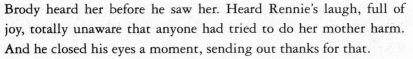

Brody heard her before he saw her. Heard Rennie's laugh, full of joy, totally unaware that anyone had tried to do her mother harm. And he closed his eyes a moment, sending out thanks for that.

He came into the backyard and saw his girls there, laughing, kicking a ball, all that pretty pale hair flying as they ran. His, and nothing had ever felt better.

"I hear some ladies might be hungry."

"Brody!" Rennie ran across the yard and up the steps of his deck. He had to drop the bags quickly to grab her instead, hugging her close.

"Hey, sunshine. I missed you today."

She held his cheeks and gave him a kiss. "Your mustache tickles. Mom said we're all going to the beach this weekend. Can we fly kites? There's a kid in my class who flies kites. I think it sounds cool. Do you think it sounds cool? Do they have pink kites with sparkles on them? If not, I could probably be okay with a yellow kite. As long as it's not green. I don't really like green unless it's pickles. I like pickles."

Elise shrugged at him as if to say, *Get used to it*. But he was, and all that droning chatter was just fine with him.

"We will find you a pink kite with sparkles. I think kite flying sounds like a wonderful idea."

He put her down and sat on the blanket as Elise began to set out all the food. How wonderfully fucking normal it was. He kissed Elise's cheek and stole an onion ring from her plate. She whacked his hand but laughed.

"Rennie," he said, looking to Elise, who nodded, understanding he planned to broach the subject of their getting married.

"Yep?" She had ketchup on her chin. Elise handed her a napkin and she mopped it up with a grin. Brody wondered if it was possible to love anyone as much as he loved Elise and Rennie just then.

"What would you say if I asked your mom, and you of course, to marry me? We'd live together and you two would be my family."

Her eyes widened and she jumped over the food into his lap. "For reals? Would you be my dad? I had one, but he wasn't very nice. He made Momma cry. Mom and I are good." She tipped her chin up proudly, and his eyes stung to hold back his own damned tears. "We're good, but we could make you happy in our family."

He hugged her, love making it hard to breathe. "Will you be my daughter? Officially? If it's okay with you, I'd like to make it official. We can file papers that make me your dad. Your last name would be Brown like mine."

She looked up at him. "Really?" She turned to her mother. "Did you hear that? He's gonna marry us both."

Elise laughed. "I heard it. It's pretty cool, huh?"

"Can I have a horse?"

Startled laughter broke from his belly.

"Get used to it. That's how she rolls."

"You can have a horse doll. And we can go horseback riding. But a horse won't fit in the backyard."

"Oh." She pursed her lips as she sat back at her place and began eating again. "A few dolls would be good, I suppose. And a pink sparkly kite."

28

"Christ. If the day before I met you, someone had said I'd be head over teakettle in love with a ballerina and her eight-year-old, going on forty, daughter, I'd have told them they were crazy. I wasn't looking for you, Elise. That I found you anyway is sort of a miracle to me."

They stood on a balcony overlooking the ocean, newlyweds for less than twelve hours. The wedding had been in Adrian's backyard. It had snowed, and Elise had never seen anything as beautiful as Rennie in her little pink dress, dancing with Brody at the reception.

Her parents had taken Rennie back to their house, where she'd spend the next week with them while Elise and Brody had a honeymoon in the San Juan Islands, at a vacation house belonging to a family friend. The house sat on a cliff with the Strait of Juan de Fuca spread out under the clear sky, the waters cold and dark.

"I tried not to fall in love with you. I did. But you're irresistible. Each time I thought I had it in check, you'd do something else to make me love you more," Elise said and shrugged with a smirk.

He drew her back inside to the bed. He'd built a roaring fire so the space was warm and a pretty glow flickered over the walls.

"It was my cock, wasn't it?"

She tossed her robe and got on the bed. "It's one of your finest features."

"I love you, Mrs. Brown." He followed her, twining his fingers with hers as he kissed her neck.

"I love you too, Mr. Brown."

He traced his fingers and then his tongue over the beautiful phoenix on her belly and side. She loved looking at it. He'd done such beautiful work, it fit her body perfectly. She looked down her body at him, at the phoenix on his back, felt that connection, looked to his wrist where he'd added her and Rennie's initials to the scrollwork in the ivy curling from the base of his hand to his mid-forearm.

He did little things that softened her inside. Filled her up with kindnesses and care until she couldn't really remember a time when he wasn't at her side. He loved her freely and openly, included her and Rennie in his life as if they'd always been there. As Erin neared her due date, they'd all become closer, and Elise and Raven had even reached a sort of mild non-hatred.

Right then with his hands on her, with his mouth on her hip, on her thigh, and then as he lay back and pulled her up and on top of him, she was filled with nothing but love and happiness, with hope for their future.

"No, not yet," he said, stopping her when she fully planned to put him inside her. "Come up here. Brace yourself on the headboard and hold on. I want to eat you this way."

Her breath stuttered as she felt a blush work up her body from toes to scalp. "I can't brace myself on the headboard if I'm not facing it."

"No, not that way. Sit on my face."

Oh she loved it when he was blunt like that. "Oh."

His pirate's grin sent a shiver through her as she moved up, bracing her hands on the headboard and putting her knees on either side of his body.

She'd never done it this way, but wow, was it good. Her thighs trembled as she lowered herself over his mouth. His beard tickled her inner thighs and against her labia. They really trembled when he licked through her pussy, finding her clit, teasing it with the tip of his tongue.

She moaned, louder than she usually did, because they were alone and no one would hear. The fingers holding her thighs tightened and she smiled, tucking away that he liked it when she was loud.

The sounds he made as he licked made her crazy. The wetness of his mouth on her, the wetness of her body against his mouth. It felt so good, it sounded so raw and sexual, she had to close her eyes to take it all in.

She rocked just a bit to get more, and he gave it to her. Urging her with his hands and mouth.

"Mmm, that feels so good. Oh god. Yes."

He stabbed his tongue up and into her entrance and pulled it out, swirling through her folds and up to her clit again. Her muscles tensed and relaxed each time he did it, until she was focused on his mouth on her pussy and nothing else. Her hands gripped the headboard tight as she rode against his lips and tongue.

Climax hit her hard. Her head fell back as she gasped and then cried out. Her entire body tingled, went numb and tingled some more, until she scooted away from his mouth because she couldn't take it anymore.

He surged up, keeping her in his lap and kissed her, hard. His mouth on hers, his tongue demanding entrance she willingly granted.

His fingers dug into her hips to keep her close as his taste, mingled with hers, flooded her system.

And then he was in her and it felt so good it set off a bone-deep climax she hadn't expected.

"Baby, Christ, Christ, that's so good. Hold on. Hold on," he whispered as he panted through the flex and clasp of her inner muscles.

After long moments, he leaned back against the headboard and smiled. "Fuck me."

"Mmm, my pleasure."

Brody nearly came each time her body came down, her cunt surrounding his cock, lava-hot and ridiculously right around him. He loved seeing the tattoo on her belly, loved knowing he'd put it there, loved knowing it connected them. She was a thing of beauty to him, something he'd never looked for but sure as hell couldn't live without now that he had her.

She ground herself down against his pelvic bone, her clit a hard, slippery knot against him. Her hips moved back and forth as she held him deep.

"Goddamn, you're the most beautiful thing I've ever seen."

Those half-lidded, fuck-drunk eyes opened to focus on him. A smile flirted with her lips and she gave in, showing a face he knew only he ever saw. The intimacy of it was shocking, straight down to his toes.

"That's funny, I think the same thing every morning when I open my eyes and see you there."

She scratched down his chest, stopping to give extra attention to his nipples. That was hot. Then she leaned forward and her nipples brushed against his. That was beyond hot. He knew she stroked her clit against him, and then her nipples too. In the last year and a half, she'd opened up to him enough that the shy woman had shown him her sensual side and now she unabashedly took her pleasure.

"Your cunt feels so good."

She groaned and he smiled. The shy Mrs. Brown loved dirty talk.

"Does it?"

"Yes. Hot, so hot. And wet. Your honey slides down my cock and over my balls. I love it when you fuck yourself onto me this way. Then again, I love fucking you every way."

"Handy."

He laughed as he pinched and rolled her nipples. "Yeah. I thought so. It's why I married you."

"Certainly wasn't for a quiet house."

"Quiet is overrated."

"Yeah. So fuck me. Come inside me before I die right here stuffed with you."

Oh. Well. He liked dirty talk too. Especially from her lips. Good god.

"Pick up the pace then. Ride me hard so your tits jiggle."

Sometime later, when the moon reflected off her skin as she lay facedown on the bed, satisfied and sleeping, he looked at her and then out the window. His life had been a series of turns, hard rights and lefts around blind curves. It hadn't always been easy, but the place where he ended up had always been a joy. Such as it was with her and his daughter.

She'd come into his life precisely when he didn't need or expect a woman, didn't need a girlfriend, much less a wife, and she'd taught him just what need was. And in the end, what it meant to have need sated, to be loved and love in return. Not such a bad outcome, even if he had to get hit by a car to get started.